FOR YEARS

TO COME

A novel

Tim Emery

Copyright © 2021 Tim Emery

All rights reserved

The characters and events portrayed in this book are fictitious. Any similarity to real persons, living or dead, is coincidental and not intended by the author.

No part of this book may be reproduced, stored in a retrieval system, or transmitted in any form or by any means, electronic, mechanical, photocopying, recording, or otherwise, without the express written permission of the publisher.

ISBN- 9798594088238

Dedicated to my wife, Pam.

Thank you for your love, patience,

and encouragement.

1

Matthew shuffled across the front porch in oversized leather sandals and the Middle Eastern headdress he was forced to wear. The shoulder-length fabric was held in place by a braided black cord and released a spicy scent of the Cairo Bazaar where it had been purchased. With a slide projector in one hand and a retractable screen in the other, the teenager navigated down the parsonage stairs, unaware his quiet life would soon ignite into chaos.

"A little early for Halloween," teased Walter Pratt as he watched Matthew pass on the nearby sidewalk. Not getting a response, the elderly janitor continued to swing open the wobbly glass door of the church message board for the second time that morning. Walter returned the cigarette to his mouth and used a crooked finger to poke at the plastic letters at the bottom of a cardboard box. "Crazy minister... switching his words again. On Sunday morning no less!" Walter changed the last phrase and read the entire message out loud to check the spelling. "Sunday June 8, 1969 - Youth Group Returns from The Holy Land - Come see the slides and share in the JOY!" He shook his head in disbelief and muttered, "Joy my ass."

As Matthew arrived at the century-old Methodist Church and climbed up each worn slab of granite to the front door, he was winded and overheated. He wanted to pull off the souvenir outfit and drop it like a spent parachute onto the bushes below. His shoulders ached from carrying the heavy equipment and he wondered why adolescence had only made him scrawnier looking in spite of the heavy snow he had shoveled all winter. He glanced down at his father's sandals and noticed that even his toes seemed unreasonably long, as though some miniature medieval rack had been used in his sleep to stretch out every knuckle. Between his spindly arms, slender neck, and the pair of white stilts for legs, Matthew appeared every bit the insecure fourteen-year-old he was.

He was about to set the projector down on the stoop to rest when the acceleration of a car up the street forced him inside so he wouldn't be seen. WHACK! Matthew cringed. The unwieldy built-in tripod of the screen collided with the side of the doorframe and gouged out a chunk of wood. He felt bad about the damage and knew that Hal Dobson wasn't going to be pleased with the loud interruption of the morning's rehearsal.

"What in the Sam Hill is going on?" The choir director worked his way out from behind the organ's tiered keyboard. He adjusted the belt on his favorite pair of pastel slacks. The wide belt matched his white loafers. Hal eventually recognized the odd silhouette against the sunlight that streamed through the church's front entrance. "My goodness Matthew, you look like a Bedouin door-to-door salesman!" Hal returned to the organ and played the theme song from the movie, *Lawrence of Arabia*. Members of the choir let out a chuckle as Matthew removed the uncomfortable headdress that had made his brown hair a sweaty mess. He tossed it over a nearby pew. Though he never cared much for the balding choir director, Matthew respected his elders and returned a polite wave.

The music stopped when Reverend Thomley entered the sanctuary with a clinched jaw and the well-defined exclamation mark of his cleft chin. The Pastor's new tan made the clerical collar appear whiter than usual.

"Would someone please explain why I can't prepare for my sermon in peace and quiet?"

"Dad, do you want the screen in the center or off to the side?" asked Matthew.

The heavy footsteps of John's wing-tip shoes echoed loudly off the hardwood floor as he crossed between the pews toward the youngest of his three children. Matthew and his grandfather once secretly joked that John looked like a combination of Sinatra, for his baby blues, Elvis, for his perfect black pompadour, and Clark Gable, for his larger than normal ears. They agreed to add a dash of gargoyle for his ugly temper.

John hissed, "Why isn't this set up?" He pointed at the equipment.

"Ah... well, it won't take-"

"Where's your brother? I told you to get his help."

Matthew knew his juvenile delinquent brother couldn't afford another confrontation with their dad so he was more than willing to take the blame if needed. "I guess... I forgot to ask."

Matthew's mother stepped forward from the choir in a burgundy robe. It added elegance to her graceful movements. With high cheekbones, long sultry dark hair, and flawless skin, Barbara looked to be in her mid-twenties rather than her true age of thirty-four. "John, there's still plenty of time to-"

"I guess we'll find out, won't we?" He locked a threatening eye on their son. "And where is your headdress? Put it on this instant." Matthew did what he was told and returned the garment to his head while John continued with his commands. "Place the screen to the right of the main aisle. Set it high so folks can see it. And make sure the projector is level. Got it?"

Matthew nodded. He knew his father always felt anxious before delivering a sermon but today seemed worse than usual. Hal Dobson flipped through sheets of music to remind everyone the rehearsal needed to continue. The Pastor checked the large antique clock above the balcony and marched toward the organ with a heightened concern for the morning's schedule. "Hal, how much longer will you need my wife?" A few snickers escaped over the choir's music binders. "You know, with choir practice."

"Ah... I... we, we should, the warm-ups..." stammered Hal. He was aware of the absurd rumors surrounding his late-night music rehearsals with the minister's talented wife.

Barbara spoke up. "Dear. We're almost done with warm-ups. Then we'll run through the lovely selection of hymns you picked." She knew from her many years in a volatile marriage the fastest way to John's heart was through his ego.

John grunted and stormed back to his office while Matthew gave his mother a cheery nod of encouragement. Matthew had reached a decision. He would do whatever it took to keep his troubled family together.

A few blocks from the church, Matthew's older brother, Bud, and his two friends, entered the alleyway behind Harmon's General Store. It had become their favorite spot to hang out and smoke cigarettes or an occasional joint. Bud was obese, with bushy sideburns and long oily black hair, which gave everyone the correct impression that he didn't care what people thought. His round face of stubby beard growth from two unshaven days resulted in an unusually mature appearance for someone still in high school. The Mexican poncho he wore everywhere was used to conceal items he shoplifted.

Bud knew the earlier situation with his brother wasn't handled well. He had absolutely no interest in helping Matty set up a slide projector that might make their father's sermon any more of a success. That is not to say that Bud didn't feel some sympathy for his little pain-in-the-ass brother, what with having to wear that ridiculous costume. In hindsight, given how angry his father was with him of late, Bud wished he hadn't joined up with his new friends and had gone to the church with Matty instead.

"You're in trouble now, fatso!" The high pitch declaration came from Donny. He was short, rail-thin, and rarely stopped talking. "What's your old man gonna say this time?"

"Who gives a shit," Bud stated flatly and took a long draw on his smoke. The Reverend's son wasn't allowed to smoke cigarettes, drink alcohol, or use curse words… ever. Smoking grass was certainly out of the question and something his parents had no inkling occurred. Bud's troubles with restrictions started at age five while playing alone under the sprinkler on the side lawn of the parsonage. Without Barbara's knowledge, her oldest son stripped off his swimming trunks and giggled all the way down the sidewalk to Roland's Drugstore. The phone call came from the store's amiable pharmacist. He informed Barbara her little "Buddy" was out front, naked. Once Buddy felt the cool breeze between his legs, his mother had a difficult time forcing him to stay dressed. Much of her attention was needed to focus on the church duties of a minister's young wife and for taking care of the younger three-year-old Matthew. Barbara convinced her father to construct a good-sized cage on his farm where Buddy spent countless afternoons. Snacking on his grandmother's sugary snacks and sleeping naked under the warm summer sun filled him with joy. His mother made it clear to the entire family, and all prying neighbors, the cage was not meant as punishment but was built to allow her son's uniquely free spirit to safely express itself. Bud's preoccupation with nudity disappeared by the start of elementary school, and the cage was dismantled. Unfortunately, his strong desire for candy, ice cream sandwiches, and donuts continued. School brought its own challenges and the Thomleys were advised to hold their husky son back to repeat third grade, which they did. Later when he flunked the eighth grade, the image of a fat, lazy, and troublesome teen was well cemented in everyone's minds. His weight only increased while his self-esteem sunk to an even lower depth.

Donny ended the silence in the alley by smashing an empty Moxie soda bottle with his new Wrist Rocket slingshot.

"Will you knock it off!" Bud hollered. "You're such an idiot."

"The P.K. is scared little brother," inserted Ryan in a quiet deep voice. "I can tell."

"Preacher's kid, preacher's kid, you're nothing but a preacher's kid!" Donny teased.

Donny and Ryan had just moved into East Fields from a rough neighborhood in Chelsea, Massachusetts. It had been six-months since their father in the Marines was reported missing in action. The boy's distraught mother told them it would be best if they moved back to the small town where she had been raised. She knew in her heart their dad wouldn't be coming home alive. The hope was for her folks to help raise the two difficult boys. She also assumed that her willful teenagers would benefit from spending any free time with the Methodist minister's eldest son. That assumption proved to be a poor one.

"Fuck you!" snapped Bud. "I'm so sick and tired of everybody calling me the preacher's kid and saying my dad is... some kind of... ah forget it."

Ryan, with his slicked-back strawberry blond hair, lit another cigarette and leaned against the rough brick wall of the store. He returned the pack of Marlboros to the sleeve of his tee-shirt and flipped it over twice. It was a cool trick his father had taught him years ago and it had the bonus effect of exposing one of his large freckled biceps. "Naw, you'll always be a P.K." He took a deep inhale, "With no balls."

Bud's anger got him to his feet. He didn't hesitate to use his two-hundred-and-seventy-nine pounds to plow over the empty cardboard boxes that separated the two young men. The physical showdown had been building for days and they collided hard. Bud forgot Ryan had been a star on the varsity wrestling team back home and with two quick moves,

Bud's right cheek lay on the store's grungy loading dock.

"Big mistake lard-ass!" Donny cheered with glee. "You don't screw with us, man!"

"Okay! Fine! Just let go... come on Ryan, you're hurting my arm!"

"My dad says guys who just talk never deliver!" Ryan nudged Bud's arm upward a little more. "It's time to put up or shut up." He released Bud with a final shove.

The embarrassed preacher's kid rose onto one knee. He gasped for breath while dirty beads of perspiration rolled down his forehead and stung his eyes. Bud had been in a lot of fights over the years and had always been able to use his weight as an advantage. He certainly wasn't accustomed to losing so quickly. He was tired. He was tired of being the target for everyone's insults. Tired of getting mistreated by so-called friends who enjoyed poking fun at his size. Punks...who never bothered to look beyond the weight and were always ready to deliver another stinging fat joke. Bud had hoped the extra pounds would protect him, like a thick impenetrable barrier between him and the cruel world. The fact was it only made things worse.

Bud felt his familiar rage coming back on and he tried to control it. It seeped down to simmer with his many fears, like a toxic stew. Finally, he spoke. "Oh, I'll put up!" He stood with effort and took off his poncho to cool down. He headed up the alley a short distance with hunched shoulders that did nothing to support his words. His extreme weight required him to swing out each leg to move forward. The odd gait also helped to keep the chaffing of his inner thighs to a minimum. Suddenly, Bud stopped. He placed his poncho over one shoulder and turned sideways, sucked in his gut a few inches, and met the scrappy brothers' glares with a smile. "Well, you boys coming?" Bud stretched out his arms like a used car salesman with nothing to hide. "Cause I got a wicked cool plan." The three amigos exchanged nasty grins and departed the alley with their better judgment left behind.

2

The long cool shadow of the church's steeple enveloped most of the crowded parking lot below. Giddy teenagers piled out of their families' cars, adorned in flowing Middle Eastern attire. The girls wore colorful gowns with matching sheer veils that kept their smiles hidden. Only their excited eyes, thick with Cleopatra-like eyeliner, could be seen above their veils. Many of the boys laughed while they struggled to keep their long headdresses from taking flight in the morning breeze.

Inside the modest church, Hal played a soft prelude on the organ and ushers assisted the older parishioners to their seats. The seniors were led down the main aisle that divided the wooden pews into two sections. Most of the older members insisted on sitting in the same pews they had claimed as their own for decades. Like their occupants, much of the pews' varnish had faded over time. Parents with small children preferred to enter on their own along the outside aisles. Sitting on the far end of a pew allowed for a quick exit if their child became unruly during a sermon, something everyone knew was a pet-peeve of Reverend

Thomley. The dusty and seldom-used balcony extended above the first six rows of pews and contributed to the church's small dark interior. The congregation was comprised mainly of conservative farmers and small business owners who could trace their roots in the church over many generations. Like so many other places of worship in New England, the church helped maintain a strong social tie that held the community of East Fields, New Hampshire, together.

Standing near the card-table in the main aisle, Matthew tried his best to resemble a stoic, Sultan guard, arms folded, and feet spread shoulder-width apart. Matthew did not feel like talking. In fact, he hated even being there. But as promised, the brand-new Kodak Carousel slide projector was exactly level and pointed squarely at the center of the screen. The church's old and heavy portable record player sat next to the projector with its lid open. The specially bought record was all set to play. Thin brown extension cords were connected end-to-end and laid precisely under each pew. Matthew secured the extension cords to the wood floor with numerous pieces of narrow masking-tape. He knew that taking simple precautions to ensure safety should be everyone's responsibility. Matthew did not believe in guardian angels, or in any angel, for that matter.

Just inside the building's front entrance stood the Thomley's eldest, Sarah. She felt uncomfortably on display in a pale-green veil, certain that her burgundy penny-loafers looked dreadfully inconsistent with the ornamental garment she wore. Despite her father's wishes, Sarah refused to purchase the authentic pointed-toe slippers, meant to go with the gown, for what she thought was today's short-lived event. She wanted to get the whole thing over with as quickly as possible and retreat to her room in the parsonage next door. At just five-foot-two, the somewhat plump high school senior handed out printed bulletins to every soul whether they wanted one or not. Like most Sundays, Sarah had already spent most of the early morning mimeographing the weekly bulletins in the church's storage room in the basement. Her dad's frequent last-minute changes required her to be fast and flexible. Sarah considered her cobalt blue fingertips visual proof of the important role she played in her father's ministry.

Of late, Sarah had given more thought to college and to firming up her declared major but could not decide between teaching English literature or pursuing a career in journalism. She was not sure if she could develop the aggressive personality to become a successful hard-hitting reporter, and felt far more at ease with the less demanding requirements of teaching high school or college literature. Sarah was certain of one thing. She wanted more from her life than what her mother had achieved. A bored housewife of a Methodist minister with three kids and no chance at a career. With her own high school graduation ceremony just one week away, Sarah absolutely sensed the mounting pressure to decide soon. As always, she wanted her ducks in a row; preferably each webbed foot shackled to the one behind.

"Sarah, oh my, don't you look... different," announced seventy-nine-year-old Edith Sloan, as she took one bulletin for her and her frail husband to share. Edith was on the town council and leader of the church's quilting club, where Sarah's outspoken father was often the topic of discussion. "How was the Holy Land, Dear?"

"Well, Mrs. Sloan, it was... *different*." Sarah pushed her eyeglasses back up the bridge of her sunburned nose. She forced a second bulletin onto Mr. Sloan. "And guess what, so is today's sermon. In fact, my father is showing slides of the trip." Sarah knew Mrs. Sloan wanted, like most everyone in East Fields, for church services to remain consistent and to provide a sense of security. Church was really the only place that had not changed much during the radical upheaval of the prior two years, and anymore surprises were simply not welcomed. Between the cold-blooded assassinations of Robert Kennedy and Martin Luther King, along with the ceaseless antiwar demonstrations and violent race riots on television every night, most folks in East Fields felt as though the entire country was on the brink of disaster. Nearly everyone simply wished their quaint town would just return to its tranquil existence of the previous decade.

"Well, I'm sure the pictures will be lovely dear," stated the crotchety parishioner through pursed lips. She turned away with the bulletin squeezed tight in her grasp and hooked her hand around her husband's skinny forearm. Mrs. Sloan whispered, "She knows how I hate it when her father changes the Order of Worship. We must remain *methodical* to reach salvation." She pressed her thin wrinkled lips together again, then spoke more fervently. "We're not called Methodists for nothing!"

"Yes dear, I know. Now please hush and sit down," instructed her husband gently. The gray-haired couple settled into their favorite pew, and Edith adjusted her frayed blue-fox stole. It clung around her gaunt shoulders like some prehistoric trophy she herself had clubbed to death. She thought about the brazen young minister and how, from day one, she had never liked him.

Malorie Wells entered the first row of pews from the far end and sat down directly in front of the towering pulpit. She was eighteen, blonde, and knowingly attractive. The aroma of the new perfume she had purchased overseas generously filled the nearest three rows like a powerful force-field that seemed to both mysteriously attract and repel at the same time. Malorie crossed her legs. Just visible above the pale pink veil, her excited green eyes showed the keen anticipation she felt for the recognition she would soon receive from Pastor John. But like two faceted emeralds, her eyes also showed the flawed jagged shadows of a painful childhood.

An hour earlier, Malorie had begged her grandparents to attend the Sunday service. She wanted them to see for themselves just how critical her role was in generating the required funds for the Youth Group's trip overseas. Not surprisingly to her, both declined. They were simply too exhausted and lacked any desire to get dressed in their finery for church. They said they really preferred to sit comfortably in their screened-in Florida room, and watch the wild birds on the feeders in the backyard. The fact of the matter, was they both wanted a cigarette, more black coffee, and a much-needed break from their enthusiastic granddaughter. Her constant, inane ramblings about the trip to the Holy Land had gotten tiresome. Rather than argue the issue, she forgave them and took the high road to the morning's service alone. As Malorie sat in the pew and listened to the organ play, she dragged a long fingernail across the red cushion and made numerous heart-shaped designs on its plush fabric.

In his office behind the altar area, Reverend Thomley opened a vintage armoire near the new paisley foldout sleeper-sofa he occasionally used when things weren't going well at home. He reached in and carefully removed his long, satiny black minister's robe, then solemnly put it on. Next, he gently lifted over his head the purple silk 3-inch-wide sash. With a quick adjustment, coming from years of dutiful practice, both ends matched perfectly at the bottom. John felt pleased with himself. He smiled at the thought of Hal playing the theme song from *Lawrence of Arabia* earlier that morning. John softly whistled the tune as he removed his own expensive headdress from the armoire and delicately placed the flowing material on the top of his head. He recalled the enjoyment of successfully haggling the merchant down to nearly half of its original price, along with obtaining a large silver and blue lapis ring for a few more American dollars. The Reverend fitted the elaborate olive green agal to hold the white fabric securely on his head. The agal's four golden cords contained small vertical rings of thread and were held together at the corners by substantial burls of fine green silk. John inspected his image, and everything seemed complete. Except for one prop. The curved Egyptian dagger, with its decorated sheath, was hidden in his desk drawer. John had bought it as a gift for Bud, but still was not sure if his impulsive eldest son was responsible enough to own it. The dagger would be a peace offering to smooth over their last heated argument before the trip. John had stressed upon Bud how important appearances were in his occupation and that every family member represented John to the larger community. He added that despite Bud's latest desire to be a filthy hippie, along with his seemingly uncontrollable problem with weight, he could at least keep his long hair clean and combed. Bud fought back angrily with his usual foul language, and ended the argument by lumbering off with a thick middle finger raised in defiance.

John opened the desk drawer and carried the dagger to the full-length mirror on the back of the office door. He decided he would give it to Bud at dinner that evening to fix what seemed like a constant struggle between the two of them. At least for a while. The minister placed the big lapis ring on his middle finger and carefully removed the sharp dagger from its curved scabbard. The unmistakable sound of metal rubbing against metal excited him. He recalled the scene in the movie where Peter O'Toole first caught a glimpse of his new Arab attire and grinned. John situated the shiny weapon near his own face and examined his limited refection in the dagger. He slowly turned around to take in the mirror's larger reflection of his entire costume. John admired his handsome profile as it extended past the headdress's long material; the impressive image was held captive within the tapered edges of the blade. He spoke in a whisper, "Take no prisoners."

The congregation's reaction to Reverend Thomley's grand entrance into the sanctuary had come in a variety of emotions, ranging from small gasps of shock to full belly laughs. The unexpected sight took everyone by surprise. Their trusted minister, with the classic white collar and black robe, was adorned with the lengthy trappings of an Arab prince. As the giggles and murmurs in the room subsided, John stood proudly behind the pulpit and gazed out over the attentive faces of his flock.

"Well then, it's good to be back." John's baritone voice easily reached the last row of pews. As was always the case, no matter where he spoke, the enthusiastic minister did not need a microphone. "Of course, the sunny weather in the Holy Land felt wonderful." He tilted his head up to the side and struck a fashion model's pose. His fists dramatically placed on his hips. "So, what do you think of my tan?"

Malorie Well's unbridled laughter from the front pew was certainly the loudest reaction amongst the audience. Other teens joined in to help soften the uncomfortable tension growing in the nearly silent church. John may have been only kidding but for the farmers in the crowd who worked twelve-hours days outside, unnecessary tans were not appreciated. "Yes, well then, let's start with a hymn, shall we?" John requested desperately. "Barbara?"

The entire congregation and choir of nine stood when Barbara Thomley walked toward the hand-carved wood railing. Below, three red carpeted steps separated the altar area from the main sanctuary. Her silky brunette hair was up in a loose bun which allowed some of the long curly strands to fall lightly around her neck. She opened her hymnal and glanced over the familiar congregation until her eyes fell on Matthew, seated in the center aisle. He had been sketching the peaceful slumber of a toddler boy curled up on the far end of a pew.

Matthew knew he had to keep the sketch simple. Between the likelihood of the boy waking up and the slideshow demanding his full attention, the detailed shading of the sketch would have to wait until later. Matthew's artistic talent had rescued him from many boring church services over the years and the standing agreement with his mother was still in effect. As long as he didn't cause a distraction, he could draw to his heart's content.

"Please turn to page forty-five in your hymnal." Barbara smiled and announced, *"This Is My Father's World."* The irony nearly caused her to laugh out loud.

John always enjoyed a good hymn, but tended to bellow so loudly that he often covered over his wife's sweet vocals. His voice was not bad; it just overwhelmed everyone else at times, much to the dismay of Hal, seated behind the organ. Little did John know that, as his favorite hymn played on and he filled the church with an overblown voice, his eldest son was doing his damnedest to break into a store nearby.

Bud pushed downward on the iron crowbar and was surprised to find how easily the rusted screws of the padlock plate were set free from the weathered wood of the doorframe. He opened the squeaking door to get him and his cronies, one at a time, into the back entrance of the darkened store.

"Far out, man!" Squealed Donny. "We're like breaking and enter-"

Bud quickly silenced him with a nudge as they stepped farther into the building. Each plastered-over window of colorful advertisements kept the good folks in town from seeing the busy thieves inside. They giggled nervously, while exploring the dark surroundings with their flashlights, and started to fill the empty pillowcases they had nabbed from Barbara's linen closet.

As the hymn ended, John held the last note longer and louder than anyone else in the church. "Thank you, Barbara... Hal." John turned back to the congregation with his carefully prepared sermon. He hesitated for a moment until he had everyone's full attention. He wanted to savor the moment. John simply loved the control that being a minister afforded him, and how he could drive home his message into the receptive minds of those in front of him, to have his words accepted as truth, concepts he could easily back up with the Holy Bible if need be. At times, it seemed as if he was an approved spokesman for God Almighty himself. Every Sunday, John assumed his parishioners would think about his sermon all week while working at their mundane jobs. Then on the following Sunday, he would deliver yet another inspirational sermon. As he placed his soft hands on the upper edges of the pulpit, he felt powerful, like one of those motorcycle riders he had noticed on the roads more often of late, those tough powerful guys in leather jackets, with their tattooed arms held high on tall silver handlebars, roaring down the interstate without a care in the world. He had his own form of power too, but John had to admit he envied their freedom of the open road. He so hungered for more excitement in his safe, predicable life.

"The Order of Worship will be changed today," announced John. "I know you'll find this hard to believe, but as the bulletin shows, the collection of the Offertory will need to wait because of the slide show." Nearly everyone chuckled. They knew how strongly he felt about the collection of cash donations and it always occurred early in the service. John's bright smile glistened white even more because of his tan. "I'm pleased to say it was a very eventful trip. I want to extend my sincere appreciation to all of you whose efforts made it possible." Quiet applause spread throughout the room as various parents placed their arms around their children's shoulders. For most members of the Youth Fellowship, this had been their very first time away from loving families and the security of their New England homes.

"The bake sales, the car washes, the quilt sales, the... oh hey, speaking of quilts, that's a wonderful banner by the way." John pointed to the polyester banner that hung low from the bottom of the balcony and swept over the middle aisle. Meticulously quilted images of pyramids, Egyptian hieroglyphics, and a hillside with three bold crosses filled the top half of the banner. Along the bottom half, large block letters made up the phrase: *'WELCOME HOME TEENS!'* John had been surprised by the new banner when he first entered the sanctuary. He was more than a bit annoyed no one had asked his permission to put it up and realized it must have been hung in secret while he was getting dressed in his office. Years earlier, when John became Pastor at the church, there were six vertical quilts that hung along the balcony railing. Over time, he had been able to get rid of four. He felt the quilts were distracting, with their cute fabric artwork and quaint messages. The *"I Am the Bread of Life"* quilt featured a perfect loaf of sliced white bread on a plate with three golden tabs of butter, complete with a glass filled with milk. To John it looked more like a magazine ad for Wonder bread or the Land O' Lakes Dairy. That banner was the first one to go. The decisive minister thought he had made it clear there would be no more quilts or banners, but obviously he had not.

From John's vantage point at the pulpit, everything on the sheer banner appeared backwards because its front side was hung with those entering the church in mind. The fabric was transparent enough that he could still read its message and concluded he had better give it some praise. "Another fine job no doubt from our own Mrs. Edith Sloan and her industrious quilting crew. All of you, please stand and take a bow." John's smile camouflaged his dislike for yet another example of the ongoing power struggle he had to endure with certain church members. He knew many were hell-bent on getting rid of him.

Six elderly women stood only when Edith Sloan finally rose and nodded to her fellow parishioners with a smug smile of satisfaction. She was so pleased that Mr. Pratt, that nice janitor, had hung the banner at the last minute. The surprised look on the Reverend's face had been priceless. She also wanted the teens to know how proud the church elders felt. The Youth Group did, after all, represent their All-American congregation to all those awfully poor foreign countries. There was no doubt in her mind that the much-deserved applause made the long hours of stitchery worth it. Edith soaked in all the attention she could, until the young, flamboyant minister stole it back.

"Okay then, where was I? Oh yes, the fund-raising. All those car washes last summer. Remember?" John grinned widely and glanced down at Malorie, recalling the hot July afternoon when she surprised him from behind a tree. She wore a yellow bikini and doused him with a bucket full of cold sudsy water. It took a few moments for John to refocus, and he increased his volume. "So, let's all give our amazing President of the Youth Fellowship here a big hand for organizing and supervising the fund-raising activities. Malorie girl, stand up! Come on now, don't be shy."

Malorie jumped to her feet with abundant enthusiasm and faced the scattered applause. John went on to sound less like a minister and more like a television game-show host.

"And it was the lovely Miss Wells here who also came up with the 'Teen Canteen' at her high school. It turned out to be the largest money-maker of all." As if choreographed, Malorie released the veil from over her ultra-white smile and deeply tanned face. She finished with an exaggerated slow curtsey as the applause died down.

Sarah Thomley shook her head. She realized it was as good a time as ever to leave her station near the front door. She took a seat in a pew across the aisle from Matthew's slide projector and glanced at her little brother. Sarah rolled her eyes at the needless attention she thought Malorie had just received. She still had a hard time accepting her father's ridiculous decision to appoint Malorie, over her, as President of the church's Youth Fellowship.

Matthew set his sketchpad aside and opened and closed his fingers and thumb as though his moving hands were their father's speaking mouth. Brother and sister snickered among themselves.

Matthew and Sarah had always been remarkably close; it started the day he came home from the hospital all cuddlesome and smelling pure. Sarah had a brand-new living doll to feed… with tiny fingers that would grasp her pinkies and pull them toward his mouth. She fell in love with the baby's contagious giggles, finding it difficult to attend school and leave him at home. Over the years, Sarah was the one who taught little Matty how to take his first steps on the front lawn and insisted that his earliest attempt at a full sentence was in fact, *"I love you Sar-ah."*

When Matthew started coloring pictures within the lines, it became clear to those who saw them that he was blessed with artistic talent. While other toddlers in the neighborhood were struggling with crude stick figures, Matthew's drawings were nearly three-dimensional and always finished with the appropriate colors. As the years went by, it was not unusual to find Matty in his room, drawing nearly exact reproductions of the animal photographs in their family's collection of National Geographic magazines. His artwork only improved, and Sarah encouraged him to accept his creative side as a valuable gift from God...something to embrace and be proud of. Throughout his upbringing, Sarah protected him and taught him the real lasting value of intelligence and creativity. She took the stewardship of her youngest sibling seriously, and as a result, felt she deserved most of the credit for cultivating his impressive drawing skills. She knew that under her watchful eye, Matty was going to become a true artist. He would succeed in a society that was not very kind to sensitive people like her youngest brother.

More recently though, during a family debate at the dinner table, Sarah could not understand Matty's continued stubborn unwillingness to believe in the value of religion. She could not grasp his obstinate refusal to agree with any of her and their father's shared viewpoints on the greatness of God. She had grown very concerned he was relying too exclusively on the *"Natural Order of Things,"* or *"N.O.O.T."*, as he called it. The concept was Matthew's own creation; an unshakable adage for life's design, where everything mankind needed came from nature and science. For Matthew, it was a logical view of the world, without the requirement of a single shred of religious content, and he would happily explain it to anyone who would listen. Even his science teacher was impressed with Matthew's unassigned research paper on his theory of N.O.O.T., and how Charles Darwin would have embraced it. At home, Matt would often quote Darwin in his debates with Sarah, pointing out that religion was nothing more than a tribal survival strategy.

When Bud attended the occasional family debates, he did not always side with his little brother. When that was the case, Matthew would quickly point out his brother's bad grades as a fine example of how the Natural Order of Things worked. That natural selection was in place, and the family should just accept it. His brother certainly had.

Despite Sarah's opposition to N.O.O.T., she was pleased her little Matty understood the comfort people derived from worshipping the Lord. He was always kind to those who disagreed with him and allowed them to voice their opinions. Sarah was proud of her younger brother and she would do anything to help him succeed and flourish.

3

Pastor John continued to pull his audience out of their habitual passive state. "Folks, we could not have taken the Youth Group if it hadn't been for all of your hard work and generous contributions. You should be very, very, pleased!" John clapped his hands loudly to get everyone motivated. It had always bothered him that so many New Englanders did not show their emotions in public, unless of course they were at a sporting event or a bar. At last, most of the parents rose to their feet and applauded, which prompted the few very reluctant parents to finally stand and acknowledge their kids as well. "By the way, Gregory Hanson from the Portsmouth Harold is here with his big professional camera. Hey there Greg." John gave a wave to the rear of the church. "I convinced him our fancy outfits would make a great front page on Monday's paper!" John noticed the changed look of interest on the faces of his congregation. He eventually glanced down at Mrs. Sloan. He smiled, deliberately, and relished her sorrowful expression. "Now I know this is difficult for some of you, but as I said before, I need to alter today's Order of Worship. First, the Lord's Prayer, of course, and then I'll show the slides you've all been waiting for."

Edith's mind raced back and forth between two strategies. The first would be particularly un-Christian because it involved the cold-blooded murder of her minister and the slow creation of a quilt crafted from his newly tanned skin. The other, a little less severe but just as satisfying, would be the delivery to the church's District Superintendent of a typewritten report. A document focused on the Reverend's numerous indiscretions; today's changing of the Order of Worship would be right at the top of the list.

John bowed his head and the obedient congregation joined in. "Our Father, who art in heaven, hallowed be thy name. Thy kingdom come, thy will be done, on earth as it is in heaven. Give us this day our daily bread…"

Inside the closed general store, Bud and his mates used flashlights to fill their sacks with cigarettes, candy bars, and cans of ice-cold beer. Bud whispered, "It's like trick-or-treating without having to walk." He quickly stuffed his mouth with the first of two pink Hostess Snowballs.

To Bud, they were like a nice pair of tasty teen tits covered in coconut. Donny opened the centerfold of a magazine he found hidden under the counter and his face lit up. He dropped it into his pillowcase. Unfortunately, the boys' petty crime escalated to a whole other level when Ryan took the iron crowbar to the antique cash register.

"...and forgive us our trespasses, as we forgive those who trespass against us. And lead us not into temptation but deliver us from evil." John opened his eyes slightly to get a read on the room. "For thine is the kingdom and the power and the glory forever. Amen."

During the prayer, Matthew continued his sketch of the sleeping toddler and paid little attention to his father's sermon, or as Matt preferred to think of it, *'a performance.'* More than anyone, Matthew felt as though he saw through his dad's thin façade, and truly hated to witness so many parishioners hanging on his every word. It was so obvious to him that his father had, over the years, completely hoodwinked the entire congregation. He knew his dad was just going through the motions. Even the trip to the Holy Land was really nothing more than a pleasant diversion from the dull tasks of running a small-town church. Matthew grinned with the thought of his grandfather who would have called the entire trip a *'boondoggle.'* His granddad had dozens of funny words and sayings that always made Matthew laugh, like *'cockamamie,'* which to Matthew, sounded nasty. He wished he could have faked an illness like he had done so many times before. The obligation to operate the slide projector meant playing sick was not an option. Matthew admired his brother's ability to make no excuses for his low church attendance. Most times, Bud just simply didn't show up and wouldn't talk about it later. Matthew also envied Bud's courage the day he told their father he had no desire to go overseas with a bunch of butt-kissing pansies. If only he could be braver and more defiant like his brother. Matthew stopped drawing and wondered if there were actual steps he could take, things that would help him become self-confident. Like lifting weights. Suddenly he was forced out of his daydream.

"Son wake up! Turn on the projector!" John called out stridently. "Doesn't he look like a shepherd boy. Albeit a deaf one." John laughed, as did most of the churchgoers. "It's a shame he was too afraid to go to the Holy Land. But I got him an outfit anyway." John raised his hands and cupped them on both sides of his mouth. "Son, it's time to find your gumption."

Matthew stared at his larger-than-life father and tried desperately to keep his anger in check. He turned the projector on and pressed the button to advance the slide, as though it fired a howitzer canon aimed precisely at his father's tan forehead.

An usher turned off the lights, and the tall, colorful stained-glass windows glowed along both sides of the dark quiet room. The fuzzy image of the entire Youth Group, posed at the departure gate at JFK airport, filled the screen until Matthew adjusted the focus dial. There was clearly a look of excitement on every face in the slide except for the blank stares of panic grimaced on those few who were terrified of flying.

"Our journey began with long flights from New York to Paris and then on to Cairo. Next slide." John gave a raised eyebrow toward his son. The new image showed half of the group on camelback while the other half stood on the hot sand below. The camels' colorful embroidered reins were held tight in the hands of those standing. Tall palm trees and the blurred shapes of the pyramids could be seen in the far hazy distance. John, in the foreground and donned in his new headdress, was mounted proudly on the back of the biggest camel. He had a three-inch wooden cross attached to a thin leather strap around his neck, letting everyone know he was a Christian. Sarah stood below him, obviously not happy with the requirement of controlling her dad's foul-smelling camel for the photograph. With legitimate concerns about the camel's aggressiveness and the possibility of it spitting, Sarah posed stiffly in a long-sleeve shirt, baggy pants, and a wide-brimmed hat to shade a nose covered with zinc oxide. To John's left, sat Malorie on a smaller camel, wearing a white tee-shirt, shorts, and a relaxed smile. For the photograph, she had leaned over and placed her rosy sun-kissed cheek on top of John's forearm.

"One of the early events of our trip was riding really honest-to-goodness camels... what a wonderful adventure!" laughed John. He faced the screen and missed the gaze of worship in Malorie's glistening eyes. "You know, dear friends, I couldn't get over how emotional I was at every moment of this trip. Even before we arrived in Jerusalem, my heart felt raw and open to experiencing new things, new feelings, new ideas."

Barbara and Hal exchanged a quick glance that confirmed they were thinking similar things about John's comment. Barbara knew for certain and had they been sitting together; Hal would have whispered they were both on the same sheet of music. The choir director loved to use that phrase whenever possible, and it drove Barbara nuts.

"Next slide."

The new image showed most of the group at the base of a pyramid, with Reverend Thomley posed in the foreground, his index finger pointed toward the top of the mammoth stone structure. John smiled at the slide and turned to face the audience. "Of course, a visit to the Middle East isn't complete without a trip to the ancient pyramids, and they were breath-taking. And I do mean *breath* taking. In fact, it was... oh wait, Matty play the record."

Matthew switched on the record player and purposely dropped the needle hard onto the shiny black disk. It resulted in a bang and scratch until the needle finally found a groove in the vinyl. The pleasant sounds of Egyptian music filled the sanctuary and Matthew winked at his father.

"Yes, well, as many of you know I pride myself on staying fit." boasted John. "After this photo was taken, I challenged the youth group to scale a few lower blocks of the pyramid. We hadn't gotten far when I was overcome with paralyzing fear. I couldn't breathe. I simply couldn't go on." John paused for dramatic effect and continued. "So, I told everyone I was fine. To not worry and to go ahead without me. I worked my way back to the ground, completely spent. I sat down and leaned against one of the huge stones, closed my eyes and tried to inhale deeply. I nearly fell asleep but then, I saw... something... and it wasn't a dream dear friends or Deja Vu. No, no, it was more, more of a vision." John looked up to the sanctuary ceiling and opened his arms wide. Below, the room held a sea of concerned faces.

Matthew yawned and stretched out both of his tired arms along the back of the pew. He tilted his head backward and blinked his dry eyes repeatedly to refresh them. He had overheard most of his father's feeble story, from down the hall, late the night before. Matthew's mother had stressed that the older church members would not want to stray from the routine sermon. Barbara suggested that showing the slides on Sunday morning would require a time limit. He could provide more details if he chose Wednesday evening instead. She also pointed out that the evening service was less formal and there would be far fewer of the older attendees. While Matthew agreed with his mother, his father did not, and their argument seemed to continue for hours. As a result, Matthew had hardly slept, and it was all he could do to stay awake in the pew.

"Slaves... pulling on thick ropes." Spoke John with emotion. "As they strained with the extreme weight of the giant stone, I felt my own arms ache with each tug of the gritty line." The minister stepped out from behind the pulpit, closed his eyes, and positioned his arms waist high. He gradually pulled sideways on an invisible rope. "Hand over hand, my palms bleeding badly. Chanting. Chanting together and working as one. Hand over hand. Hand over hand." John called out in a slow trance-like rhythm. "Aiii-ya, Aiii-ya, Aiii-ya." He suddenly dropped to his knees and slammed his hands against the side of the hollow pulpit. The earsplitting sound of his new oversized lapis ring smacking the wood caused nearly everyone to leap with surprise. A baby awoke with a jolt and let out a scream. "The mammoth stone broke free and slid down the steep ramp... crushing our bones to bits!" John pressed the side of his face against the wooden front edge of the pulpit. "I knew then... I had died in that moment." John whispered quietly with eyes closed. "I know... now, I was one of those slaves in a past life."

He opened an eye to witness the reaction of the extremely shocked crowd. Other than the baby's whimpers, not a peep was made until a few people cleared their throats with the anxiety of not knowing what was coming next. John abruptly got up on one knee and with even more urgency, declared, "Reincarnation dear friends! Would our creator, our heavenly father, really give us only one life to live?" John stood and continued. "To learn life's difficult lessons only to die and be buried in the cold ground? It just doesn't make sense." He stepped forward. "Now I know many of you won't embrace it dear friends, but remember what Jesus said, 'Seek the truth and the truth shall set you free!' Don't you want to be free?" John stepped back behind the pulpit and rapped the top of it with his knuckles, then pointed to the nearest stained window. "What if there is more truth out there than our ordinary lives are showing us? Shouldn't we move beyond stale doctrine and worn-out traditions and search for the real answers?"

The baby settled down and the sanctuary grew silent again. Outside, a strong breeze caused the treetops to sway.

The highly motivated preacher stepped out from behind the pulpit with more vigor. "Shouldn't we open our minds to the unlimited possibilities all around us? Why even the government is planning to land on the moon this summer. For Pete's sake! Land on the moon! The MOON! That just blows my mind, as the young people say." He glanced at Malorie and both laughed effortlessly.

John continued to smile and walked down to get closer to the overwhelmed members of his church. He paced back and forth in front of the pews; his loud footsteps echoed throughout the sanctuary. And like the eye of a hurricane, his footsteps fell eerily silent on the carpet of the aisle, until his shoes hit the hardwood floor again. "And on television news lately, a fellow insisted he saw a real U.F.O.! And what exactly is an out-of-body experience? How can I have one? How can *you* have one? Oh, oh, and what about speaking in tongues? Heck, what do our dreams mean? Do we really have colorful auras surrounding our heads?" He allowed his words to flow quickly with the numerous concepts he had recently researched at the public library. "And did you know, over in India, they say a Swami can levitate!" John was excited and the speed of his words accelerated. "I would love to do that. And... what about Jesus walking on water or turning water into wine? The laying-on of hands? Healing the afflicted. Why can't we perform miracles too? Oh, and how about those mind-expanding drugs. Perhaps in a controlled environment they could be useful in reaching enlightenment. Who really knows?"

"Well I *KNOW* I can't listen to this nonsense!" announced Edith Sloan angrily. She stood up abruptly, with perfect ramrod posture, the handles of her handbag clinched in rage. "And I highly recommend all of you do the same!" She stepped out into the aisle with righteous indignation, flung the limp tail of her stole over her shoulder, and turned back to face her husband.

"But they have slides," whimpered Marty. Silence. Under her relentless glare, he stood and dutifully followed his wife out of the church. As if on cue, the entire quilting club rose to their feet and were joined by others, mostly seniors, as they exited their pews and headed for the exit.

"Don't run away!" shouted John as he ran partway up the main aisle. "Why are you so afraid to ask these questions? Shouldn't we live each day as an exciting adventure?"

Matthew advanced the next slide and removed his hot headdress. He started for the front door, knowing his father had finally gone too far. Matthew was not going to stick around for the big finish; he passed his dad on the way out.

"Good son, good." John patted Matthew's shoulder. "Go bring them back!" John reached the first step of the altar stairway. "Don't you see everyone? We're more than just mere sinners." He turned to face his audience. "We can do great things in life if we just shake off the chains of ignorance and seek something MORE!" He took another step up. "We need to let go of our fears." John reached the top step. "To experience a life filled with joy and passion!" Suddenly the emotional clergyman turned and sprinted to the altar; he held his arms out and spun in tight circles. His black robe and long white headdress twirled together like taffy twisting in a boardwalk shop. He stopped suddenly and gazed toward the ceiling. "I want to seek the truth so the truth can set me free!"

Malorie hurried up the small stairs, past the wood railing, her pink sheer gown hiked-up on her golden legs. She dropped to her knees at John's feet. She stretched her slender tan arms up toward her beloved Pastor and cried out, "So do I John, so do I!"

The wails of the terrified baby intensified again. Barbara bolted upright and hollered, "Hal, play something! Anything!"

As Hal pounded out the first anthem he'd learned, *"Onward Christian Soldiers,"* wispy gray smoke curled up from under Matthew's headdress. The absentminded teen had inadvertently draped it over the critical air-vent on the front of the hot projector.

John reached down and helped Malorie to her feet. With him in the lead, the pair walked towards the screen. John pointed to the new image of the youth group posing in front of the tomb where Christ was supposedly laid to rest. To be heard, John needed to shout over the baby's cries, the Egyptian music, and Hal's antics on the organ. "And what about the resurrection? We were at the tomb. We felt its power!" John moved in front of the screen and shielded his eyes from the projector's bright light. He was joined by Malorie, who did the same. He looked out into the crowd and finally hollered, "Damn it! Would someone please shut that kid up!"

Because of the intense heat trapped in the projector, the slide quickly melted outward from the center. A projected bubbly shadow moved, superimposed over John's and Malorie's bewildered faces. WHOOSH! Matthew's headdress shot up in flames. Those seated near the ignited projector turned and screamed. An older usher removed his polyester suitcoat and with the best of intentions, rushed toward the fire. He swatted at the flames with the jacket but that only increased the flow of oxygen. The fire grew hotter and higher. Suddenly, his jacket ignited too. The frightened man bolted up the center aisle, whipping the coat over his head like a cowboy's lasso set ablaze. The burning jacket snagged the *'Welcome Home Teens'* banner. Its synthetic material instantly ignited and dropped gooey melted balls of flames. Hal's hands came down on random keys of the keyboard as the mini bonfires grew on the carpeted center aisle. Most everyone crowded into the side aisles to escape the center aisle's growing inferno. A quick-thinking young man jumped from one pew to another toward the source of the blaze. Unfortunately, he slipped off the last pew and hit the floor hard. Though dazed, he was able to grasp a leg of the card-table and toppled it over. The projector slid onto floor and became a large melted blob of burning plastic and glass. The record player laid broken on its side nearby. The black shiny record shattered into pieces.

The church's sprinklers, installed twelve years earlier, had never been used. They abruptly released a spray of cold rusty water in Zone One, soaking the altar area and the perimeter of the building's interior. It missed the main aisle, Zone Two, where the projector had fallen. Another brave soul succeeded in tearing down the burning banner as it split in-half. The two separate pieces fell onto the highly combustible material of the pew cushions below. The cushions ignited on both sides of the main aisle with thick noxious smoke. Dark plumes of smoke raised eerily upward, like evil black demons standing for an unholy communion. If the intense blaze reached the balcony, the tinderbox of a church would be engulfed in an inferno.

John lifted the lengthy fabric of his water-soaked headpiece and placed part of it over his head. The rest covered Malorie's head like a droopy wet dishtowel. Hal scrambled out from behind the organ with a music binder held over his glistening scalp. He headed toward Barbara. She had just raised her choir robe over her head to block the water, and had not realized the hem of her dress was hiked up with the choir robe, her sheer stockings were in plain sight, held in place with the delicate white straps and clips of her garter belt, where a stark contrast existed between the nylons and her creamy white legs. Though he hated doing it, Hal pulled her dress back down to its normal position. Together, they hurried along the side aisle behind John and Malorie. The large panic-stricken mass remained tight in their slow-moving stampede.

Matthew had exited the church, unaware of the fire. He sat down on the cool granite landing and relaxed. Free of his headdress, Matthew gradually felt his core temperature fall, while he watched the slow-moving seniors depart the parking lot. He glanced down at the worn stone staircase and wondered how many shoes it took, over the years, to have made such deep indentions. Matthew imagined all the unhappy teens, like himself, who were dragged to church against their will over the past century, forced to sit through Sunday after Sunday of pointless sermons. He thought about his dad's current sermon and knew the theory of reincarnation was pure hogwash. Matthew was certain there was nothing to experience after death. No heaven or hell. No God. Just the end of the road. His train of thought completely fell off the tracks when the organ music inside changed. Matthew stood and turned to the building's entrance to see the front doors flung open. Gray smoke swirled around the first of the frightened parishioners. They exited with tear-filled eyes. Each one coughed hard to clear their lungs of the poisoned fumes. Everyone breathed deeply to take in any clean air they could capture. Matthew could not get an explanation from anyone of what happened, so he finally entered the dark structure himself. The dense acrid haze nearly overwhelmed him, so he held the billowy fabric of his retired altar boy smock over his mouth. Matthew quickly crouched lower, to find the air near the floor much easier to breath. He headed farther inside. He soon caught a glimpse of two men who had just extinguished many of the flames emitted from the smoking... slide... projector.

"Holy shit!" The stark realization of what had happened nearly caused him to black out.

"Thank God you're all right!" screamed Sarah, who grabbed Matthew's shoulder from behind, then spun him around. She hugged him so hard that whatever air was left in his lungs was fully discharged.

"I'm okay, I'm fine, just let go Sarah," gasped her little brother. "Where's Mom and Dad?"

Sarah took his hand, stayed low, and pushed their way past numerous others headed for the church exit. Along the way she sadly noticed smears of wet ink from her soaked bulletins had stained every surface blue where they'd landed. Sarah eventually spied her father's head above the crowd. "There's Dad, come on!" She coughed violently and pulled Matthew across the front of the nearest row of pews to reach the far side of the church. She stopped abruptly. Matthew saw the reason. Held up behind the slow throng of church members, their father had his arm tight around Malorie's shoulder. Hal followed closely with his fish-white forearm wrapped around their mother's waist. Her robe had cinched up her dress again and much more of her left thigh was exposed. The nylons strained at their clips as Barbara caught the questioning eyes of her children. She forced Hal to let go just as the Zone Two sprinklers unleashed their spray.

The moment seemed to last a lifetime, as if it encapsulated the precise moment when they realized all of their lives had just changed forever. Barbara quickly pulled down her soaked dress. Sarah turned to face Matty and saw his confusion. She reversed direction so fast it took a great deal of effort for him not to fall. Within moments they blasted out the front door into fresh air and bright sunshine. Like most of the congregation, the Thomley kids hunched over and coughed hard to clear their constricted airways.

When John and Malorie finally emerged from the church, the distant wail of a siren approaching caused a small impromptu celebration on the front steps. "Yes, it's okay, I'm fine!" declared John. "Don't worry." He then realized the crowd had cheered for the siren of the soon-to-appear fire trucks and not for him.

"Thank God, the firemen are-" John called out, then doubled-over with a deep cough. Malorie lovingly patted his back until Barbara broke free of the crowd and used her ample hips to jostle the young blond beauty aside. Barbara took over the duties of helping John to stop hacking, although her back slaps were a tad bit less restrained.

She leaned forward and whispered, "What is it with you and fire?"

"Not now, for Christ's sake!" John coughed hard once more. She helped him to stand erect and did whatever was required to bring appearances back to normal. Within moments, John returned to his old invincible self. "Please everyone, keep moving!" roared John. "Let's clear the steps for the brave firemen!" He escorted a young mother and her two toddlers down the stairs to the safety of the sidewalk below.

The intense sound of the siren had grown more extreme. Everyone turned toward the street's far corner only to see a police cruiser with flashing red and blue lights approach. As if in slow motion, the car passed by and John's eyes engaged those of his oldest son in the back seat. Bud raised his handcuffed hands and smiled weakly.

Matthew, who had seen it all transpire, made his way down to his father's side and happily gave into temptation. "Looks like N.O.O.T to me, Dad."

4

"Religion isn't meant to be exciting John," stated New England District Superintendent, Stanley Dunn. The dark somber office had only one window and it was blocked by two heavy, green velvet curtains. The tarnished antique lamp on the tidy desk provided the only source of light, and its harsh glare spilled down on a thick file folder. '*Reverend Jonathan Eugene Thomley, Junior*' had been neatly handwritten in ink across the tab. Dunn tossed his copy of the Portsmouth Herald onto the desk, with its bold front-page headline: '*Celebration Turns to Tragedy!*' Below, the large black and white photo showed firemen with hoses entering the smoked-filled church.

"Yes Sir, I just thought if…"

The Superintendent abruptly raised a pudgy hand. Stanley Dunn disliked any type of confrontation with the ministers he supervised, and was certain the plan he was about to present the young couple made sense for everyone involved. With his own retirement less than a year away,

Dunn just wanted everything to run smoothly. He needed to maintain a low profile during the final months of his career.

Barbara sat to John's left in a hard-narrow antique chair she knew was not built for people with hips. She shifted her weight and recalled that the last time she had seen Superintendent Dunn had been last year at a church-sponsored Christmas dinner. She was forced to sit next to his talkative wife. Today, from across the desk, Barbara stared at his large oval face, with its teeny-weenie mouth. She wondered when the last time was his wife had passionately kissed those thin unattractive lips?

"John, you're forgetting that your congregation looks to you for guidance. You are their shepherd. You should be focused only on traditional Wesleyan teachings." Dunn picked up a note he had written earlier that morning to underscore the seriousness of John's situation. Dunn cleared his throat and shifted into his own sermon-type voice. "Wesley, the founder of our church, himself, once asked this about his ministers. And I quote. *'Have they a clear, sound understanding; a right judgment in the things of God; a just conception of salvation by faith? Do they speak justly, readily, clearly? Are believers edified by their preaching?'"* Dunn glanced up at John through his thick white eyebrows.

"Reincarnation, indeed." He dragged the file of paperwork closer to himself. "You need to know the Bishop is not pleased. And quite frankly, that's all I care to say about it!" He opened the dense file, which since the fire, had nearly doubled in size with angry letters from numerous church members calling for John's immediate resignation. Dunn turned his attention to Barbara. "Well then, Mrs. Thomley. Before we discuss the next step in John's ministry, let's talk about your children for a moment."

Barbara wasn't surprised by the portly man's implication that the success or failure of their children was really her responsibility. She could read the look in the superintendent's beady eyes. If the children had truly been her primary concern, a big part of the recent scandal could have been avoided. Over the years, she had learned what the church expected of a minister's wife, and she had grown to hate every bit of it. In the beginning, it felt wonderful to be serving others, and she genuinely enjoyed the role, although many in the congregation considered her much too young and attractive to take her seriously. But now, it seemed that hurtful gossip and blatantly false statements about her inability to control her eldest son had reached a level she could not accept. Barbara felt she was awfully close to telling the church leader she had genuinely reached the end of the road.

Dunn adjusted the round, golden, wire-rimmed reading glasses on the tip of his nose, and reclined back to read from his swivel chair. It creaked under its user's weight, as if its own retirement could not come soon enough. "I have a report here from a Mrs. Mable Berger, your youngest's Sunday School teacher. It states some serious issues."

"Mable can be a bit difficult, sir." John broke in.

"Like folding a fitted sheet," Barbara muttered under her breath.

"Yes, well, anyway." Dunn quickly read from the typed report to keep from smiling. "Number one. *'Matthew Thomley has not made the required transition into the Youth Group.'* Number two. *'He continues to be unwilling to attend Sunday School.'* Number three. *'Matthew apparently doesn't believe in God.'* Is this true?"

"Of course, he does." John stated. "But I think it's religion itself he's having trouble with." John turned to face Barbara. "Unfortunately, the boy's grandfather swayed Matthew away from the church."

Barbara broke in. "Come on John. Yes, the war changed my father's beliefs, but he didn't press them onto Matthew."

John glared at his wife. "Sure, whatever you say dear. But I know for a fact it was your father who led our son away from Christ." He turned to address Dunn. "I also think Matthew enjoys getting folks upset with crazy concepts about God and…" John's words trailed off given how they must have sounded. "But hey, did you hear our daughter is speaking at her high school graduation? She's the class Valedictorian. In fact, since I'm giving the invocation, and I'll be on the stage anyway, I get to hand her the special diploma. She's thrilled!"

Barbara shook her head with the knowledge that graduation day was not going to belong to her intelligent hardworking daughter. Not when there could be an exciting John Thomley production to be had.

"I'm sure she is, John" stated his jovial boss with a wink toward Barbara. He knew of John's tendency to grab attention, having seen it himself firsthand at various church functions. Particularly at each of their Annual Conferences. Dunn searched through the file for the daughter's name. "Has... uh... Sarah, decided on a college?" Barbara barely opened her mouth to answer before John sat up straight and launched into another attempt to control the conversation.

"She's applied for numerous scholarships and some look like a sure thing. She was even thinking of studying at West Virginia Wesleyan.

Chip off the old block, you know." John pretended to throw a football. "Go Bobcats!"

"Of course." Said Dunn. A long awkward moment of silence filled the room while the Superintendent revisited the file. John exchanged a glance of apprehension with his wife because they both knew what was coming. "And your oldest son?" Dunn read the name dramatically out loud. "Jonathan Eugene Thomley the Third." He removed his glasses. "My goodness, that's a lengthy title to carry about."

"That's why he goes by Bud!" Barbara blurted out the words much louder than she had intended. It only fueled her anger. "And yes, he's the petty thief you called this damn meeting about!" The two men stared at her completely astonished. "That's right, isn't it? So why don't we just skip all this crap and get to the-"

"Ah... sir, the good news is that the owner of the store that was robbed, is a valued member of our congregation." John provided a meek smile. "Well actually, he's not technically a member, but his wife is. A wonderful, lovely supporter of mine... and the church of course. They own a great deal of real estate in town, and are actually quite wealthy." John's thoughts seemed to drift for a moment. During the hesitation,

Barbara shifted again in her chair. "Anyway, her husband won't be pressing charges."

"On one condition." Barbara said as she stood and smoothed the front of the conservative gray dress she always wore to these types of meetings. "Her husband wants Bud to enlist in the army for Pete's sake!" She walked straight over to the window. The thought of her oldest son in the dark jungles of Vietnam filled her with dread. She had to see sunlight and suddenly threw open the heavy drapes.

Both men shielded their eyes. John directed his words at Barbara with increased irritation. "For your information, darling. He's a decorated veteran of both World War II and Korea." John turned to the Superintendent. "He and I had agreed the army *would* have been perfect for Bud. But apparently, there's a problem. The army won't take him because of his weight."

Barbara's face showed her surprise. "When were you planning to tell me that bit of news?"

"It was resolved this morning while you were at the hairdresser." John's smirk was quite noticeable. "Fortunately, Mrs. Harmon convinced her husband to compromise. The charges will be dropped and there will be no jail time." John smiled at his boss. "Instead of the army, she, I mean they, will pay for his complete tuition this summer at Camp Crossroads." John curled his fingers and delivered the universal sign for quotes. "They say it's the best camp for *'overweight'* boys in all of New England." The room grew silent. "I think this could be the answer," stated John.

"Well, I've certainly had my own battle with the bulge." Superintendent Dunn patted his round belly. "So, Mrs. Thomley. I gather you're onboard with all of this?"

"Well, I know five mothers in our congregation alone who have lost sons to this stupid war. So of course, I'm relieved." Barbara turned her face and gave her husband an intense glare. "But do you really think some... fat camp will make up for how you've hurt our son?"

John stood and pointed at his wife. "You see Stanley, this is precisely what I have to put up with! She constantly undermines me. She's the one who has no idea how to raise children. In fact, she-"

"That's enough John!" Dunn raised his voice. He hated raising his voice. "Please, both of you sit down." The Superintendent refused to allow the conflict to escalate. He placed his elbows on the desk and clasped his hands together. "I have to agree with John. This camp could very well turn things around. And it will be far safer than the army."

Dunn smiled at Barbara and leaned back in his chair. "It's certainly worth

a try. Anyway, I trust you two will do what is best for your children.

Meanwhile, the construction folks have told me it will take most of the

summer to repair the damage to the sanctuary." Dunn turned and focused

intently on John. "The Bishop believes a leave of absence would be best."

"A leave of absence... from the church?" asked John, with genuine

fear in his voice.

"Or from each other?" Barbara questioned optimistically.

Dunn suppressed a laugh. He liked this minister's wife. "Well,

perhaps a short break from each other would be beneficial as well. In any

event, it's just for the summer. I want you both back here at the start of

September with a renewed commitment to the church. And to your

marriage. Think of this as a little faith-lift." The Superintendent winked.

He hoped to have lightened the mood, but the couple remained

motionless, lost in their own thoughts of how the news affected them.

"Well then, it's all settled." He closed the Thomley file. "I'll see

you both at the end of the summer, refreshed and with John ready to

preach." He stood, walked to the door, and opened it wide. The couple headed for the exit; their eyes cast down to the floor as if the answers to what the future held were somehow woven into the carpet. Dunn smiled and slapped a meaty hand on the minister's shoulder. "And John. When you do preach in the future... a little less *fire* with your brimstone."

5

Matthew woke and noticed the old-fashioned leather suitcase still sat empty by his dresser. Today was the big day, and he had not even packed. He had tried to convince his parents he should stay back with his grandmother on the farm for the summer, but they ruled against it. Helen had slowed down quite a bit, and would not have the energy to keep up with a teenager. Matthew understood and accepted their decision. Still, he hated the idea of going on any road trip that did not include his mother.

That morning, Matthew's only desire was to linger in the room that had become his most favorite place in all the world... where he could read anything, he found interesting, and experiment with various drawing techniques. The cozy bedroom was filled with books of all kinds and sizes. Some were stacked on the floor in neat piles and others lined up in bookcases along the walls. At the foot of his bed, a low bookcase still contained the picture books his mother and sister had taken turns reading to him as a child. *"Make Way for Ducklings"* and *"Ferdinand the Bull"* were two of his favorites, along with *"A Fly Came By,"* which always made him laugh. On another bookcase under the window sat three sizable art history books held upright by a half-dozen instructional manuals on drawing and sketching. All were gifts that Sarah had given him over the years.

Matthew crossed both arms behind his head and stared at the ceiling. He was thankful that school was out, and tried to imagine what starting high school in the fall would be like. Bud had warned him to stay low, that seniors just loved to harass pussy freshmen. His brother made it clear on several occasions that he wouldn't have Matthew's back. Bud wanted him to experience a few of life's hard knocks as he had. Time to toughen up. Bud even teased that he may drop out of school altogether so than he wouldn't be able to protect Matthew, even if he wanted to. What Bud didn't know, was that Matthew's artistic talent had already won over nearly all the kids in his eighth-grade class. Even the mean ones. The new high school freshman felt confident that his talents would work with the upperclassmen as well.

It had started at lunch period on the second day of school, the year before. Matthew was sitting alone at a table in the cafeteria, drawing on the handmade cover on one of his textbooks. The school required all textbooks to have protective covers, and like most kids, Matthew used the brown paper from grocery bags as an inexpensive way to comply. He decided to add illustrations based on each book's subject, and selected the Revolutionary War as the theme for his U.S. history textbook. The bloody battle on the front cover was complete, with its fiery cannonball blasting through a battalion of British soldiers in retreat. Matthew just finished adding the fine details of Paul Revere's galloping horse along the book's binding when Randy Larson arrived. With his thick neck and massive arms, he was by far the toughest boy in East Fields Junior High.

"You draw that?" asked Randy.

Matthew nodded nervously. They had never spoken before.

"Do mine." The imposing boy tossed his science textbook onto the table and sat down to inhale his lunch.

It did not take long for Matthew to sketch out an exciting montage of Randy's favorite sport. In the center, helmets clashed over the line of scrimmage, with sharp jagged lightning bolts emitting from the impact. Inserted on the lower right corner of the cover, a field-goal kicker's foot sent a football skyward, just beyond the reach of the lineman's outstretched fingers. At the cover's top left, a black and white striped referee held both his arms straight up high, with the goal post looming behind.

Within a week, the young artist was detailing so many books at lunchtime he barely had time to eat. News spread, and soon every popular student in his class had to have at least one custom-drawn *'Matthew Thomley'* cover of their own. Even the school's hippie art teacher took notice of his talent and insisted Matthew join her Art Club immediately. While he certainly enjoyed the newly found attention, Matthew could not help but wish he had a more impressive medium than brown grocery bags, taped onto textbooks. Then he recalled from his art history books that even the great Michelangelo himself had to spend four painful years flat on his back in the Sistine Chapel.

"Matty, it's time to get up!" His mother called from the kitchen. "We're all packed and ready to go."

Matthew rolled out of bed in his outgrown pajama bottoms and walked down the dim hallway that led to his parent's bedroom. On top of their neatly made bed, where his father had not slept since the fire, sat a massive leather suitcase like the one in his room. This one was much larger, more like a trunk, with three straps cinched tightly with tarnished metal buckles. Seeing the heavy looking suitcase, once owned by his grandparents, filled Matthew with a finality he had not expected. His stomach began to churn. He abruptly made his way back up the hall to his sister's impeccably clean bedroom. He wanted to discuss fixing their parent's turbulent relationship.

The lavender colored room housed Sarah's extensive owl figurine collection, which filled nearly every nook and cranny. For his older sister, owls embodied intelligence and had become her personal mascot at a noticeably young age. Though he did not quite understand her emotional attachment to the peculiar birds, it certainly made birthday and Christmas gift-giving easier.

Matthew discovered Sarah, barefoot, dressed in her black graduation cap and gown in front of the full-length mirror, rehearsing her speech. The bunched index cards held behind her back were slightly damp with nervous perspiration. Though she had the material completely memorized, she still struggled with achieving a slower delivery. Matthew realized immediately that it was fortunate he had only peeked around the door, instead of barging in as usual. He decided he would talk to her after the day's ceremony.

Matthew peered into his brother's mess of a room across the hall where brilliant sunshine had just shot in under the pull-shade. It shone directly onto Bud's ragged face. He was in a deep sleep, so the sunlight and his brother's presence did not seem to matter. Matthew examined his brother. He thought the long bushy sideburns looked ridiculous, like so many Union generals in the Civil War. In Matthew's mind, the style of mutton chops had never been a commendable choice but he knew these sideburns were important to his brother. He also knew Bud's hippie look was not created to display his support for civil rights or to protest the war. His brother's recent transformation had nothing to do with spiritual growth or improving the environment. Bud had only one motivation: To simply piss off their father, a cause Matthew felt was well worth undertaking. Their mother was not too concerned about Bud's appearance. She understood her oldest son's need to become his own man. She did, however, point out often that Bud's dirty long hair wasn't helping his acne. Matthew studied Bud's skin more closely and wondered if he were to sketch his sleeping brother, would he include the scars, blackheads and pimples, or go for less detail. He considered his brother to be basically handsome, with his grayish blue eyes and the strong jaw hidden somewhere under the sizable double-chin. Despite the weight, there was no denying that his brother had a certain magnetism, and Matthew envied his brother's confidence. His easy sense of humor had resulted in numerous friends. He took a moment to visualize his brother as slender and groomed, without the weight and the sadness it brought. Matthew knew Bud would unfortunately need to lose a lot of fat and clean up his act if girls were going to take it beyond friendship and show any romantic interest.

Matthew glanced around at the dozen or so empty candy bar wrappers and dirty plates scattered across the floor. His brother's room didn't have an assortment of books like Matthew's, but the tattered Playboy magazine peeking out from under the bed was a part of a prized collection. Without Bud's knowledge, Matthew borrowed one from time to time.

"Hey, we need to talk about Mom and Dad" Matthew whispered. His brother turned over with a moan, and continued his sleep without much concern. Matthew recognized Bud would rather embrace his stained pillow than face their family's uncertain future. Matthew took a deep breath to keep his anxiety in check and headed down the first few steps of the narrow back stairway toward the kitchen. He stopped at the myriad of vintage black and white photographs he had asked his mother to hang on the wall of the staircase. Matthew considered himself the family historian; he was fascinated by the photos of relatives with whom he shared a bloodline. His favorite, though still painful to look at, was the last photograph taken with Glen, his grandfather. The Polaroid photo was snapped by Helen, his grandmother. It showed Matthew at age-twelve, standing on the rear axle of his granddad's Farm-All tractor. Glen was dressed in his unofficial uniform of Dickies brand khaki work pants, with suspenders and a tucked-in white tee-shirt. Matthew's slender arm was wrapped halfway around his beloved grandfather's stocky neck. Matthew closed his eyes to recall the menthol smell of the Aqua Velva after-shave Glen splashed on each morning for Helen's benefit.

Matthew peered closer at the photo. Behind the tractor's black, rubber-coated steering wheel, their faces were filled with the obvious contentment of each other's love and trust. Each summer, Matthew would spend countless hours working with his gentle Granddad, weeding the vegetable garden and pruning and shaping the Christmas trees that always sold lightning fast at holiday time. He loved woodworking together in the shop, making frames for his artwork. They would sit together on the tractor and plow the fields, where occasionally Indian artifacts would be exposed like rare precious gifts on top of the dark, turned soil. They often went fishing at a nearby covered bridge. One colorful fall, Matthew sketched the structure from various perspectives, and later turned the drawings into Christmas gifts for his family. They enjoyed a bond that often exists between grandparents and grandchildren, where the pressure of raising the child correctly belongs to the child's parents and not to the earlier generation. Within their world of mutual acceptance, even the simplest mundane tasks were a pleasure. Each warm hazy summer day on the farm faded into countless moments of easy laughter and serenity.

Until the unbearable late August morning when Matthew was tenderly woken early by his mother, who told him that his Grandfather had died in his sleep. During the long painful weeks that followed, no amount of consoling would get Matthew out of his room. Finally, it took the start of the new school year and John's stern insistence to force Matthew to stuff the painful grief deep inside. The loss became the most defining moment in his young life and caused unstoppable heartache. Whatever faith Matthew had in God up to that point was completely shattered. He fully understood, in the days that followed, why his grandfather had lost his faith after the war. Matthew saw firsthand how unfair death could be, robbing people of their love and joy. How could there be a God? He felt abandoned and furious at the world, where reading and drawing alone in his room became the only distractions from the empty loss of his Granddad.

In the stairwell, Matthew reached out and lightly touched the picture of them with his fingertips. "Intracerebral Hemorrhage." He uttered the cold clinical words he would never forget. Matthew stepped down the remaining stairs and peered around the kitchen's rear entrance. His mother stood at the sink, dressed in a long pink bathrobe and her favorite pair of slippers. They concealed the painful bunions at the base of both of her big toes. She had always felt extremely embarrassed by the two angular bulges and often joked they were her giant, *"Paul Bunions."* Barbara rinsed each dinner plate that had soaked overnight, and stacked them on the wire rack to dry. She reached up to check on her extra-large curlers, then lowered both hands onto her neck to rub out the strain of the past week.

Matthew worried about his mother's health and the frequent

headaches that so often forced her to lie motionless for hours until they subsided. He encouraged her many times to get checked, but her response was always the same, *"don't be concerned my little lifeguard."*

What Matthew did not know, was that during the six-months prior to his being conceived, Barbara had seriously considered taking her life. Regardless of her love and concern for her first two children, she had become filled with an agonizing despair. She felt she had no other option. Barbara felt trapped in a loveless marriage, overwrought with regret for the choices she had made. She sought comfort in food and excessive sleep, and as her weight increased, so did the hurtful gossip at the church. Barbara tried the newly invented diet pills her doctor prescribed, but the medication only intensified her mood swings, which contributed to her deepening depression. Her concerned parents urged her to find renewed purpose in her role as mother and to make amends with John for the children's sake. Barbara finally agreed with her parents and decided to make the effort. One more attempt. She begrudgingly surrendered to the only matrimonial obligation her mother said, would restore harmony to the family.

To everyone's surprise, the unplanned pregnancy changed things completely for the better. Barbara saw it as an opportunity to start over and she regained her proper weight. Many church members witnessed the results, and saw the event as a spiritual renewal for both the Thomley family, and their church as well. John was thrilled with his wife's new outlook and was not shy in implying that he was the agent of change in the matter. Four-year-old Sarah sensed the positive changes in her mother, and could not wait to hold the new baby. When asked if he wanted a little brother or sister, a frowning three-year-old Buddy relied, *"I want a pony."* Despite Bud's equestrian desires, Matthew's birth went smoothly without complications. Barbara was overjoyed with her newest child and loved to kiss and coo over his perfect fingers and toes. Caring for her infant provided her with a new lifeline to happiness and purpose. The marriage survived, too, and Matthew became Barbara's priority. John was forced to accept the arrangement to keep peace in the family. Over the years that followed, Barbara still had brief relapses with depression and migraines, but never again contemplated suicide.

Matthew turned and retreated up the stairs. He wondered if his mother had the strength to be out in the real world without his help, a world vastly different than the small town in which she was raised.

Outside the parish house, Walter Pratt shut off the mower and wiped his forehead with a grass-stained handkerchief. The scent of freshly mowed clippings filled the now silent neighborhood, as the town's resident curmudgeon headed toward the church next door. Walter was more than pleased that the demanding minister and his family members (particularly the heavy one) would be gone for the entire summer. In fact, Walter had just shared that opinion with his friends at breakfast, downtown. No amount of weight loss would change that fat hippie kid. Walter was convinced that Bud was rotten to the core because he, himself, had caught the sneaky bastard stealing the church offerings last November, right out of the metal tackle-box hidden in the Pastor's office. Each customer at the large round table in the Chat-n-Chew Dinner had nodded their heads in agreement while Walter continued his caustic assessment of Reverend Thomley's fall from grace.

John stepped off the curb and taped the last of his handmade signs on the inside of the 1959 Rambler station wagon's rear window. Each of the three signs had large, bold lettering, which clearly stated the messages the Pastor wanted conveyed to everyone on the road. The sign on the rear driver's side window read: *"WE LOVE YOU!"* The one on the passenger rear side window announced: *"SEEKING THE TRUTH!"* And the largest sign, attached to the back window, encouraged travelers to: *"HONK FOR PEACE!"*

The tan and white station wagon had three suitcases under a large green canvas tied to the luggage rack on the roof. Matthew's small suitcase would be thrown into the way-back with him. The car's dashboard was completely overwhelmed with travel books, various maps, two packages of Fruit Stripe chewing gum, a bag of black licorice, sixteen semi-filled S&H Green Stamp booklets, and a tattered copy of *"The Prophet"* by Kahlil Gibran. The book had become overdue at the Portsmouth Library, but John had no intention of ever returning the dog-eared copy. The car looked to be in surprisingly good shape, considering its age, and had minimal rust on the body. Other than the dented right front fender, a result of Sarah's learning to drive, the newly decorated Rambler was ready to hit the road. Though hard to start of late, John felt confident that the car could make the entire trip if he kept a close eye on the fluids.

With dishes done and the refrigerator emptied of perishables, Barbara returned to her bedroom. She sat down at the vanity to remove her curlers and noticed Matthew in the mirror. He leaned on the door frame until his mother got up and opened her arms wide, inviting him over for a big hug. A hug both desperately needed. Matthew wrapped his long arms tightly around her. Barbara understood him better than anyone on earth and accepted all his sensitive quirks without judgment. She knew how deeply the loss of her father had affected him.

"Honey, do you remember Granddad's saying about hard times?" Matthew nodded reluctantly and continued to look down, still embarrassed by the pain he felt in missing him. Barbara noticed again how tall her youngest had grown but did not say anything about it. She looked up lovingly into his eyes. Matthew recited the phrase in a near murmur, as though each word physically hurt to let it out.

"The brook would lose its lovely song... if they took away the stones." Both hugged again and Matthew whispered in her ear, "I hate the stones." They giggled and stayed in a warm embrace until John's urgent voice ricocheted up the front stairwell.

"Let's go family! I've got places to see and people to meet!" The screen door slammed shut behind him.

Like most buildings and homes in New Hampshire, the packed high school gymnasium had no air-conditioning. The crowd relied on a few industrial fans near open doors to provide a cross-breeze. From their hard-wooden bleacher, Barbara and her sons had a good view of John on the stage, adorned in his minister's robe and white collar. Nearby, Sarah looked apprehensive on a folding metal chair with her gold braided honor cord and large Valedictorian medallion draped around her neck. She was squeezed in tight between the Principal and the School Superintendent, as if she were some invaluable gem, they both wanted to claim as their own. John sat on the Superintendent's left side, next to the Mayor, and waved to the few members of his congregation in the crowd who still appeared friendly enough to return a smile.

Matthew had on a white short-sleeve shirt with a colorful silk tie his father had lent him. His mother tied it for him, but it still extended well below his waist. He was extremely proud of his older sister. He felt nervous for her as well. What if she froze up and could not speak? The pressure he knew she was under filled Matthew with a queasiness he was not sure he could handle. Meanwhile, Bud, sat next to him in a triple-X dress shirt his mother had bought for the special occasion. Given the oppressive heat in the gym, he was happy his signature poncho was left in the car. Hungry again after a bountiful pancake breakfast, Bud now craved a smoke and an ice-cold drink.

Without warning, Barbara stood and addressed the two boys in a voice far more formal than needed. "Gentlemen, I'm going to locate the lady's room." She looked different to Matthew. Her eyes appeared more joyful and shiny with anticipation. For an instant, he felt hurt. He wondered why leaving him seemed to make her happier than she had been in years. Matthew let the feeling go as he watched her in high heels step down carefully on the steep blenchers. Once Barbara got to the gym floor, her pace quickened to the right until she disappeared.

"Does it bug you at all that our family is falling apart?" Matthew questioned Bud in a loud, uneasy voice.

"It ain't falling apart, Dink. And keep your voice down."

"Then why is she leaving us for the summer? I'm just saying-"

"You're just scared." Bud leaned in closer to his younger brother. "Look, Mom and Hal are just friends. They've got some stupid music act they'll do for the summer. It's no big deal." Bud rolled his program into a make-shift telescope, and used it to spot any cute chicks entering the bleachers across the gym. "Don't sweat it Matthew. She'll get it out of her system and be back when summer is over. So will Dad. It's not like he can do anything else but preach." The brothers exchanged a knowing smile. "And big-brain Sarah will be in college and I'll be so thin you won't even recognize me."

"Fat chance." Matthew stated under his breath.

"Good one." Bud grinned and re-directed his program telescope toward the stage to spy on their father. "You really afraid they're gonna' break up?"

"Yeah."

Matthew answered so softly Bud got concerned. He put down the program and faced his little brother. "Do you know something I don't?"

"Well... you weren't at the fire."

A long silent moment passed, and Matthew finally blurted out, "Sarah and I saw Mr. Dobson with his arm around Mom. She looked like we'd caught her doing something." Matthew took a deep breath in and let it out. "What if they're-"

"No way. He's bald."

"Look, I've got a bad feeling about this. About him," Matthew said.

"What do you want me to do? Break out of fat camp and drag her home?" Bud gazed down at the steps of the bleacher and recalled their mother's quick exit. "Besides, there's something you should know about mom that-"

Thump! Thump! Thump! The rarely cheerful high school Principal, with a fresh crewcut and the same pale blue suit he always wore, tapped on the microphone at the podium. His everyday sober voice sounded unusually upbeat. He did little to disguise the enthusiasm for his family's upcoming summer vacation at Rye Beach: Corn dogs, cold beer, and long naps on the sand.

"Welcome everyone to the graduation ceremony of the class of 1969." The audience clapped and cheered, while many of the underclassmen loudly stomped their feet on the wooden bleachers. The excitement of the moment surged through the graduating class on the gym floor as they rose from their folding chairs and chanted, "Seniors, Seniors, Seniors!"

Bud turned and hollered at his brother, "we'll talk later!"

Reverend Thomley's eloquent words got the ceremony underway with the religious tone expected for such an event. Many familiar with the Pastor were more than a little surprised how brief he'd been. As was always the case, the dry speeches from the other dignitaries extolled the importance of higher education in achieving life's goals. For some seniors in the audience, the day's diplomas would be their last.

Sarah's upbeat commencement address went quite well until the very end, when her focus strayed. She had been distracted by Malorie Wells, who had been engaged in a lively conversation with one of her friends seated nearby. Luckily, Sarah located Matthew in the stands, and he gestured toward the back corner of the gym floor. Their mother had just stepped out to make herself more visible. Sarah locked in on her mother's smiling eyes. She understood her mother's need to get away, if only for the summer, and knew a much-needed adventure might be the perfect remedy for her mother's sadness. A sadness that Sarah knew was her fault.

Barbara's loving expression immediately filled Sarah with all the confidence needed to continue. Barbara wished she could have stayed for the entire ceremony, but the plan was to keep gossip to a minimum. Meekly, the Pastor's wife used the cover of the steady applause to retreat through the gymnasium exit. At the door, she gave Matthew a small wave, who then nudged his brother to look as well. But in the split second it took for Matthew's eyes to return to the door, she was gone. His mother had just hurried outside and got into Hal Dobson's brand-new sports car.

Back on stage, the Principal began to call the student's last names alphabetically. Each graduate arrived at the podium with an earnest expression, while their parents suppressed the need to yell in celebration. Near the end of his list, the Principal proclaimed over the microphone, "and next, our school's very own Valedictorian, Sarah Ann Thomley!" The audience clapped, and the Superintendent handed Sarah's specially framed diploma to John on his return to the podium. "And her father, Reverend Thomley, will now present her diploma." The Principal relinquished the lectern, and John adjusted the microphone so he could look back toward Sarah.

"We put a lot of hard work into this, didn't we honey?" John returned the microphone and his attention back to the audience. He smiled broadly. "How many of you believe a commencement ceremony is the end? The end of high school?" Scattered hands shot up among the seated graduates on the gym floor. Numerous students applauded and cheered. "The truth is, *'to commence,'* is really meant to start something new. A new journey. A new adventure. You seniors are *'commencing'* on new paths and hopefully you'll have some exciting times along the way." John turned and glanced at his daughter. "Are you ready for an adventure, darling?" The minister returned to the crowd. "For us, all the effort was worth it. We now have three colleges offering full scholarships! Praise God from whom all blessings flow."

Courteous applause filled the gym while Reverend Thomley shook hands vigorously with the Principle, the Superintendent, and the Mayor. He returned to the podium. Obviously energized, John announced a little too loudly, "as a matter of fact, we're leaving right now to visit each and every campus!"

Sarah had not seen that coming. The shock overtook her quickly as her mind spun with basic logistical concerns. What about the photographs with the Mayor? The hugs of friends and congratulations from the faculty? Did her stupid, overbearing father have any idea of how serious this was? Today was supposed to be *her* day. Least of all, what about her five-dollar deposit on the return of her rented cap and gown? She searched out over the crowd for her mother's smiling face, but it wasn't there.

"Come on honey, we have to go," commanded John with a frantic wave of his hand. Sarah finally stood and trudged toward her father with the knowledge that most everything she had dreamed of for years had just slipped away. She limply took the framed diploma from her dad's hand as he leaned in to kiss her cheek. Instead, he whispered into her ear, "Smile at the nice folks and follow me." Before father and daughter left the stage, John located Bud's questioning face in the stands and gave him a quick head jerk in the direction of the exit. It occurred to John he had missed an opportunity and stepped back to the microphone. "Oh, I forgot to mention, my son Bud, the big guy there in the bleachers, will be attending a famous weight-loss camp this summer." The pride in John's voice lingered over the air waves of the public address system. Bewildered applause mixed with the occasional loud wise crack about Bud's weight followed. The positive tone of their father's announcement surprised both brothers. As they left the bleachers, Bud waved to those who had clapped and flipped off those few who had teased him. The three uncertain siblings followed their hard-charging father out the main door and to the front parking lot.

Sarah took off her gown near the car. Her confusion had already transformed into a simmering rage that didn't go unnoticed by her youngest brother.

"Gee, good thinking, Dad. We're gonna' beat the crowds... all that traffic and stuff." Matthew's kind effort to provide his sister with an explanation for the early departure did not work. He could tell she did not buy it, which left him at a loss for words. Sarah tossed her cap, robe, and framed diploma through the open rear side window of the station wagon. Once in the front passenger seat, she slammed the door, clinching her arms tight over her heaving chest and glaring straight ahead.

"Matthew, climb into the way back!" John ordered. "Bud, get in the back seat. We're leaving right now, and I don't want to hear another word!" The stern tone in their father's voice conveyed what each sibling had known from individual experience... pushing him any further would result in dire consequences. John got behind the wheel, started the engine after a few attempts, slammed down the gas pedal and surprisingly drove around to the rear of the school. He stomped on the brakes by the cafeteria's rear doors, put the car in park, and jumped out. He ran around to the passenger's side. "Sarah, get in back with Bud." John entered the school's kitchen still wearing his long minister's robe. Sarah had never seen her father quite so agitated, and did as she was told.

Within moments, John stormed out of the kitchen door with an army duffel bag on his shoulder, and his robe wadded in a tight bundle under his other arm. He quickly opened the car's rear door and threw everything onto Matthew's lap. His father was clearly flustered as he closed the bulky tailgate and rushed to the driver's door. Malorie Wells made her way out of the building and plunged excitingly into the front passenger's seat in tattered jean shorts and a newly purchased, tie-died halter-top. John glanced over the car's roof to search the empty delivery area for anyone who might have been watching. Though Malorie's elderly grandparents had approved the two-week tour of college campuses with John and his daughter, he strongly felt that the fewer people who knew, the better. Once behind the steering wheel, the excited Pastor yanked the white-collar tab from his shirt and tossed it onto the cluttered dashboard.

John stated firmly, "Not a word. Not a single word." The station wagon bolted forward without a soul in town witnessing their covert departure.

6

Hal Dobson's red Triumph Spitfire convertible cruised the highway much faster than Barbara felt was necessary. She worried that the yellow silk scarf over her hair should have been tied tighter, with the top down. Between the ceaseless wind-noise and Hal's frenzied voice, Barbara frowned, knowing one of her infamous migraines was stomping its hooves and ready to charge.

"This beauty has rack-and-pinion steering, and dual-carburetor, and hits 60-miles-per-hour in 12.5 seconds. What do you think of that?" Hal's gloved hands squeezed tightly around the small steering wheel.

"It's fast all right."

"Oh yeah, Barbie Girl!"

Hal adjusted the rear-view mirror to check on the status of Barbara's oversized suitcase. The mammoth bag would not fit in the trunk, and required being tied to the car's more decorative than functional luggage rack. He wished she had owned a small sleek Samsonite like he had in the trunk. Hal worried that the rack's meager chrome bars might not hold up under the weight and if the bag itself, with its straps, caused undue wind resistance. Then he noticed his image in the far-left corner of the mirror's reflection. He liked the way his dapper tweed cap kept his toupee securely in place. The sunglasses made him feel like a British secret agent, and he imagined nearing a heavily guarded Soviet checkpoint. "You know, if we had to stop suddenly, this latest model has larger brake calipers. Pretty cool, right?"

Barbara continued to search her new, extra-large leather purse for her make-up compact. She did not hear Hal's question. Oversized purses had become all the rage, and she just had to own one, although the bigger size made locating small things more difficult.

Hal assumed that Barbara hadn't heard him, and dropped the question. He had not felt this good in a very long time, and allowed himself the rare opportunity to gloat a bit. Not since his messy divorce was finalized a year earlier had he done much of anything to move on with his life. It only confirmed his ex-wife's opinion that Hal was an absolute bore and afraid to take chances. This summer he would let go and live it up. He tugged his cap down a smidgen and smiled at how his ex-wife would react if she could see him behind the wheel.

Earlier in the week, Barbara had told Hal about the summer repairs to the church and of the directive from church leadership. She also mentioned her own desire for a leave of absence from John and the kids. Hal was thrilled and wasted no time getting involved. He contacted a fellow musician from his college days who currently ran the entertainment department at the swanky Mendelson's Hotel in the Catskills Mountains. Hal hoped his old friend would know of a lounge somewhere in New York City, the Catskills, or perhaps the Pocono Mountains in Pennsylvania, in need of a small musical act. Instead, completely unexpectedly, Hal received a gracious invitation to audition for Mendelson's summer lounge job. Apparently, their regular guy had just been lured away by The Accord, another local resort. Hal saw this opportunity as a sign of fate. Though the gig would only involve weekday afternoons, it would still be a chance of a lifetime for Hal to perform again in public. He could not wait to nail the audition.

Mendelson's Hotel would certainly be packed with wealthy guests for the summer and perhaps some famous celebrities as well. He also read in the back of a travel magazine that the entire Catskills resort area had become a thriving hot spot for singles. He even saw ads that offered discreet swinging for couples. In Hal's mind, that was just frosting on the cake, though he failed to mention any of those details to the minister's wife. In fact, there were many things Hal had failed to address. Like how the scent of her perfume stayed on his suit's fabric for hours after sitting side-by-side at the piano. How he loved the beautiful pale skin of her slender hands. How aroused he became when their fingers accidentally touched the same keys. The man was smitten, and he knew it. Unfortunately for Hal, she did not feel at all the same way.

Hal drove on; his inner showman contemplated how fortunate it was that he and Barbara had ended each choir rehearsal with learning a new popular song. Since the church was not the appropriate location for belting out modern music, Hal's musical instrument store in downtown Portsmouth worked out perfectly. They drove to his shop after every choir rehearsal, and over the course of the past year, they had amassed an extensive repertory of current hits. *"I'll Never Fall in Love Again"* was Barbara's favorite solo, and he did a good job with the sexy tune, *"Lay Lady Lay."* When they sang songs together, their voices blended extremely well, and he knew that they were finally prepared for real exposure.

From her purse, Barbara removed the plastic, clear tube of orange Breck Concentrate Shampoo, her large can of Aqua-net hair spray, and a recently purchased bottle of UltraLucent Fluid makeup. She shoved her over-sized container of Anacin pain relief tablets aside and grinned. "Ah, here it is!" She removed the compact from the bottom of the vast purse, but found its lid would not click open. Though she hated doing it, Barbara used a long, polished pink fingernail to spread it apart. Only then did the black and white photograph, folded to fit inside, drop out. It nearly flew away before she nabbed it against her shoulder. It was a Thomley family Christmas photo from years earlier. It had been sent with their annual letter to every living relative and congregation member. Barbara flipped the photo over and recognized Matthew's neat handwriting: *"Don't forget us."* Barbara blamed the wind for the tears.

Inside the rear of the Thomley station wagon, on a stretch of Route 9 just south of Granite Lake, Matthew used Malorie's duffel bag as a backrest. He had placed it against his own suitcase and the cardboard box that held two cans of Quaker State Motor Oil and a bottle of brake fluid. He tried to draw on his sketchpad to take his mind off his mother's absence, but the car's bumpy ride made it nearly impossible to do so. Matthew crossed his long legs in the cramped space in the backseat and stared at the back of his father's head. He could tell from his dad's silent treatment that it was going to take a long time before Matthew's negligence would be forgiven. He had sincerely apologized numerous times for the fire, but it seemed to only make his father more upset... a consequence that Matthew had dealt with before. At age eleven, he informed his dad that he did not want to be an Acolyte any longer. He was done with lighting candles and wearing the silly white smock. John pointed out how embarrassing it would be for him, as the minister, for neither of his sons to participate in church activities. John stressed that people would gossip, so his quitting was out of the question. The fact was that Matthew was an introvert. Nothing at all like his outgoing father. Why couldn't his dad understand he simply did not crave attention and wasn't at all comfortable in front of large groups? Matthew stopped asking and agreed to be the dutiful son. He dressed in the billowy smock and assisted his father every Sunday morning for another year-and-a-half until he could not stand it any longer. He doubted his father ever forgave him.

Matthew removed his dad's long tie and unbuttoned his shirt's top button. He adjusted the lumpy duffel bag and leaned back. He decided it was probably best to stop apologizing for his mistake, and just allow Bud's brush with the law to distract from the disaster in the church. Matthew smiled. The idea of his brother's weight keeping Bud out of the Army and out of harm's way was truly ironic. Survival of the fittest was one thing, but survival of the fattest was going to take a while to prove.

Matthew's thoughts turned to Sarah and how she must be feeling about the pretty girl in the front seat. At times he could sense Sarah's stone-cold indignation behind the hardback novel she held at eye level. He put his head back and closed his eyes. His mind was filled with concern for what the future had in store for his family. How far was his dad planning to go with that Malorie person? Did their father really think his own kids had not noticed the new positive outlook? It had been only a month ago that John slept-in late every weekday, avoided most of his responsibilities at the church, and snapped even more at their mother. And while the trip overseas made John easier to get along with, Matthew knew it could all change instantly. He closed his eyes and tried to imagine his mother. Would she get the singing job? And where would she go if she did not? Would she just go home? Would her friendship with that creepy choir director grow deeper if they did get hired? Would it become more than just a friendship? He hoped not. Matthew knew he could probably ensure his father's faithfulness by staying close by and disrupting any of his dad's advances with Malorie. That was not the case with Hal and his mother. Matthew still could not understand her insistence on being apart for the summer. Didn't she understand they needed to stay together if their goal was to remain a family? Was he the only one worried about these things?

Matthew tried to gaze out of the left rear window of the station wagon where just enough space existed between the large "We Love You" sign and the vertical edge of the rear door. He wanted nothing more than to rid his mind of the dull pain of worry. He wished the meager view of the passing countryside were wider. That was ...until a blue semi-truck with billowing dark exhaust invaded Matthew's field of view. The driver's calico beard of red, gray, and brown revealed a toothless grin. He reached for the handle of the big rig's horn.

"I love you too, boy!" The trucker pulled on the air horn repeatedly as he passed, and its deafening sound blasted into every opened window of the Rambler. Matthew did not hear the actual words but certainly got the intended message and slouched even lower. He pulled his dad's black robe over his head and tried to disappear. John, on the other hand, happily waved his arm cheerfully out the window and returned three short toots of his own.

Bud had his head tilted back on the rear seat when the truck driver's antics suddenly woke him from a deep sleep. He felt himself slipping ever closer to his dark side, where mounting rage would not listen to reason. Then the realization him that fat camp looked damn good compared to this crazy road trip he was on. Bud felt hungry and wondered what kind of crappy low-calorie food they would force him to eat.

Sarah lowered her novel with the truck's passing, and the loud interruption only proved her theory that the idiotic signs her father placed in the car were an invitation for trouble. As was bringing that bubble-headed blonde seated in the front: Sarah's seat. It was crystal clear to her now what forced the early exit at the school and just how sneaky and premeditated her father's devious plan had been. She started to wonder if the visits to her colleges were going to happen at all or if it was just a convenient ploy in an even larger deception.

"My God I feel wonderful!" announced John, followed with numerous quick turns of the steering wheel. The car swayed from side to side. His kids loved that when they were young, but now three hateful snarls greeted him in the rear-view mirror. "Oh, come on now. We're on the open road, nothing but smooth sailing ahead. Except I can't hear very well." John rolled up his window. "We have plenty of gas." He smiled at Malorie. "Good company. Hey everyone, close your windows so we can all talk." Malorie cranked up her window while John resisted the temptation to lay his hand on her long tan leg. She sensed his longing and returned a slow flirty glance.

"Okay, that's it! Pull over, I'm out!" Screamed Sarah. "I can't take anymore!"

"Oh, for heaven's sake, you've been moody ever since the ceremony." In the rear-view mirror, Sarah witnessed her dad's blue eyes shift from her to Malorie. He winked. "Now let's just get along and enjoy this beautiful scenery."

"Scenery? All *I* see... is my little brother missing his mom and... the Cretin here, being sent to some stupid camp where he's bound to starve to death!"

"You wish," Bud broke in.

"Shut up, I'm not done!" Sarah yelled at her father. "I see you in a mid-life crisis... hellbent on balling a girl my own age! A classmate, no less."

"That's enough!" declared John. He swiftly pulled the car over to a sudden stop on the side of the road. "You can't talk to me like that. I'm your father."

"Well she's certainly not our mother!" Sarah took the thick novel she was reading and flung it toward John. The book's rigid cover caught the top of the seat back and fell to the floor at Bud's feet. John rammed the gear shift on the steering column into park and turned to face his unruly daughter.

"Now you look here young lady, if you think-"

"What did you expect Dad?" Bud piped up. "First, you screwed up her graduation-"

"Stay out of this, it doesn't concern you" John fired back.

"Yes, it does. Everything you do concerns me." His voice dropped in volume as he opened his window for some fresh air. He stared at the other side of the road. "But you're so full of shit you don't see it."

John Thomley turned off the engine. "I will not have you talking to me like that." He got out of the car and slammed his door.

Malorie pivoted in her seat and sounded off at Sarah. "See what you've started?" She turned back with a scowl and faced the windshield.

Sarah suddenly leaned forward, grabbed a handful of Malorie's golden locks, and pulled back with all her might. The maddening image of Malorie having been gossiping during her important address filled her mind's eye. She yanked even harder. Malorie's head rocketed backward over the top of the front seat.

"John! Help! They're gonna' kill me!" She pleaded hysterically.

John grasped the driver's door handle. Bud reached forward and pressed down the lock just in time. He locked his own door, and then rolled up the window and nearly caught his dad's fingertips. John bolted for the station wagon's rear door, only to find his youngest had already locked it. Matthew also secured both Sarah's and Malorie's doors by stretching forward along the right side of the car. He nearly got punched by both struggling girls on his way back. Meanwhile, the raging madman yanked unrelentingly at the rear door handle. The frightened teen pressed himself tight against the back of the rear seat. Despite the fear, he felt oddly powerful. Matthew thought perhaps he was finally getting courageous after all. He sat back with a smile and watched the family mutiny unfold.

Bud leaned awkwardly over the front seat and used his shoulders to shove his incensed sister and her victim to the right. His breathing became more labored as he reached forward to turn the ignition key. John continued to rant, and pounded loudly on the driver's side window. The chaotic situation caused Malorie's terrified screams to intensify in volume.

"Goddamn it son, open this door!" John's loud voiced added another layer of confusion. He didn't hear the car's starter grind repeatedly and fail.

Bud tried again and again with no success. The recognition that they were stranded washed over everyone at the same moment. Sarah released her death-grip on Malorie's hair. Matthew unlocked the rear door. Bud collapsed backward and tilted his throbbing head on top of the seat back. The exciting rush of adrenaline disappeared, and the sad realization that he wouldn't be leaving his father on the roadside filled Bud with hopelessness.

John tapped softy on the window. "All right son let me try. You just flooded it. It's okay; I'm not going to hurt you."

The temperature of the car's interior had climbed, and perspiration continued to pour from Bud's forehead. "I think it's the starter." He unlocked the driver's door and opened his own, then shuffled around the back of the Rambler to stay clear of his dad and continuing till he finally reached the front of the car. Bud opened the hood to search for anything in need of repair. Could there be a loose cable or a broken wire? If he had just paid more attention to the greasy teacher in his automotive shop instead of ditching class, he would know what to do. Bud was extremely disappointed with himself. He felt like crying.

After frequent attempts at turning the key without results, John joined Bud near the open hood. Meanwhile, Malorie had exited the car and walked a short distance along the wooded roadside. With each step, she rubbed feeling back into her scalp and wondered if she had made a huge mistake going on a trip with such a crazy family. She may have been raised by old feeble grandparents, but they had never tortured her.

Sarah and Matthew piled out of the car to find a level area of grass about ten feet from the pavement. They sat exhausted in the limited shade of a young tree. Sarah contemplated Bud's gallant attempt at defending her disappointment over graduation; she could not remember a time when he had actually stuck up for her like that. Their relationship had always been complicated… based on mutual survival in a home filled with tension. They also distrusted one another, aware of each other's weaknesses and how they made for perfect targets. Sarah mainly poked fun at her brother's weight until her own teenage body rebelled with wider hips and an appetite she couldn't curb. Over time, her jabs focused more on his failing grades, as he, in turn, ridiculed Sarah on her fuller figure. Their interaction relied entirely on abusive remarks, barely disguised as playful teasing. In fact, when Bud started wearing his Clint Eastwood poncho, Sarah was quick to point out that since he was neither *the good,'* nor *'the bad,'* he must be *'the ugly.'* Her brother did not let on how much that hurt but saying something would have required him to be vulnerable, and that did not fit his tough-guy persona.

"So where is the starter anyway?" inquired John, hunched over the mysterious engine.

"Beats me. I think it's…" Bud was about to say more when a distant low rumble caught his attention. He leaned out, around his father, and looked up the county road to locate its source. John bent farther over the left front fender and continued his inspection for anything in the motor that might have the word, *"STARTER"* inscribed on its top. Perhaps he just needed to tap on it with something hard to get it working again. He wondered if the glove compartment contained a tool he could use for that purpose.

Bud eyed a bright-colored shape of some kind approach on the hazy horizon. The heat of the blacktop caused the slow figure to appear like a strange glob of colorful wavering liquid. Suddenly, two additional images appeared over the hill's crest and magically join the first.

John quit his probe of the engine and turned to see his reckless son in the middle of the road, both hands above his eyes to block the sun. He was about to reprimand Bud on the lack of safety, but instead turned in the direction of whatever had captured his son's attention. John placed a hand across his own sweating brow and witnessed the same multicolored shapes oscillating down the hill. They eventually transformed into a caravan of three vividly painted vehicles. John mumbled, "Holy Christ... what the..."

When the lead bus came within forty yards of the car, its two front tires turned onto the dusty shoulder until the brakes squeaked to a complete stop. Someone honked the bus's horn five times, and John figured it was a friendly response to his *"Honk for Peace"* sign on the rear of the station wagon. It took a few moments more before the loud reverberating engine turned off, and for the two other vehicles to park in a single line behind the first. The roadside dust settled onto the cracked windshield of the lead bus. Combined with the sun's glare, the inhabitants were completely invisible to the Thomley family. A full minute of tense anticipation ticked by before the bus's side door finally opened. By then, Bud and his father had walked about half the distance between their car and the decorated vehicle.

It stood before them like an immense piece of wacky mobile art, crudely covered in thick coats of various colors of house paint. The front fenders were navy blue and painted with white flower petals, each with jagged ends that burst out from the rims of the rusted headlights. Green painted stems extended down from the lights, with leaves that curled around each fender. The stems ran wildly across the bus's vast, peeling, violet-colored hood. The vine-like stems continued down the silver-painted grill and toward an actual ceramic clay pot. It was stuffed with plastic white daisies. The large pot was secured with numerous strands of rusted wire onto the red bumper, dented from many years of service to the Marion County Public School District.

The vehicle's roof was painted a sky-blue. Faded, puffy clouds scattered across the top of the bus, and flowed over the rounded front above the windshield. There, in black lettering on a white rectangle background, appeared the words:

"NEW HARVEST FARM"

The door of the lead bus folded open like a massive psychedelic phone booth. Custom made, size-15 leather moccasins, laced up in front to just below the knees of their owner, emerged from the bus's door. They landed flat on the road's shoulder. Dust fragments floated up from the soles, past the faded blue-jeans with assorted suede patches and stopped just shy of a green velvet vest. Shirtless, the young man's face had a long, reddish-brown beard. The two long eagle feathers stuck in the top-hat's headband exaggerated the owner's height of six-foot-five.

"Hey gang. I'm Tower."

Bud snorted a laugh and John squeezed his impulsive son's neck.

"Yeah, I get that a lot." The good Samaritan grinned. "And don't bother to ask if the weather is fine up here. It is." He pointed at the car. "So, you folks need a jump?"

Bud spoke up. "It's more than the battery. I'm pretty sure…"

"That's okay son, I'll handle this."

"I was just gonna' say…"

"Enough." John stepped forward with a taut smile to shake the strange giant's hand. "I'm Reverend Thomley. I'd welcome your help if you can spare the time." The minister took a half-step back. This was his first interaction with a real certified hippie, and he wasn't entirely sure how to act.

Tower gave Bud a friendly wink of acknowledgment and reached out to engulf the minister's small smooth hand with his own enormous calloused one. He instantly switched from the conventional handshake into the more modern thumb grasp. John went with the change, but appeared a bit confused. He had never shaken hands like this with anyone.

"A Reverend… that's far-out." Tower sensed his confusion and pulled John in for a bear hug.

By then Matthew had walked over to join the group. Sarah stayed on the grass. She wanted her little brother to take part in the male camaraderie without the presence of her own ever-growing resentment toward their selfish father. Sarah hoped the delay would soon be over, and the peculiar man with the top-hat would get the car started. It was bad enough that her father hadn't outlined the travel plans with her, but now it was anyone's guess when they would actually arrive at the first college. Sarah laid back on the ground and placed her bent forearm over her weary eyes. She regretted losing her temper and pulling Malorie's hair. Confronting people had never been her approach to solving problems and she had always prided herself on keeping a check on her emotions. She relied on logic and reason to stay above the fray. Sarah's thoughts turned to the itinerary she had implemented for the Holy Land. It had been detailed, complete, and successful. It was followed by everyone, with no questions asked. This afternoon her dad had once again shown his obvious stupidity by not requesting that she do the same for this equally, if not more so, important journey.

Tower placed his massive hat onto Matthew's head, only to have it slip down and rest on the end of Matthew's nose. He returned the hat with a smile. Tower placed it on top his own thick, tumble-bush head of hair, then joined Bud under the car's hood to begin the process of diagnosing the problem.

John turned to face Matty, only to find his youngest son stood stiff; the boy's gaze transfixed on the front of the bus. A young mother had appeared with a hungry infant clamped onto her ample bare breast. She waved back with a confident smile and sat down on the front bumper near the pot of fake flowers. The wide-eyed Pastor returned the wave nervously, then succeeded in spinning Matthew back toward the protection of the family station-wagon.

Tower had just closed the hood with a bang when Malorie strolled back to the car. Not to be left out, Sarah wasted no time in getting up on her feet and joining the roadside conference. They both wanted to know the vehicle's status, but more importantly, both needed to find out who the strange tall hippie in the funny hat was.

"I agree with your son. This dinosaur is dead. Extinct. Kaput."

John stepped forward. "Can I impose again and ask you to stop at the next service station? Tell them we need a tow."

"I'll do ya one better, man. We own our own tow-truck. It's really old but it still works. We also have a mechanic back at the farm. Well, not a real mechanic, mechanic, but he knows enough to keep these old heaps running. I'm sure he could get yours going again." Tower quickly raised and lowered his eyebrows and pretended to flick an imaginary cigar of its ashes. With a Groucho voice, he leaned toward John and gestured in the direction of Malorie and Sarah. "And these out-of-sight chicks must be your daughters?"

7

Tower studied the vibrating reflection of the empty road in the bus's side mirror and determined it was safe to pull out. He glanced over to confirm there was plenty of room to clear the station wagon. As the bus eased past, Tower pulled back on the lever of the fold-away door. "Tow-truck is on the way boys!"

Bud, in a sour mood, returned a tired peace sign while Matthew waved excitingly with both hands. John and Malorie made themselves comfortable in the first bus, followed by Sarah in the second. Prior to boarding, Sarah pleaded with her father to consider the boy's safety. She grew incredulous when he insisted that she was being silly and that her brothers would be fine. He felt certain there was no need to worry and told her to simply take the advice the tall easygoing man had already given her. *"Just go with the flow, babe."*

Tower's kind offer to dispatch their tow-truck when they returned to the farm was wholeheartedly welcomed by John. It was followed with an invitation to stay there for free while the automobile was repaired.

Except for new parts, it would not cost John a red cent. Perhaps more valuable in John's mind was the unique opportunity to visit an actual hippie commune and explore their spiritual beliefs.

"Dad's a moron" announced Matthew from his perch on the hood. A silver Corvette slowed down to read the *"Honk for Peace,"* sign and blasted its horn as it passed by. Matthew waved at the driver and continued. "There's only one box of graham crackers, one can of fruit cocktail, and some packets of that Carnation Instant Breakfast stuff. We have no milk, so how does he expect us to make that?" Matthew unrolled the first of two paper bags Tower's wife had given them. "I guess we're forced to eat whatever…" Matthew had barely reached into the bag when the flap of wax paper inside opened. The pungent aroma of aged goat cheese sandwiches overwhelmed them both.

"Christ... what the…" exclaimed Bud and reached over the car's right front fender. "Here, hand me that shit." Bud threw the two cheese and alfalfa sprouts grenades far off into the tall roadside grass. "What's in the other bag?"

Matthew held his breath and timidly removed a simple loaf of bread. "Smells okay. Here, you try."

Bud tore away a large hunk from one end and then grinned through a mouth bursting with crust. "It's all brown inside too. But tastes good." He handed the strange-looking loaf back to his brother and made his way around the car to open the rear door. Bud crawled in and removed the two signs from the side windows, followed with the third on the rear door. He rolled them all into a tight cylinder of resentment, then folded that four times into a compressed wad and tossed it into the woods. Still chewing, Bud sat down on the front passenger's side with his feet flat on the ground. He leaned completely back onto the bench seat. It was cooler inside the car, and he felt better now that his father's stupid signs were off the station wagon. The rarely traveled stretch of road, with its wooden telephone poles and sagging wires overhead, lacked buildings and billboards. With nothing really to look at, Bud figured a nap would help pass the time.

Matthew hopped off the hood and lay in the back seat with one foot propped up on the opened door's armrest. He enjoyed this time alone with his brother, and his thoughts drifted to happier days when they had been close as kids. They would often explore the fields behind the parsonage and fish for bluegills at the nearby park. Sometimes they simply climbed trees by the post office. With cap guns in hand, they would often play Sheriff and Outlaw inside the scary dark church (until the time Barbara discovered Bud about to hang Matthew from the balcony railing). To his credit, the Ace Bandage would have certainly stretched the moment Bud kicked the folding chair out from under his seven-year-old brother. Then in his early teens, Bud outgrew their friendship and their fun adventures ceased. Without any warning, he started hanging around with boys his own age, like the three Morris brothers who lived in a rundown trailer by the cemetery. Though little Matty tried to tag along, he was often left behind. That was the first summer Matthew spent every day with his grandfather.

"Any left?"

Bud's voice startled Matthew, and it snapped him back to the present moment. He raised what remained of the tattered loaf above the seat and his big brother snatched it away.

"I thought you were sleeping" Matthew said and crossed his legs. He was still very hungry, but knew that Bud wanted the rest of the loaf for himself. "Hey, was I breastfed?"

"How the hell should I know?"

"Most likely not. Although it's an excellent example of the Natural Order of..."

"Not today Matty. Hey, hand me the jug."

Matthew sat up and reached over the rear seat into the way back of the station wagon. He found the handle of the plaid metal Coleman container. Matthew's mouth encircled the nozzle and pressed the button to allow the ice-cold cherry Kool-Aid to wash down the taste of the bread. "I'm waiting..." stated Bud.

Matthew wiped his mouth and extended the new cooler to his brother. "At least Dad bought this. I told Mom to buy one for her trip too but she-"

"Always the Mama's boy." Bud held the nozzle six inches above his opened mouth and a stream of bright red fluid arched flawlessly into the target.

Matthew struggled with a good comeback. "Yeah, well, it's ah, better than a… nobody's boy."

"What the hell does that mean?" Bud shot back.

"Well, you haven't exactly made it easy for them. Like taking down Dad's signs just now. Not to mention your failing grades and-"

"Oh, like you should talk. Practically burning down the church." Bud placed the jug on the floor mat and snickered. "I heard the guy's *"Blazer"* didn't help the situation."

"So funny." Matthew decided to take the argument up a notch. "Yeah well ...did you know even grandpa thought you were a lost cause?" Matthew giggled.

"When did he say that?"

"It was a few years ago. We were talking about you. You were in trouble again at school or something. And all of a sudden, grandpa picked up the morning paper and delicately tore the middle of the front page all the way down in a straight line. Not on the fold. Down the middle. He said, *"This is what most regular folk are like. They follow the rules, get along, and stay the course. But your brother is more like this."* He turned the second page sideways and tore a jagged line. No matter how many times he tried, he could not make a straight tear. He said, *"Bud will always go his own crooked path, and there's not much anyone can do about it."* So, what do you think of that?"

After a long pause Bud spoke with pride. "Sounds about right."

"I suppose." Matthew leaned forward and peered over the front seat. "Are you worried about this summer?"

Bud popped the last small bit of bread into his mouth and mumbled, "naw, I'll survive."

Matthew decided to finally say the words he'd held tight for years. "Ah, no offense, but I always figured with Dad, if I just did the opposite of you, I'd be fine. You know, don't talk back, get good grades and stuff. Stay in line."

"That's smart." Bud smiled slightly. "As usual."

"Why don't you study? You're plenty intelligent but ...you never seem to try." Matthew's eye's brightened with a vivid memory. "Remember that time our homework wasn't done by dinner? Dad grabbed your thick math book. Smacked your head hard with it? I was so scared, I thought I was going to be next."

"Naw, he's never gonna hit you, Matty." Bud removed the folded map from the dashboard and opened it across his chest. "He loves you, hates me. It's pretty simple."

Matthew sat back. "What if you just tried harder? You know, in school."

"That ship has sailed, little brother." Nearly a minute elapsed before Bud spoke again in a murmur. "Teachers don't explain a thing. Kids teased me about being fat. Or for flunking. I'd beat them up and get expelled... then fall behind with schoolwork even more. Did the old man ever step in? Hell no! All he does is put more pressure on me. To make it harder. I've never been good enough in his eyes!" Short of breath, Bud stopped for a few moments. "And did ya see the way he treated me when the hippie guy talked? That guy spoke to me *first*! Ah fuck it." Bud's eyes had a hard time reading the map, so he wiped them quickly. He ran his index finger along the map's blue line of highway. "Besides, why should I make it easier for them?" Bud sat up with effort and glanced toward the roadside's thick forest of trees. Further in, each trunk of coarse bark seemed to get closer to the one next to it. Just one impenetrable black wall of timber. With a mood just as dark, he laid back down and whispered faintly. "They're all fuckin' liars anyway."

Matthew leaned forward again. "What? I can't hear you."

Bud faced his brother. "Matty, I've gotta' tell you something."

"Let me guess. You're Mom's and Mr. Dobson's love child."

Bud gave his brother a stern glance. "I'm serious here so shut up and listen." He tried to gather the map along the folds but could not; he stuffed it back onto the littered dashboard. He struggled to reach into the left front pocket of his jeans and finally removed a Zippo lighter. "A while ago Mom told me some things." With effort, he slid off the front seat and the vehicle adjusted for the shift in weight. Bud untied the canvas on the car's luggage rack and pulled the handle of his suitcase until a final hard yank freed it up. He carried it to the front hood and opened it wide. Bud was out of breath, but with some effort, raised his voice so that Matthew could hear him from inside the car. "I kinda' promised her I... wouldn't tell you this, but, well, it's time, I guess.

Matthew got out of the back seat and joined his brother near the side of the car. With a slight panic in his voice, "what? Tell me what?"

Bud's smile became a smirk. "For a kid who knows everything, you really don't know shit." His laugh got whisked away with another tailwind of a passing car. Bud smiled. With their father's signs gone, there was no honk. Matthew felt a chill come over him. He thought perhaps it was the car's cool draft. Or he sensed his uncomplicated view of the world was about to be shattered. Bud's voice got louder. "Good old' Dad. You know, *"Mr. Do as I say, not as I do."* What an asshole." He removed a pack of unfiltered Camel cigarettes from the suitcase. Bud knew his secret addiction to smoking had reached the point of no return. "So, you ready to grow up little brother?"

"Come off it already!"

Click. Bud lit up. He grinned with a sudden idea and filled his lungs with smoke. He placed the cigarette lengthwise along the crack between the car's hood and the fender. Bud interlocked his fingers and brought his palms together. He steepled his two index fingers, then blew the smoke into his clinched hands. "Here's the church. Here's the steeple." He turned his hands towards Matthew. "Open the doors and see all the choking people." His thumbs opened to reveal his dancing digits in a haze of thick smoke. Bud laughed out loud until his own coughing took over.

Matthew tried not to laugh but finally did. "Can you get on with it?"

Bud picked up the cigarette and took another drag. "Well Matty-boy, this whole thing goes back-a-ways. Way, way, back." Bud returned the pack of cigarettes to his shirt pocket, then latched his suitcase and placed it on the ground. At first, he slid onto the hood in short stages to minimize any dents. Then the front shocks surrendered to his weight. "Screw it!" He arrived at his destination with a wake of indentions on the surface of the hood and rested his back against the warm windshield. Bud took another long inhale. Shrugged his shoulders as if to say, *"Oh well."*

"You've heard Dad talk about the house he grew up in? The one that-"

"Sure. Burned to the ground. He was in high school" Matthew replied. "Yeah, I've heard it a bunch of times." Matthew wanted to climb onto the hood and join his big bear of a brother, but the cigarette smoke hurt his eyes. "So, what's your point?"

"Well, there's more to the story. What Dad didn't say was that he and mom were dating in those days." Bud took another slow pull on his smoke. "After the fire that night, Dad's folks got a small hotel room just for themselves. Truth is, his parents were fairly sure that Dad had left something cooking on the stove. His old man blamed him for the fire and was very pissed off." Bud shifted onto his side and looked directly at Matthew. "But here's the kicker. Guess where Dad slept that night? Right on the sofa in Mom's living room." Another inhale on his smoke. "Anyway, between the excitement of the fire and all, Mom's parents fell right back to sleep. Everyone was out cold except for... Mom. So, she decides to sneak downstairs and crawl in with Dad."

Matthew's eyes opened wide. He blinked repeatedly to process the new information.

"They did the dirty deed right there on the couch! And nine months later our smart-ass sister pops out." Bud laughed heartily and rolled the Camel between his fingers. He gazed at the thin red line near the growing ash. He took another drag. "Christ, a fire. Go figure." Bud's exhale carried the shadowy fumes up into his nostrils. "Anyway, Mom told Sarah all this about two years ago so Sarah wouldn't make the same stupid mistake she had. Like who would want to screw our sister? The Owl Queen. Who... who?" Bud's impersonation made him snicker. The cigarette returned to his lips and dangled as he spoke. "Of course, old serious Sarah hears all this and figures she's a mistake. Wasn't planned for, or shit, even wanted." Matthew stared past his brother with distant eyes. "So little brother, don't you get it? They had to get married. Bet it changed their plans for the future, big time." Bud leaned back against the windshield. "His folks must have been so ticked off. Hers too." He swept his open hand in an arch, from left to right. "Today's headline... 'YOUNG MINISTER GETS FARM GIRL KNOCKED UP!'"

Dazed, Matthew leaned down against the car's hood. Placed his forehead on folded arms. His voice carried a faint word. "Why?"

"Horny, I guess." Bud flicked his cigarette butt onto the road.

"No, not that! Why did Mom tell you?"

Bud put his head back and closed his eyes. "Sarah started acting weird. Kept hinting she knew some big bad secret. She wouldn't say what. So finally, I forced Mom to tell me what the hell was going."

"Why didn't she tell me all this... stuff?"

"Crap Matty, let's face it. You don't handle change so good."

"Well. I don't handle change so well." Matthew's eyes moistened.

Bud turned and faced Matthew. "Exactly!" Bud savored the moment of being right until he saw Matthew's troubled expression. He had not expected to see so much anguish in his brother's hazel eyes.

"Why are you telling me now? I mean, I can't-"

"Cause maybe Mom and Dad aren't right for each other. Don't you see, man? They had to get hitched. Chances are they weren't even in love back then. They sure as shit ain't now." Bud put his head back and closed his eyes again. "Maybe we were mistakes too. Maybe they're just waiting for *you* to get old enough." Bud paused. "You know, so they can finally get divorced." Bud's tone lightened up and he smiled. "Hell Matty, maybe it's NOOT."

Matthew was not amused. "Is Dad going to... cheat... with that Malorie girl?"

"Christ, I hope not. She'd be nuts to get it on with an old married man." Bud craved another smoke but decided against it. "Come on Matty, would it really matter if they got divorced? They're both miserable."

Matthew's temples throbbed. He had to lie down or possibly throw up. He made his way to the car's backseat and piled in. Bud rolled noisily off the hood and grabbed his suitcase again. He located a hidden Baby Ruth candy bar in his luggage. Tore open its wrapper. Then leaned into the car and peered over the front seat to check on Matthew.

"You look beat little brother. Here, have this." Bud spoke with a tenderness he rarely expressed. Matthew refused the candy bar. "Hey, why don't you take a nap, Matty? You're gonna' be okay. Just forget things for a while. I'll wake you when the tow truck gets here."

Matthew placed his head on the rear seat and brought his knees up toward his chest. He needed to get small and tight. He thought about Sarah and how painful it must have been for her to hear the news. For her to wonder if she had been genuinely wanted. Or, if they resented her, for always reminding them of what had happened. Matthew agreed with his brother; their parents may not have wanted them as well. He wrapped his arms around his bent legs. Smaller. Get compact. Despite what his mother had always said about him, Matthew worried he was just a mistake too. Within a few moments, his troubled mind relinquished its ability to stay awake.

Bud devoured most of the candy bar as he sat sideways on the front passenger's seat. His wide feet were flat on the roadside shoulder. He leaned to his left, and gently retrieved the unfolded map to figure out which direction would be best if he hitched a ride. He, like both Matthew and Sarah, had received a cash gift of fifty dollars from their grandmother, Ruth. She told them all to enjoy the *"mad money,"* and their summer away from home. Bud tossed the last bite of the candy bar into his mouth. His grandmother's generous gift of cash would come in handy up to a point, but there certainly was not enough to make a run to Canada, let alone Mexico. He realized too, that going back to the parsonage was really the only option that made sense. He would have the house all to himself. A friend could shop for his cigarettes and food. It would be lonely, but a hell-of-a-lot better than being a prisoner of a fat camp. The issue of not attending the camp would no doubt come back to haunt him, but he figured he would burn that bridge when he got to it (fires being a family tradition now). Bud smiled. Hopefully, old man Pratt, the church janitor, would keep to himself. Hopefully, he would never see Bud hunkering down in the parsonage. Of course, all this meant leaving his little brother behind, and that was a concern. Bud saw Matthew as not just the baby of the family. Matthew *was* a baby. A pussy. He had no skills in self-defense and wasn't at all brave. Matty had always been treated special for his artistic talent. His sensitivity. But Bud considered those as disadvantages in the real world. He worried that his little weakling brother wouldn't know what to do if he got into a dangerous situation. Sure, Matt's clever sense of humor would be helpful at first. But at some point, the charming jokes would fail, and his brother's sensitive side would be taken advantage of. He'd be hurt. Maybe even killed. The weak always got thinned out of the herd, as Matty often declared.

"Shit!" Bud muttered to himself so as not to wake his little brother. He imagined all sorts of gruesome outcomes if he left Matty behind. Many were based on horror stories that he and his buddies would tell each other around their illegal campfires. Tales of bloody slaughter in vehicles stuck in the woods. Where a sharp hook scratched the paint along the side of the car. When all sorts of evil tricks would tease the frightened victims inside the automobile until their merciless fates unfolded.

Bud withdrew the one coveted joint hidden in his pack of Camels. He absolutely loved getting high for the way it made his worries fade away with each hearty toke. The thick doobie in his hand had been a last minute going-away-gift from one of his few friends in school. His pal had warned Bud that the new weed was strong as shit, and to be careful. He called it, *"Acapulco Gold."* Bud had no idea what an Acapulco was and thought it was a stupid name. He lit up anyway and laid back on the seat.

Closed his eyes and inhaled deeply. Soon, gray billows escaped upward from the car like urgent smoke signals, warning of the difficult days ahead.

In the lead bus, John was seated next to Malorie on a tattered sofa without legs. He declared with a loud voice of genuine delight, "I'm as happy as a clam at high tide!" For the past twenty-minutes, John had informed Tower and his wife, Serene, of the amazing events of the last few weeks. Included, were the highlights of the Holy Land adventure and the exciting details of his heroic leadership during the dangerous church fire.

Malorie found her attention swayed by Serene, who sat behind the driver's seat directly across from her. As the young hippie-girl continued to nurse in plain sight, she made a pantomimed invitation toward Malorie to hold the baby. "I've never held one." Malorie cautiously made her way across the floor of the jostling bus with apprehension and a smile of uncertainty.

"Tell ya' what, Ebb is back there in the crib." Serene pointed toward the rear of the bus. "Just pick him up and support his head with your hand. Then we'll switch because he hasn't eaten yet." John looked surprised and held up two fingers. Serene nodded yes with a warm smile. Malorie returned nervously with a sleepy blond boy bundled in a soft handmade quilt. She gently sat down next to the barefoot mother.

Serene appeared to John as being around twenty-three years old or so, boarder-line pretty because of the lack of makeup and her brown hair was badly in need of a shampoo. Her long-braided pigtails were tied off at the ends with thin leather string and beads. Her feet were callused and dirty, so John assumed she wasn't much for wearing shoes. In contrast, Serene appeared to Malorie as simply lovely. Someone who radiated with the joy of having her beautiful twin babies in her life.

"Just lay Ebb here, that's good. Now put your hand under Flow's head, perfect." She had to chuckle at Malorie's tentative movements. "Malorie you're a natural at this. You just need a little practice, that's all. Better be careful John."

"What's that?" John replied. The two delighted young women laughed and waved him off. They sat side-by-side and giggled away at the healthy babies. John smiled uncomfortably and stood to take a closer look around the vehicle's custom interior. The inside of the bus was noticeably dirty but overall, it was just as impressive as its multicolor skin. Every square inch seemed designed to serve a function. Beautiful tapestries from India draped overhead across the ceiling and hid the pink fiberglass insulation glued against the roof. The colorful pieces of fabric traveled down to where they ended neatly behind black cotton netting secured to the walls. The netting held everything from pots and pans to fresh oranges and books. Numerous wooden shelves with railings held a dozen or more Mason jars filled with nuts, seeds, brown sugar, beans and assorted grains. Planks of weathered barn-wood siding ran the length of the bus's interior. Midway in the bus's front section, the wood siding supported a table with three large brass hinges. John assumed it could be folded down when not in use. The small cast-iron, potbelly stove, with its soot-covered chimney pipe connected to the roof, was bolted to the floor along a wall, which separated the living room area from the bedroom in the rear. John lightly parted the tie-dyed curtain and took a quick peek at the tall platform bed. He noticed the handmade, built-in drawers underneath. He released the curtain with the realization that someone in the group knew how to work with wood, and had certainly planned the design well ahead of the construction. John thought for a moment about his own lack of skill with hand-tools, and wondered why he hadn't inherited any of his father's natural abilities. It had always bothered him that Barbara knew more about tools and home repair than he did. He often had to suppress strong feelings of insecurity around her because she had grown up on a farm, and knew how to work with nearly any tool.

John raked his hand through his thick hair and decided it would be better to bring his attention back to the present. His throat was dry from speaking over the loud rattling of the bus, and he needed to find something cool to drink. John noticed again how extremely dirty the floor was. Clumps of dried mud everywhere looked like small islands among a sea of empty sunflower-seed shells. Old breadcrumbs, pine needles, and twigs were captured deep in the dozen or so shag carpet samples that ran the length of the bus. John assumed their dark spots were wine stains because of the numerous empty wine bottles scattered along the shelves and ledges. Nearly every bottle had a candle of various length and color on the top. Abundant wax had melted down along many of the wine bottles, and their wicker wrapped baskets held layer upon layer of wax. John took a closer look around and noticed that a gray grime clung onto every surface. He disliked how dirty and unkempt the bus appeared and hoped the accommodations at the commune would be cleaner. John noticed the kerosene lamps, each with a round reflector behind its fluted glass. They sat on their own wooden shelves, secured with stained leather straps. There was no doubt the soot-covered lamps contributed to the interior's oily sheen. He imagined how each must have had provided hours of glowing warmth for night-time nursing.

The vivid image of Serene breast-feeding popped back into John's mind, along with her earlier statement regarding Malorie and motherhood. He had pretended not to hear the comment because the subject caused a definite pang of panic in him. John had absolutely no intention of their seemingly mutual attraction going anywhere near marriage. Certainly not in the making of a baby. Granted, his relationship with Barbara was falling apart... had been for years. But the last thing he wanted was to start over with someone new, let alone a person young enough to be his daughter. On the other hand, he did enjoy the attention of a beautiful woman. He liked the look of approval he received from Tower when Malorie was introduced to Serene as John's *"close"* friend. John certainly felt younger with Malorie at his side. He enjoyed the way she hung on his every word, as she did on those long flights overseas. Her willingness to learn from his vast experience and knowledge. Something Barbara had certainly discounted long ago.

John continued his self-guided tour. He realized the upcoming journey may be his last chance to truly live for the moment. To try anything and everything new that came his way. If a sexual relationship developed with the young women, should he just let it happen? Maybe. Provided no one got hurt or expected more to come from it? John smiled. They had already kissed passionately in the dark hallway of the hotel in Cairo. Her young firm body felt amazing in his arms. When her full lips parted with his, the sudden awareness that he had not kissed a woman other than his wife of eighteen-years only increased the excitement. John could not help but imagine how incredible it would be to take things further with Malorie.

By now, John's thirst had gotten quite distracting, so he lifted the lid to the dented metal cooler under the table. Melted ice-water kept a dozen or so rounded cubes bobbing on the surface. A lone bottle of RC Cola swam among three bottles of beer. Always the teetotaler, John grabbed the soda out of habit, and then dropped it. The minister removed a beer, and thought about the numerous dinner parties in the past where he would politely deny any alcohol. *"Lips that touch liquor will never touch mine,"* John would declare. That phrase never failed to get a good laugh at social events. He used the rusted bottle opener that was built-into the end of the cooler. He took a tentative swig. Cold and refreshing. John was surprised by how much he liked the flavor and gulped down half the bottle. He leaned back and noticed on the tabletop near him an oversized magazine. The cover showed part of the moon in the lower left corner with the blue earth floating in space above it. The title, *"Whole Earth Catalog"* was printed in a white font at the top of the $4.00 Spring publication with the smaller subtitle, *"access to tools."* John picked it up and thumbed through it. Articles ranged from new building techniques and tying knots to guitar making, camping, and self-hypnosis. Most had black and white illustrations and directions. He skipped over many topics that appeared too complicated, like mathematical snapshots and a detailed advertisement for a Volkswagen technical manual. John had never seen, in his life, such a hodgepodge of information in one magazine.

The advertisement for the manual triggered a concern for getting back on the road himself. The plan had always been to visit Keene State College for just an afternoon and spend the night in an inexpensive motel near the campus. He and Bud would be in one bed, and the girls in another, with Matthew on a couch or the floor in a sleeping bag. It so happened that Keene State College's mascot was the owl, and Sarah thought that had to be a sign. John considered it to be a fine liberal arts school, but not his first choice for his daughter's continuing education.

Next, they would drive south towards Amherst. Along the way, they would drop Bud off at his camp. John smiled. It would be nice to finally have his demanding son squared away for the summer. Sarah loved the idea of attending Amherst College in the hometown of her favorite author, Emily Dickinson. It had an excellent English Department, but John did not think its large size would be the best environment for his reserved daughter. He had a difficult time understanding her fixation with literature and her unwillingness to study something important like theology, as he had. The United Methodist Church had allowed full clergy rights to women years ago, so that door was open. But Sarah was not interested in being a minister. Given her trepidation of public speaking, and lacking her parent's gift for singing hymns, John decided it was best not to push her in that direction.

John had always been extremely close to his only daughter, but it seemed she had pulled away from him over the last few years. He assumed that it was her teenage hormones at work. Of late, though, she barely spoke to him unless John started the conversation. Even then, it was filled with so much tension, that in some ways, she reminded him more of her guarded brother than of his sweet amicable daughter. John thought about the oldest son with whom he had never felt a close bond. A colicky baby, Buddy made evenings nearly impossible for anyone to sleep. That stressful experience went on for more than eight months, and toward the end, it nearly brought John and Barbara's marriage to the breaking point. Even the members of John's golf foursome could see how the little tike was affecting John's game. One sunny afternoon on the 18th hole, they presented him with a miniature set of red leather boxing gloves for his combative son. John shared in the laugh, but as time went by, the appropriateness of their gift hit home, for the fight was on. His second child seemed to always be getting into trouble, and in need of more and more discipline. When Bud reached his early teens, John felt strongly that his son was squandering his potential and was not working hard enough to improve himself. John stressed the importance of getting good grades like Sarah, and Bud's future depended on it. The minister so wanted his son to be successful and accomplish more in life than he had. But the harder John pushed, the less Bud tried. Despite John's repeated scolding and harsh punishments, nothing worked. The hostility between them only intensified with each angry confrontation. John admitted that there were occasions when he had been too tough on Bud and not stern enough at other times. Being a father had not come easily. He was himself an only child and had barely known his own dad. So how was he to parent such a troubled kid? John took another swig of beer and thought about Bud's immediate future. Despite the *"Guarantee of Satisfaction"* on the camp's color brochure, he wasn't convinced that a summer of limited calories and strenuous physical activities would really make any difference in Bud's behavior. At this point, John honestly did not care anymore. He recalled a phrase he recently came across in his reading. "Hate isn't the opposite of love, it's ambivalence." John agreed with the statement despite the guilt he felt. He had to admit, it was just easier to have his dependable wife pick up the slack of the couple's child-rearing so he could meet the demands of the church.

The church had been and always was his focus, even though he had become so bored of late. The same old tasks required of being a minister were ultimately killing him. The wedding ceremonies were not so bad, but when he had to comfort the sick in the hospital at all times of the day and night, with all its nasty smells, it was awful. And especially the funerals, consoling the weeping mourners and trying to explain to sad family members how their loved ones were in a better place with God All Mighty in heaven. And the hardest chore by far was counseling married couples. As though he was some great source of knowledge when it came to wedlock. Wedlock. John detested the word. The image of Barbara's angry face poked his mind's eye. He could not go on with that woman. He may have impressed her early on, but it was obvious that she didn't love him anymore. And it seemed that she had found a sneaky way lately to remind him of that every single day as though he was entirely to blame for her unhappy life.

The minister placed the beer bottle on the wood table and decided to take a more positive outlook. John knew for a fact that Malorie was smitten with him. Impressing people had always been important to John, as was being the center of attention. He felt most alive when speaking in front of a large audience and influencing folks with his natural talent for public speaking. It had been his early career path; and perhaps more importantly for John, the path of least resistance. From a young age, John noticed the way that adults in town respected and admired Reverend Murphy, the friendly, easy-going minister who brought him under his wing. As the lead Acolyte, John had the opportunity to receive encouragement and fatherly advice from the elder Pastor that he wasn't getting at home. He enjoyed wearing his own special white smock and tending to the candles on the alter. He often played important ceremonial roles in front of the congregation, and felt genuinely special. It also seemed to John that compared to the long hours of labor his own dad toiled at the Portsmouth Naval Shipyard, being a minister and speaking on Sunday mornings was an easy job.

The demands of building submarines for the war required his electrician father to leave home before dawn; and rarely did he make it home for dinner. As a result, John and his exhausted father were never close, and he relied more on his gregarious mother for shaping his emerging personality. At the age of ten, and completely unexpected by his parents, an extrovert Johnny Thomley asked if he could give the prayer at a multifamily potluck held at the christening of a submarine. Dozens of people were simply in awe at the ease with which the blessing flowed, with plenty of volume, from such a confident and well-spoken boy. He delivered a truly inspirational prayer that made use of various religious themes, and then brought some to tears at the end by touching on everyone's heartfelt American patriotism. From that day forward, each family meal at home started with Johnny's self-assured words of prayer. He relished the attention and respect it provided him. By his early teens, he dropped the name, *"Johnny,"* and insisted on being called *"John."* Soon he knew the bible better than most adults. Rarely did a local high school sporting event or celebration in town start without a notable John Thomley prayer. What started as a simple way to get noticed, became his special gift. Prayers led to outright preaching and though he never truly felt God's presence per se, or heard the "calling" to do the Lord's work, he found preaching resulted in a great deal of positive comments from family, friends, and the public at large. By seventeen, he had become the youngest Lay Minister to give inspiring sermons at various Methodist

Churches in the area. Many local folks called him the new Billy Graham. The older church members even compared him to Billy Sunday, the famous, early 20th century evangelist. Perhaps best of all, there was no limit to the excited teenage girls who were drawn to his bright smile and undeniable self-confidence.

But as fate would have it, despite John's charismatic personality and superb speaking skills, the fame and fortune of becoming a popular evangelist himself never materialized. Instead, he became a simple pastor, a reluctant family man, and someone extremely bored with his duties as a small-town minister.

John sat quietly in the strange colorful bus and yearned for something new and out of the ordinary. He wanted to feel inspired and witness some form of tangible proof of the God to which he had dedicated his entire life. Did God really exist? He needed a sign.

John finished the last gulp of beer and felt its subtle effects. He returned the empty bottle to the cooler. On his way to rejoin the happy young ladies he stopped and sniffed one of the kerosene lamps. John determined he did not much care for the smell. There were other aromas that John had identified the moment he'd boarded the bus. Incense and patchouli oil... he had both experienced in the Middle East but there was one other unique scent he could not quite place, so John decided he would ask Tower when they reached the farm.

8

Thirty feet behind the lead bus, the second vehicle rolled along nicely due to its new tires and recent alignment. Tower had told the minister's daughter she would enjoy the more comfortable ride of the step van. After a brief introduction to Serene, and to her older sister, Ruth, an anxious Sarah Thomley reluctantly boarded the 1963 Ford. With its sliding doors on both sides, it had once been owned by the Gottfried Baking Company. It delivered Golden Crust bread all over Manhattan, until its transmission was thoroughly cooked. Bought at an auction and repaired, the step van was later painted in wild colors and converted into the commune's most reliable errand runner.

Sarah sat on the handmade passenger's seat that did not exist in the van's prior life as a bread truck. Nor did the numerous tassel strands that hung from the roof, or the gold shag carpet glued on the top of the dashboard. Sarah crossed her right leg over her left knee, and adjusted her weight to the side. She wanted to study Ruth behind the steering wheel without her knowledge. Sarah ascertained that the driver was probably in her early to mid-twenties and single, as there was no wedding ring or tan line on her finger. Sarah figured that Ruth must really love her faded denim overalls, for they were completely covered with dozens of various patches, which seemed to hold the threadbare fabric together. She surmised that the driver's lean arm muscles must have come from years of intense manual outdoor labor. Sarah also noticed Ruth's old work boots were caked with dried mud.

"Take a picture... it will last longer." Ruth stated.

"Oh, I'm sorry. It's just that, I've never seen... a woman in overalls."

"Well, get used to it."

The curtains between the two front seats parted. Through the truck's narrow entranceway to the rear, a smiling woman with short auburn hair emerged. She was dressed in a long paisley panel-skirt, a white baggy blouse with some stains, no bra, and strange cork-soled sandals.

"Don't mind Ruth. The general takes a lot of getting used to. Of course, she's an Aries. The first sign of the Zodiac, so she tends to charge ahead like a ram. I'm a Libra, myself. Very much into balance and harmony, but we can be gossipy at times. I'm working on that. Anyway, I'm so sorry I missed the introductions, dear heart. My stomach's such a wreck today. Guess that makes me gossipy and gassy." She ended with a loud guffaw.

"Gee, I hope you feel better. I'm Sarah." She held out her hand.

"I'm Aurora." The friendly twenty-eight-year-old women shook Sarah's hand with long fingers covered with dirty band-aids and tarnished silver rings. Both her wrists had numerous wide turquoise bracelets that clanked whenever she moved her arms. Sarah liked the interesting woman immediately. She loved her extra-large, hooped silver earrings and the friendly openness she sensed. She made Sarah feel welcomed and right at ease.

Sarah asked, "Is that your real name?"

"Oh God no, it's Estelle. Now tell me, do I look like an Estelle?" Aurora threw her hands dramatically into the air and shook them, her loud bracelets added to the show. "Aurora is my Harvest name." Sarah nodded with a half-smile, not sure where the conversation was headed. "Well, all new members-"

"Gotta' be on the farm at least a month," announced Ruth.

"Don't mind her, she's uptight about rules." Aurora leaned in toward Sarah, but continued without decreasing her volume. "Some say... that if it were up to her, she'd schedule spontaneity on Mondays, between two and four."

"Come on, that's bullshit!" inserted Ruth.

"Relax, I'm only kidding. Okay, so, where was I? Oh yeah. All existing farm members, including the kids... my amazing daughter, Breeze, is one of them, who by the way, you are just gonna' love. She's a Pisces, so she's filled to the brim with intuition. But she does tend to put the needs of others ahead of her own. So typical of Pisces." Aurora grinned widely and continued at an even faster pace. "Anyway, back to Harvest names. Able says that when a truly committed person goes through a spiritual rebirth, they should change their name to represent their new life. Their new vision. And since the farm is all about transformation, requiring everyone's involvement, we *all* get to write down a special name we genuinely think fits the person best. My favorite is Able, of course. It rings so true. As a leader, Able is *so* able." Ruth wanted to scream but stayed focused on the road ahead. "Another is

Terra. He's our head gardener, and his name in Spanish means *"earth."* It's perfect! Tower's nickname in high school was Lurch. You know, from 'The Adams Family,' television show." Aurora lowered her voice. "You Rang?" She giggled. "Tower does it much better than I do. Anyway, don't you think Tower is a much stronger name? More regal?" Sarah nodded. "So, all the slips of paper get thrown into a big old copper kettle. And the new member, who is blindfolded by the way, gets to pull out their new Harvest name." Aurora laughed again. "I was just thankful that whoever wrote 'Aurora' didn't include 'Borealis.' Can you imagine having to answer to that? I just love mine. It's like the universe gets to decide."

"What if a person doesn't like the name? Can they-"

"No." Ruth inserted gruffly.

"So far, only one member hasn't-"

"Screw you!" Ruth fired back with anger.

"No one cares that you've kept your real name. You're way too uptight Ruth." Ruth pressed her lips together to remain silent. "Did you meet her sister, Serene?" Sarah nodded yes. "She is so peaceful and centered. Her Harvest name fits her to a tee. And what a strong earth mother she is to her blessed twins. Actually, to the entire commune."

Sarah's eyes conveyed her sincere attempt to make sense of everything that had been said at such a fast pace. She was not entirely sure what to make of her new outgoing friend.

"Oh dear, you don't know anything about the commune. How it started? How could you, darling? Well I'll tell you the story, it's so romantic."

Ruth gripped the wheel harder and shook her head in disgust. The obvious display didn't stop Aurora from continuing.

"So anyway. Serene and Ruth's father left the farm to them when he passed away a few years back. May he rest in peace. Okay, it was Able's idea; he's our spiritual focal point. It was his idea, along with Tower and Serene, to start the commune. And, well... Heir Dictator here is making damn sure it stays in the family." Ruth did not turn to make eye contact. Her only response was a raised middle finger.

Aurora let out an ample laugh. "Well, I knew Able ages ago in Brooklyn, when he was Barry Rifkin. Back then, he was just a nice Jewish boy. A nobody really. You know, just another jock on the block who loved sports, right? Anyway, to make a long story short, when I decided to leave the Kibbutz-"

Sarah had to interrupt. "The what?"

"Kibbutz. Oh, you wouldn't know what that is either." Aurora squeezed the young girl's hands. "Don't worry, silly me. A Kibbutz is a community in Israel. Like a commune, sort of. But with more rules. It's much stricter than the farm." Aurora waved her hand toward the driver. "Ruth, you'd just love it there. They even use timecards."

"Do you ever shut up?"

"So, when I got prego, in my senior year of high school, my folks were, of course, horrified, cause well, what would everyone think." Her smile faded. "Anyway, they sent me over to this Kibbutz thing they had heard about at their synagogue. Supposed to be a good home for troubled girls like me. But the place, oh my god, such a hard life. Everybody worked like dogs! We were all expected to '*Make the Desert Bloom.*' As if that weren't bad enough, they wouldn't let me take care of Breeze." Aurora leaned against the threshold of the van's interior doorway and burped. She rubbed her hand across her uneasy stomach. "Of course, that wasn't her name then - but honestly, can you believe it? They actually thought she belonged to the entire group. That the raising of kids should be shared by everyone as though every adult there was her parent."

"How terrible that must have been for you," said Sarah. She stood and gave her seat over to the fascinating woman.

Aurora kicked off her sandals and sat with folded legs. "Thank you, sweetheart. Well, there was a big building called *'Bayit Yeladim'* where Breeze had to sleep, away from me, for a whole year. Thank God, at least I got to breastfeed her." Aurora eyes began to tear up. "I swear they kept us separated so young mothers like me could work the fields instead of caring for our children." She wiped her eyes on the sleeve of her blouse. A silent moment passed. Sarah was not sure what to do and not quite certain if physical contact was appropriate. Finally, she leaned forward to give Aurora a tentative hug. Aurora did not hesitate and pulled the surprised teen down onto her lap. She held Sarah tight against her abundant chest. "Darling, you can image how unhappy I was. So, I finally got enough cash from my grandparents to take *my* child out of there. Caught a plane home to New York."

"What did your parents say?"

"What could they say? I was eighteen by then. And two days later, we left. Hitchhiked across the country, just the two of us!" Aurora let go with another of her signature squeals of joy.

Sarah needed air. She grabbed the side of the interior door's opening, and pulled herself to a standing position. Aurora extended her hand. "Here, help me up princess. I need to lie down. And I'll fill you in on everything that has happened. By the way, when's *your* birthday?"

It was painfully obvious to Ruth that the two had hit it off as they headed back through the beaded curtain. Aurora had done it again. She won over another friend for life. Ruth drove on and soon realized how hurt she felt. And pissed. What if she didn't want to change her name? Ruth was her grandmother's name. It meant a lot to her dad that she had it. Ruth leaned over the steering wheel to relieve her lower back pain and imagined what it would be like if she was the only one on the farm. The farm would be free of all those fast-talking intellectuals. After all, why shouldn't it, Ruth thought. She had worked the farm successfully after their father's death, while her flaky sister only wasted good money on college tuition and books. If Ruth's own grades in high school had been better, maybe she could have gone to college too. Hell, just one of those business classes at night school would be more practical for running the farm. Better than the useless philosophy classes her sister took. Her undisciplined sister. The one who never really cared about the farm until she started balling Tower. That ridiculously tall basketball jock. With all his stupid impersonations of people who Ruth had never heard of. She couldn't believe it when they decided to quit school and showed up on the farm with their high-and-mighty college professor in tow. It was not long before their long-haired friends appeared, wanting to join the goddamn commune. On her *family* farm, for Pete's sake. From Ruth's perspective most of them were just spoiled rich kids who thought it would be so *"out-of-sight"'* to live off the land and get high. But she knew hard work firsthand. What it meant to get up at sunrise every single day. No days off. Sure, money was tight, and she even thought about selling off some of the land to get by, but that was something her father would not have wanted. When they mentioned Able's plan to get ordained as a minister of some sort, and then qualify the farm for a property tax exemption as a religious community, she finally agreed. It had always been the huge annual taxes on the land that made it so hard to get by anyway. Ruth did make it clear the group had to not only get rid of the taxes, but also generate real revenue to keep the farm intact. And if she pressed folks a bit hard, it was just her desire to keep the family farm going. Of course, she knew people joked behind her back, but she never thought of herself the way Aurora put it. *"You're way too uptight."* In her opinion, she had been open to just about everything.

Ruth cracked the knuckles of both hands. She checked the speedometer. She noticed in the side mirror of the step van that the bus behind her was lagging again. Ruth thrust the sliding window backward to allow her arm to stick out in the wind. She spun it in frantic circles and screamed at the top of her lungs, "Come on you lazy shitheads, pick up the pace!"

The caravan's last vehicle had a wide set of authentic Texas bull horns mounted on the front of the hood. Its entire body was filled with areas of gray and red primer to prevent the numerous rust spots from spreading. Occasional bright patches of the original school bus yellow popped out like happy dandelions. The primer provided the perfect background for hand painted peace signs of gold and silver. It was the commune's first and oldest vehicle, used as a temporary kitchen until the actual one was constructed. The bus had no suspension to speak of. Its seats had been removed, so that four industrial steel shelves could be attached to the floor and ceiling inside the bus's left rear corner. The shelves held cooking supplies, cans of fruit and vegetables, and numerous containers for water. A large propane stove and lengthy Formica countertop for food prep filled the remaining space up to the driver's seat. Two of the three army surplus cots that ran lengthwise along the right side of the bus supported their exhausted male occupants in a well-earned sleep. On this trip to Maine and back, the old bus served well as both mobile bunkhouse and chuck wagon, but everyone knew its future traveling days were numbered.

Behind the steering wheel, Terra wore a blue bandanna to keep his long, stringy red hair out of his eyes. His scant beard consisted of wiry hairs that had grown out in slight curly patches. Patches that would never connect. Terra had caught Ruth's crazy hand signals, and they made the shirtless twenty-two-year-old crack up. He increased the speed until the gap between the two vehicles closed to ten yards or so. Terra settled back into the hard seat for the last hour of what had proven to be a profitable journey. Although it required digging with shovels in the hard ground of Maine, the commune's second Maine Blueberry Project had been a huge success. He hated to admit it, but Ruth deserved all the praise and credit. As he drove on, Terra kept his eyes from drooping shut by mulling over the days that had led up to the trip.

He had just turned the farm's garden soil with the larger of their two tractors. Terra then fertilized the soil with rich compost. No chemicals were ever used. Terra disked the soil just as he had been taught in his college agricultural program. After the soil rested for a few weeks, he would use the much smaller tractor built by the Case Company in 1956. Its front wheels were set wide apart so that the entire orange-colored machine could straddle two rows at a time. It would pull a wood wagon that held seeds and young seedlings that were tenderly planted by all the members of the farm. The day was exactly what many of the members had always dreamed about. People with a shared commitment, living and working together. Good folks achieving tangible experiences in blending spirituality with labor. There was joy in a groovy life that they would not have found on their own. It was at the end of that perfect day of planting when Ruth stood up in the dining hall. She spoke about the blueberry business up in Maine where they had been hired to pick berries the summer before. How the company was offering a pretty decent hourly wage to plant new Highbush plants on multiple acres. The land had been cleared of trees, and was now ready to be planted. Ruth pointed out that since there was not much to do while their own vegetable garden germinated, she figured why not make some extra bucks. They could save even more money if they prepared all their own meals on site and slept on the buses. Ruth wanted to go and that left five openings, providing an extra person went along to handle the cooking.

Serene stood up and said she liked the idea of getting off the farm. She volunteered to cook if no one objected to the twins coming along. Her pregnancy had required so much bed rest that any new surroundings would be a welcomed change. For her, it was settled then. Serene would cook, while the kids played at her feet, and Tower, well… he would just *love* to plant bushes. The small dining hall had erupted with laughter. The new family-man was quite well known for dodging all manual labor if he could get away with it.

Terra recalled that was the moment that Aurora had stood up and volunteered. She stated that an adventure would be fun, and that her daughter could really use a break from her overbearing mother. More laughter occurred, until a long uncomfortable hush developed among the communal members. It had become painfully obvious that there would not be any more willing volunteers. In the three years of its existence, the busy commune had never slowed down enough for a break of any kind. Since the garden was planted, and the only construction project underway was on hold, anyone who did not go to Maine would likely get to sleep-in and pretty much hang out. He hated to do it, but Terra finally stood up and announced that he would go. He figured since the demanding garden would not allow him to take a day off until late fall, he might as well head north and enjoy something different. He would be happy to go, so long as the garden was weeded, and plants got watered in his absence. Terra went on to remind everyone that since he was really the only dude in the whole commune with any real knowledge of plants, the folks in charge up in Maine would consider him an added benefit in hiring the group. Terra took great pride in his role as the group's agricultural guru. After all, it was he who obtained a degree in animal husbandry and gained hands-on experience raising crops on the college farm, near campus. He pointed out, yet again, that his credentials added true value to the commune. He could deliver more than just good intentions. Not like some of the others.

Terra's dirty bare foot pressed down on the bus's petal to accelerate. His tender big toe displayed its dark purple nail from the injury he'd sustained the day before. It would be a constant reminder for a long while of how stupid it was to lift a huge stone by himself. Asking for help had always been hard for him. Nevertheless, Terra grinned with satisfaction. He knew the trip up north was worth the hassle. He wanted to celebrate. They had made some good bread and hadn't spent any of it, except for gas. Terra could not wait to get home to check on his sweet young plants and tender seedlings both in the rich garden soil and in the protection of the new greenhouse dome Terra had practically built by himself.

9

Hal drove up the steep hill that led to Mendelson's Hotel. He continued to the right of the impressive, landscaped circle, where flowers flowed like colorful ribbons among the groomed bushes and trees. Straight ahead, the busy valet parking area was filled with guests; their expensive cars besieged by an army of young bellmen dressed in dark brown polyester uniforms. It was his plan to stay at the hotel the first evening and to be in fine form for the ten o'clock audition the next morning. Whether they got hired or not, Hal figured that he and Barbara should enjoy the fancy accommodations for at least one night.

The hotel's primary entrance, with its tan stucco walls and Tudor-style exposed timbers, had a European charm. Two modern wings of rooms flanked each side of the main building, and a large coffee shop on the lower right led to the new indoor pool. The pool area was housed within high glass walls, and the deep end included an underwater window for guests to view the divers. Complete with a golf course, ski-lodge, large ice-skating rink, Olympic-sized outdoor pool, tennis courts, and its own post office, the resort had become a favorite vacation destination among the affluent members of New York's Jewish community. Famous celebrities who stayed at the "big M," as it was commonly known, included Danny Kaye, Milton Berle, Henny Youngman, Kim Kovak, Paul Newman, and Zero Mostel. Baseball legends Mickey Mantle and Jackie Robinson mingled with fellow guests. Often, Rocky Marciano used the boxing facility on the hotel grounds to hone his skills.

Hal was directed to pull his sports car to the right and park near the front door while Barbara quickly untied her scarf to fix her hair.

"You look fine." Hal dismissed her concern as he unfolded from the automobile. His legs were stiff from the long drive, and he wondered if it had been a mistake buying such a small car. "You can freshen up in the room, Barbie Girl."

Ever since they had left the high school graduation, Barbara noticed a change in Hal's personality, which exposed a side she had not seen before. He seemed more confident, which was nice, but also impatient at times. She hoped the choir director she called her good friend hadn't completely lost his sensitive side. She also hoped he would stop calling her, *"Barbie Girl."*

Hal received a claim stub for the car, and was told that their luggage would arrive at their rooms shortly. Once inside, Hal knew he'd need to remove his cap. It was doubtful that the toupee would still look good without some major adjustment. They climbed up the curved, modern stairway, which brought them into the main lobby. The check-in counter was on the right, and the bell desk to the left. Laughter came from another lobby further back inside and Hal suggested, "Why don't you see what's so funny while I check us in." He secretly wished they could share one room, but knew it would be pushing his luck.

Barbara would have preferred going directly to her room, but her curiosity was piqued by the loud laughter that came from the adjacent lobby. She ventured in and discovered that almost everyone faced the far side of the cozy space of the original lodge. She loved its knotty-pine walls, stone fireplaces, and trophy deer heads mounted above the mantles. Without being noticed, she watched a tall, energetic man her age conducting a rousing game of *Simon Says* in front of twenty or more standing participants. She noticed that he had a nice smile and seemed to enjoy his job, despite the obvious repetition inherent in the game.

"Simon says raise your arms above your head," instructed the leader. "Now, drop your arms." Five guests instantly did as they were told and then it was pointed out that Simon had not told them to do it. Giggles erupted. The ousted players took to their seats, surprised at losing so soon.

Barbara laughed. She felt happier in that moment than she had in a long time. This light-hearted, first impression of the resort made her excited for the summer job. She allowed herself a moment to imagine what it would feel like to meet someone new at the impressive resort. Not so much for romance, although that would be exciting, but more for being a new, someone, herself. After so many years of marriage, she was certain that John simply did not know her anymore. She had changed. She had grown. He only knew the past Barbara, the frightened eighteen-year-old he had to marry so that he could become a minister without scandal. John had not noticed the many changes that had occurred in her; the maturity that comes with the passing of years, being a mother of three unique children who reflected her own strengths and faults, and being forced to learn how to be a better person. Did he even notice the slow transformation that had made her special? She felt as though he only saw her through the filter of his own preconceived notions, a fixed and rigid mind-set of his own selfishness. All of which held her captive and unable to fully be her new self.

Barbara scanned the crowded lobby with its numerous older couples enjoying themselves. She wondered how their marriages could have lasted twenty or thirty, even sixty years. Could anyone really view a mate of so long without the constant expectation of what had come before? Barbara just wanted to be seen and loved for who she had become, without the judgment of the past weighing her down. She wondered if this summer may be the right time to explore that exciting possibility. She felt a tingle of excitement that comes from accepting whatever new experiences loomed ahead, with open arms.

As she watched another round of *Simon Says*, Barbara thought about the way society had drastically changed over the past four years. So many women just like her were encouraged to now let go of the strict codes of conduct their mothers had lived by. She recalled the Miss America Beauty Pageant from the previous year, where hundreds of feminists had gathered outside on the boardwalk in Atlantic City. They protested society's expectations of beauty by burning their bras. John thought the protest was laughable; Barbara did not agree. She understood their desire in taking a stand, of wanting to be accepted on their own terms. Suggestive messages were everywhere in movies, magazines, and on television. The roles of women and their new relationships with men were being redefined in American culture. Now with birth control just a matter of taking a pill, why wouldn't women in America want to seize their moment of freedom? Barbara smiled with the realization that she was certainly willing to give her freedom a try. Besides, what opportunities would she have in the little town where she grew up? Where she knew everyone. Where life as a minister's spouse felt like a prison sentence. For the last five years, the fishbowl of her existence seemed to have offered no possible escape to explore anything new. Barbara wanted to feel genuine passion. She and John had sex in those early months after their wedding, but it lacked real passion. It always felt awkward and filled with self-doubt. Something she was obligated to do. Making matters worse, the demands of motherhood and John's studies at seminary resulted in little time for intimate encounters. Barbra was extremely curious about sex and had hoped that being married would allow her the opportunity to explore her desires. It just didn't happen.

Barbara sat down and allowed herself to daydream again of the one and only time she was with a man before John. It had been an incredible moment and a wonderful memory she returned to often. She was a junior in high school. It was early December and Jay Mitchell, a senior, who worked on and off for years at her family's farm, was cutting down Christmas trees her father had planted along the Squamscott River. Barbara's mother instructed her to take the boy's bag lunch to the worksite without giving the task a second thought. In her mother's mind, Barbara was still the shy seventeen-year-old who simply loved to sing in church and the school choir. Her daughter seemed content to do her chores on the farm, and appeared not to be at all focused on the opposite sex. Her hardworking parents had no sense of Barbara's intense curiosity regarding what the quiet, handsome young man, down by the frozen river, had to offer.

On that snowy day, with its low gray clouds and frigid wind, Barbara surprised Jay with a snowball to the center of his back. They had known each other since she was in fourth grade. And over the years, as he worked most summers on the family farm, their friendship had grown stronger. It seemed to her that they were destined to become something more than friends. It did not take but a moment that cold day for Barbara to find how easy laughter, followed by bashful glances, could lead to a passionate kiss. And it did not end there. His unique scent, mixed with the aroma of pine from the cut trees, heightened the anticipation in Barbara. She visualized Jay's shirtless, tan torso from the previous hot summer and how the golden straw had clung along the deep V-lines leading down his narrow waist and into his jeans. Barbara knew that if she had undone his belt that day, his trousers would certainly have dropped to the ground unless they got hung up on something. *"What then?"* Barbara breathlessly returned to the memory of that winter day when he tenderly kissed her neck and moved his lips lower, toward her breasts. That was the exact moment, lasting forever it seemed, when an unfamiliar roar filled her ears and made it nearly impossible to get air. At first, she thought it was just a strong gust of wind that had blown in from the icy river. But then he pressed her body against the side of the tree-filled wagon, and her knees became unsteady. The roar intensified when her dungarees were gently opened and moved apart a few inches by her confident friend. Their warm breathing grew deeper, and just as his hand gently slid under the hem of her underwear; a low, uncontrollable moan escaped from her delicate mouth.

Then everything stopped.

Barbara's unfocused mind suddenly realized that the wonderful roar in her ears had been replaced with the chugging sound of her father's old tractor. As it approached, she hastily did-up her pants and returned her plaid shirt to normal. Their bottled-up giggles, and the numerous stray pine-needles in her hair did not go unnoticed by her easygoing father. His only mistake was mentioning the encounter to Barbara's very Christian mother, Helen, over coffee the next morning. From then on, Helen put a stop to all special deliveries of lunches. In fact, Barbara was not allowed to date until the end of her senior year of high school. Her stern mother finally granted permission when she met the polite, well-spoken minister-in-training who everyone was talking about. Helen approved of the two meeting, and loved the idea of her daughter becoming a minister's wife, if that was God's will. In the meantime, Barbara's curiosity of men, and the strong desire to be with one again, had reached a level of intensity that she could barely keep at bay.

An abrupt announcement about tennis lessons blared from the hotel's PA system. It brought Barbara back to the crowded lobby. Her distracted mind filled with hopeful questions. *"What if she could find the right person this summer, someone with a sense of humor? Someone who would be tender and kind for a change? Did she have the confidence to drop her guard and be intimate again? Could she let herself go, and share her hidden sexual desire with another? What about her marriage of eighteen-years? How would the kids feel about her ending the marriage?"* One thing was certain, there would be no following of the rules. No listening closely for what Simon says or what John says. No attention paid to what the congregation or the church Superintendent would say. And certainly, no credence to what her mother said. It was now high time for everyone to hear what Barbara had to say.

She arrived in the main lobby just as Hal left the Bell Captain's desk with two room keys and an opened envelope. There was a look of absolute dread across his colorless face.

"There's been a change of plans." Hal grasped her arm and quickly led her to a less congested corner of the lobby. "I've got a note here from Manny. Says to call him from the lounge the minute we check in."

"Has the audition been canceled?"

"No, no, just moved up!"

"Hal, take a deep breath like we do in rehearsal," urged Barbara.

Hal inhaled through his nose, then exhaled. He read the handwritten note out loud. "Hal, I've got an early morning meeting in the city. I must leave tonight. This works out better because I want to see you with an audience present. Get set up and have Tommy, the bartender, call me from the lounge. Sorry about the last-minute change. Manny."

"You've got to be kidding! I'm not dressed... son-of-a-bitch!"

Hal was taken aback. He had never heard Barbara swear, and was thrilled that the minister's good wife apparently had a wicked side after all. Hal reluctantly returned to the problem at hand when a bellman entered the lobby nearby.

"You there... young man."

"Yes sir?" The bellman rushed over.

"Point us in the direction of the Pink Kitty Lounge." Hal nodded a thank you and crossed the wide lobby with a stride Barbara struggled to maintain. It was not until he passed to the right of the bell desk, and stopped abruptly in front of the hallway's left wall, that she finally caught up. "Look, it's Red Buttons!" Hal could not contain himself. He pointed at the thirty or so framed, black and white photographs of celebrities that filled the entire passageway. "There, Debbie Reynolds with Eddie Fisher at their wedding here at the hotel. I bet there's another wedding picture of him and Elizabeth Taylor too." Hal laughed. "Oh brother, this is exciting." He turned and saw the sign he wanted. He grabbed his disheveled singing partner by the hand and led her quickly down the stairs. They walked through the darkened hallway that led to the Pink Kitty Lounge.

Barbara had never seen such sleek, modern surroundings. A vast room with so many pink vinyl chairs, and pink carpet that in places that extended over to the reflective walls, impressive surfaces of tall gleaming mirrors and shiny chrome trim. A stuffed Pink Kitty with lifeless eyes hung upside-down over the bar, as though the intoxicating vapor of booze had destroyed its mind. *"Hot Fun in the Summertime,"* by Sly and the Family Stone, played loudly from the colorful jukebox pulsating near the far end of the bar.

Hal leaned in close toward Barbara's ear. "This is it. The famous

Pink Kitty Lounge." Hal waved hello at the smartly attired bartender in his black vest, white shirt, and extra-large bowtie made of pink velvet. "I'm fairly sure that Manny wants us to fill the afternoon time slots. See that glass bowl on top that spectacular piano? It's gonna' be stuffed with tips, Barbie Girl!"

There were over a dozen patrons at the bar's mirror-like surface, along with a distracted young couple making out at a nearby booth. The majority of the hotel's guests were either basking poolside, getting a tan, or taking late day naps in anticipation of dinner and a show. The bar's jukebox switched to *"Crystal Blue Persuasion,"* by Tommy James and The Shondells. Barbara asked the handsome bartender with the thick mustache and friendly eyes where the lady's room was located. While she made a beeline for its door, she accepted the simple fact that there was not enough time to track down her luggage and change into an evening gown. She could at least fix her hair. Meanwhile, Hal showed the note to Tommy, behind the bar, and made his way to the elevated grand piano in the corner of the lounge. Angled outward, the glistening, white grand piano was positioned to encourage impromptu sing-a-longs with the clientele who would sit on the numerous pink barstools along its two sides. Hal sat down and swung the long arm of the microphone stand around until it stopped in front of his mouth. To his right stood a beautiful Vox Continental combo organ on a chrome, Z-shaped stand that would allow him the ability to play all the latest hits. Hal turned the *Connie* on (as the pros called it) to warm up, while he waited for Tommy to unplug the jukebox. Hal cleared his throat and switched on the microphone.

"Ladies and gentlemen, you're in store for a groovy treat this afternoon. Please sit back and relax." His hands danced along the keyboard with a flourish of notes. "With yours truly, Hal Dobson, accompanied by the smooth, sultry voice of the ever-so-talented, Barbara Ann Thomley."

Barbara heard the modest applause through the lady's room door as she applied a final, thick coat of ruby red lipstick. She caught a glimpse of her small wedding ring and removed it. A slight grin of satisfaction appeared. Barbara gave her hair a final brush and turned sideways to check her profile. "Oh, what the hell!" She reached under her clingy sweater and removed her bra, then stuffed it, and the ring, into her purse. Barbara entered the lounge with head held high, and her back straight. She flung her leather bag behind the tall amplifier, and grabbed the microphone off its stand. Tommy the bartender finished his call to Manny and gave the duo an enthusiastic thumbs-up. Barbara confidently took her position along the curved indention of the piano, which caused Hal to miss a few notes. The sight of Barbara's obvious excitement to be on stage filled him with glee.

10

Word of the caravan's return spread quickly among the members of the community who had stayed behind on the farm. Most had gathered on the dirt parking lot next to the children's playground. It served as the meeting place for their daily afternoon swim in the river nearby. Long-haired men wore ragged jean cutoffs; their pockets peaked out like white flags of surrender to the heat. Many of the women wore long tee-shirts over their simple cotton underwear. With its knotted rope swing and abundant shade, the secluded river provided a perfect location for cooling off and skinny-dipping.

The three vehicles rumbled along the farm's entry road with dogs of assorted breeds barking at the wheels. Shadow, a large black Labrador, led the pack, followed by Fetch, an Australian shepherd with one blue eye and one brown eye. Next, Scooter, with his short dachshund legs, managed to keep up with Alice, the excited terrier. Boon, a ten-year-old basset hound with tattered floppy ears, brought up the rear. Though it was only three-thirty in the afternoon, the excitement over the evening's homecoming party had energized the entire gathering, including the dogs. It reached its peak when the first bus came to rest and its door folded open.

"Tell Mrs. Calabash we're home!" Tower exclaimed in his best Jimmy Durante voice. They all cheered while John and Malorie smiled apprehensively and followed their friendly host down the steps of the bus. "Would've been here sooner, but we rescued this far-out minister and his family. And his special companion." Tower winked at John and led him and Malorie into the middle of the crowd. "Let's all give 'em a warm New Harvest welcome."

Immediately hugged by the nearest members, John and Malorie were overwhelmed by the amiable group's outpouring of affection and collective body odor. Tower enjoyed the visitors' reactions, until he noticed off to his right, above everyone's heads, that Terra had just stepped out of the last vehicle.

Not far off, Able stood under the canopy of a large tree at the top of the hillside lawn to observe the arrival. His sleeveless denim shirt kept him cool in the shade. The three-inch-wide leather watchband gave him the popular Roman gladiator-turned-hippie look. While most of the other men on the farm had full beards, he was clean-shaven with a long ponytail of thick black hair. It hung down between his broad shoulders and nearly touched his handmade belt. Able witnessed Tower make his way toward Terra with the tall man's familiar lanky stride and customary grin. The commune's spiritual leader smiled with affection. He had missed Tower, his easygoing young friend.

Terra had just rolled each of his shoulders in circles to stretch out the last painful hour of the road when Tower approached. He placed his hand on Terra's left elbow and squeezed gently. Able was too far away to hear the exchange, but noticed the body language of both had changed immediately. With his arms crossed tight against his chest, Terra shouted something at Tower, then stormed away with a noticeable limp.

Able walked over and gave Tower a robust hug. "Welcome home, brother. I missed you." The two men released their embrace, but remained standing close together. Tower informed his older mentor of the day's events. He mentioned the far-out signs the minister had in the car's windows, and that his two sons were still waiting to be picked up. He hoped Terra would help. Tower just figured that he would be willing to go back with the tow-truck to get them. Able could see the hard work in Maine and the long hours of driving had been a drag on the commune's most fun-loving family member.

"I thought since Terra knew where the car sat, he was the best choice. Guess I screwed that up." Said Tower.

"Look, you're all beat." Able smiled. "Don't worry man, I'll go."

"You just got home too, right?" Tower focused intently on Able's brown eyes to get a read on his emotional state. Able had been gone for the two weeks as well, having returned to Brooklyn to tie-up a messy divorce. The entire commune worried that Able would be required to hand-over full custody of his only child to his ex-wife. As it turned out, the judge agreed with the wife's aggressive attorney, that quitting a tenured job as a professor was one thing, but to then start a radical commune with students, and with no real income, showed a horrible lack of sound parental judgment. It was finally decided that Able's three-year-old daughter, Emma, should remain in the city with her mother and not be allowed to play flowerchild in the woods of New Hampshire.

"It didn't go well." Able uttered the words in a sad whisper.

Tower saw the torment in the man's fixed gaze, but did not press.

He knew in time that his friend would talk it out.

"Where's the car?" Able needed to change the subject.

"It's about forty-miles away on Route 27. I'm pretty sure Serene can tell you the exact spot. But why not send Smooch instead since he's all rested and shit."

"Smooch pulled his back again. Poor guy." Able smiled up at Tower. "Hey, it's no big deal, I'll go. Don't sweat it."

They both turned and watched the minister happily interact with the three remaining members of the group. The rest were headed for the river. "Could it be... he's older than thee?" Tower's playful rhyme made both men laugh. Other than Aurora, Able at thirty-one, was at least ten years older than most everyone else on the farm, and they all dug teasing him about it.

"Does he know the truck only has room for his sons?"

"Yeah, we rapped about that" replied Tower. "Seems he's on a mission, Bro. Doesn't really need to pick up his boys. Just wants to see the farm. Wants to discuss God and shit." Tower grinned. "Hell, maybe we *should* trade places." They shared a chuckle. Tower avoided all things religious, whereas Able pushed from the very start for the commune to have a strong spiritual foundation. He proposed the members be given total freedom to explore all religions and philosophies they wanted, as long as it didn't upset the group's overall happiness.

"I've got the towing covered." The two men exchanged another hug and Able teased Tower. "Good luck with that spiritual shit." Both parted ways with familiar laughter.

Tower returned to the lead bus and found John still engaged in lively conversation. It seemed to Tower that Malorie was a bit detached from the discussion. She was certainly weary of Shadow, the dog who had just driven his snout into her crouch. To Malorie's right laughed Blaze, a tan, shirtless, physically fit carpenter with an undoubtedly handsome face and long golden hair. Blaze always made it a point to personally welcome all females to the farm.

"Don't worry babe... because dog spelled backwards is…?" Blaze followed his question with a bright white grin that peaked out from under his bushy blond mustache.

"Oh yeah, that's comforting." Malorie replied with a laugh and another shove down on the dog's bulky head. She found the young man's smile and crystal-blue eyes extremely appealing. Malorie also found it exceedingly difficult to look away because a strong sense of something deeper than attraction had moved her. This was their first meeting, but it did not feel that way at all. It was as though they had always known each other, and Malorie could not understand the reason.

Tower stepped in and nudged the friendly animal aside. "Hey Blaze, do me a solid. Take Shadow and help Terra unload. He could really use your help since everyone else seems to be headed to the river." Tower turned away, then snapped his fingers. "Oh, I almost forgot. Tell him Able will be going back for the minister's boys."

"Sure man, I guess so." Blaze was a bit confused about the message, since he knew nothing about any boys. He spoke to Malorie in a soft voice. "Well, I hope to be seeing ya' round the ole homestead." Blaze grabbed the dog's faded red bandanna and led him toward the opened rear door of the last bus.

"We get a lot of strays" Tower stated.

"Dogs or people?"

"Both, I guess." Tower grinned. He was impressed with her insight. "Don't worry, Blaze is harmless." He pointed to the old white farmhouse a hundred-yards away, with its colorful flowerboxes in all the windows. "That's our pad, there. It's the original farmhouse, built way back when. Ruth says it dates back to the American revolution. All I know is that every doorway is way too low, and the wood floors get colder than a witch's tit in winter. My old lady and I have the front part, and Ruth has the rest in back. The second floor is Able's pad." Tower faced Malorie with a reassuring smile. "We'll find a place for you to crash when the boys get back. Meanwhile, I know Serene could use some help bathing down the twins, if you're cool with that?"

"Oh, I'd love to. And thanks, by the way... for everything."

Malorie walked toward the farmhouse, and Tower felt a tinge of guilt, stating that Blaze was harmless. Nothing was further from the truth. When it came to pretty chicks, the farm's Nordic Tarzan often got his way. Tower glanced to his left. He was relieved to see that Aurora, near the step van, had the minister's emotional daughter under her control. He could tell from the affirmative wave in his direction that Aurora had the situation covered. She would keep the teenager occupied for at least a while. It was also cool to see that Aurora receive a welcoming hug and flowers from her daughter. Their nasty argument before the trip to Maine now looked resolved.

Tower called over to John with a pleasant expression that did not expose his true feelings. "Hey Rev, how about that quick tour?" Now that Tower was home, a hot shower, a bottle of Mateus, and a nice joint was all he craved.

John sensed a real connection to the young people he had just met. He walked toward Tower with bright eyes and a happy smile that said as much.

"What a wonderful group. Such a sincere willingness to share their spiritual insights. Not at all like my closed-minded congregation at home. In fact, I've been known to mock their selfishness from the pulpit." John bowed his head and raised his voice dramatically. "O Lord, bless me and my wife, my son John and his wife; us four, no more." He glanced up and winked. "Amen."

Tower nodded with a blank look. He had not been in a church for years, and wasn't sure how to respond. He changed the subject. "Oh, hey, you might want to lose those nice dress shoes. It gets really muddy in spots." Tower began to unlace his knee-high moccasins.

"I would... but... I think I'll just leave them on." John was embarrassed of his extremely sensitive feet.

"Suit yourself." Tower sat down on one of the wood benches near the dining hall. "But remember, the bottoms of our feet are the only direct connection to the earth. I feel more grounded when I'm barefoot. Balanced and rooted." Tower grinned and tossed his leather footwear under the bench. "Man, I just love to feel the muddy earth between my toes." He flexed his dirty suede-stained toes up and down, then stood and steered his guest toward the extensive vegetable garden located down the hill. As they walked, he updated John on the plan that Able was to bring his sons and car back to the commune. Now that Tower was a new dad himself, and loved every tender minute with his twins, it seemed a little weird that the minister wasn't more concerned about the boy's safety.

"What's your group's theology?" John asked as he struggled to keep up with Tower's long strides. "Is there a doctrine you believe in? You know, like a religious glue or something that keeps you together?"

"That's a tough one to nail down. Most of us come from pretty normal backgrounds. I suppose Christian and Jewish, mostly. Able isn't a big fan of organized religions. He encourages us to cherry-pick the best of any beliefs or philosophies that ring true. A lot of us are meditating and exploring Buddhism, some Hinduism too, with a little yoga thrown in.

Guess you could call it an *'unorganized'* religion." Both men smiled.

"Terra, he's our garden guy, he does Tai Chi on the big lawn every day at sunrise. Looks to me like he's directing traffic in slow motion." Tower grabbed a woven bushel at the start of a row of young green pepper plants. He shook his head in disbelief at the immense number of weeds thriving at the base of each small plant. It was obvious that the farm members who stayed behind had done little in keeping up with their chores. Tower stifled his annoyance and returned his attention to the tour. "Folks here are free to believe in whatever makes them happy. Some people have left because we're not political enough, what with Civil Rights and whatnot. Able wants the farm to have more of a spiritual center. Not focused on solving society's problems. He says, *'What gets your attention, gets you!'* We're asked to not get drawn into the anti-war movement either." Tower stood up to relieve the tightening in his lower back. "That's been hard for some folks to let go."

"What's your faith?" asked the minister.

"Well, religion isn't my bag. I've always been kind of confused about that stuff. Like that saying about the meek shall inherit the earth. Versus the one about God helps those who help themselves. So, which is it, man? Does stuff come to those who wait, or should we get pushy and make things happen?" Tower shrugged and returned to pulling weeds. "For me it's just easier to live one day at a time. You know, treat people the way I want to be treated."

"Luke 6:31" John interjected. *'And as ye would that men should do to you, do ye also to them likewise.'"* A few moments of silence passed. "You're an atheist then?"

"I guess." Tower switched to his stuttering Jimmy Stewart impersonation. "But I... I do like Christmas though. You... you... know, decorating cookies, put... putting up the tree, opening gifts and all. Guess that makes me... an *egg-nog*-stic."

John's joyful laughter filled the garden. He liked this young man and his untroubled manner. "Oh, I'll have to use that in a sermon."

"Hey man, it's a commune. What's mine is yours." They continued down the narrow path, careful not to step on any young vegetables. "Our turkeys are gonna' dig these weeds." Tower continued to pull the unwanted plants in silence while John wrestled with his next question.

"But doesn't your group need a shared belief?"

"I gotta' tell ya' Reverend, I'm really not the one to rap with on that." Tower pulled up another handful of weeds and dropped them in the bushel. "When I met Serene in college, I had a full basketball scholarship. Had everything my folks ever wanted for me. My future was set." Tower gazed back at the farmhouse. "But I dug her, and she dug me. We'd get, well…" Tower's voice trailed off as he brought John over to the greenhouse dome. "This is where we start all the seedlings. Inside, the tomato plants should be ready to transplant to the garden. Have you ever tasted a tomato right off the vine? Now that's a religious experience!" John laughed. "Really. At harvest time I always keep a saltshaker in my pocket." The men entered the wood-framed structure covered with thick plastic sheeting. Despite the exhaust blades twirling above, every young tomato plant, on every table, laid on its side, dying for lack of water. "Shit! I can't believe this! Terra is gonna' freak the fuck out!" John was noticeably taken aback by Tower's choice of words. "Sorry man. Someone dropped the ball and shit. I mean… stuff is gonna' hit the fan." Tower scowled. He started watering to save the plants and take attention away from the swearing. He took a deep breath and slipped back into his classic tour narration. "So, okay Reverend, this greenhouse is a scaled-down model of a much bigger dome we hope to build for a new dining hall. We built this one to better understand how the overall design works. There's a far-out scientist named Buckminster Fuller-"

John interrupted. "Yes, I think he was featured in some sort of magazine I saw on your bus. It had an interesting name on the cover."

"Yeah, Whole Earth Catalog. Very cool magazine. They just did a spread on him. Everyone here refers to him as Bucky. Amazing dude, actually. He created this design. Named it a "geodesic dome." He figured out that triangles withstand pressure better. They're twice as strong and use less materials. Plus, the inside air can circulate, which is really good for plants… provided they're watered."

John smiled. "Who is this Able fellow?"

"Well, he's really into studying a lot of different Eastern philosophies. I'm sure he'll tell you more when you all get together."

"Is he the leader of your group?" Inquired John.

"He doesn't want to be seen as a leader per se. Says he's more of a vibrational sounding board." Tower pulled on the hose to reach the far table of plants. "Able says the farm works because he's focused on spiritual concerns. The heaven. And Ruth, Serene's sister, reflects the earth. She runs the farm and, well... quite honestly, seems to get off on bossing the rest of us around.

Tower turned off the faucet and led his guest out of the muggy dome. They crossed over a creek on a low wooden bridge, and Tower pointed toward the nearby canning shed. He mentioned the improved laundry room on the building's far side, but John didn't show much interest in checking it out. The pair ended up at the backdoor of the commune's kitchen. Tower noticed all the trash barrels were overflowing. One barrel was on its side, with three of the farm's six cats face down on the bounty of ripe-smelling leftovers. It was obvious to him that the dreaded chore of trash-run to the county dump had been ignored as well.

"When Serene's dad was alive, this housed heavy-duty farm machinery. It took our first winter to renovate it. Turned out okay, but sometimes when it gets hot... man… the diesel smell just creeps out of the floorboards and rafters big time. That's a real bummer when you're trying to chow down."

Tower brought John into the kitchen of industrial ovens and stainless-steel sinks, with its numerous shelves of large pots, pans, and mixed-matched plates. A too-thin blond girl of nineteen, in a full apron with no shoes or bra, lifted the lid on a large pot of simmering lentil soup. Under a sheer, tie-dyed tank-top, her bare shoulder blades struggled with the wooden paddle as she stirred the thick brown mass; its steam released a hearty aroma. John stepped closer to the stove and noticed her raised underarm was unshaven. He had never seen a female so pale, and with hair under her arms.

"Well young lady, that certainly smells good." John hoped his cheerful words obscured his surprised reaction. She returned a smile.

"Oh man, you must be starved" inserted Tower. He stepped into the walk-in pantry and shouted, "Hey Feather, where's all the G.O.R.P?"

"Gone man. Everybody's been hitting it pretty hard." Feather noticed John's confusion and provided the answer. "Good old raisins and peanuts."

"Here, grab a couple." Tower carried over a wicker basket of apples. "These Granny Smiths will hold you over till your boys get back. Then we'll all eat supper." Both men grabbed a few apples while Tower introduced Feather. "This is Feather. The world's greatest dulcimer player." John looked confused. "It's kinda' like a harp that sits sideways on a stand. You just hit the strings with little, padded, hammer-like things."

"It's a little more complicated than that, Tower." Feather's irritation was on display.

"Feather. Why, that's an interesting name." John said.

Tower replied. "You know, light as a feath-"

"Enough!" Feather cut him off and pretended to threaten him with the wet paddle. Her attempt at humor faded as she continued with a diatribe of complaints. She explained how bummed out she was to be stuck tending to the soup. How hot she was, and that she hated being the only one missing out on the afternoon swim at the river. She pointed out how unfair her workload was in comparison to the others.

"Well sister, we all do our part." Tower knew Feather was always emotional and loved to complain. Her family came from old money, and she'd never worked a day in her life until she joined the commune. Not to mention her high-pitched voice drove him mad. He also knew she loved to talk about spiritual shit, and if he did not keep their interaction brief, the tour would last much longer than he wanted. As they said their good-byes and headed out of the kitchen, Tower noticed numerous stacks of dirty dishes in the sink. The opening in the wall where family members dropped off their used plates and silverware after each meal was packed. He kept his displeasure to himself and took John past the self-serve buffet counter and into the dining area. A variety of old wooden chairs and five narrow tables filled the room. In the center of each table sat a compartmented pine wood tray filled with small pottery containers of honey, brown sugar, brewer's yeast, apple cider vinegar, toothpicks, and calcium vitamin supplements. John could smell the diesel.

"This is where we eat. When we hold our parties and considerations, these tables go out on the side porch and we throw big pillows on the floor."

"What's a consideration?" John asked.

"I guess it's like your church service. Twice a week Able reads aloud from a book he chooses, like the Tao Te Ching or a book on philosophy, and we consider the message. We meditate in silence for fifteen minutes, then hold a group discussion. I've learned a lot from considerations. Best of all, it doesn't feel like church. No offense."

"None taken." John smiled and spotted the various musical instruments in the corner. Three guitars, a variety of handmade drums, and what he assumed was Feather's dulcimer on top of its wooden stand.

"Oh yeah, music is a big deal here, and we do a lot of singing. There's around nineteen adults and I think eight kids all together, so it's getting kinda' cramped. I have a hard time remembering the exact number cause it changes a lot. We'll probably need to bump out that wall over there or just build a whole new dining hall. Because of the diesel smell and all. There's a limit to what incense can hide."

"How many members do you ultimately want?" John asked, then munched on his apple.

"No more than thirty. We've found more people mean *more* personalities. And man, personalities... they do tend to clash." Tower shook his head and let out an ample laugh. "But we did come up with the ABC's to avoid in communal living." Tower used his dirty fingers to count down each word. *"Accusation, Blame, and Criticism."* Tower paused to spoon-out some honey onto his half-eaten apple. "Of course, Able added the more 'positive' ABC's. *Accept, Bless, and Clarify."*

John nodded. "I like that."

"Back at Keene State, Able taught both psychology and philosophy. He says the two are interrelated. Says it takes a peaceful mind to understand what the best philosophies have to offer. The dude's brilliant, man. He's got a doctorate in psychology and really knows what makes people tick. That's come in handy, 'cause the farm seems to attract some wacky folks at times." Tower paused to grab a toothpick from the nearest table. When the piece of apple skin was pried from his front teeth, he continued. "Sometimes we get visitors on the weekends and during the summer who just want to try communal living and to meditate. They're cool. They jump right into chores. Pretty mellow. But others are lazy and don't offer to help at all. Most are heads or freaks who just want to get high. They don't stick around for long cause of Ruth. I tease her that she puts the *ruth* in ruthless."

"Gentlemen. These are for the party tonight, but I think we can spare some." Feather announced as she entered the dining hall. "Freshly baked carob cookies." The napkin in her hand held two round golden treats that looked delicious. "We're having ice cream too."

"Oh no, that's okay. Really. We should get going," replied Tower.

"Take them for later." She placed the napkin into Tower's immense hand and turned back toward the kitchen. "See you at the party."

"You do not want to eat these. Folks say they taste like chocolate chip. They do *not*." John nodded, and followed Tower into the annex located just inside the dining hall's front entrance. A long coat rack on the right provided a space for winter jackets along with a shelf below for shoes and boots. On the left wall, a large chalkboard displayed a welcome home message written in colorful chalk. "This is where we leave messages and announcements. Able is a big believer in open communication. If someone has a beef about something, he or she can briefly state the issue here. It will be discussed by everyone at the next family meeting. I'm tempted to write down how much I hate carob."

John chuckled, then suddenly his face became serious. "Tower, there seems to be a fair amount of discord among the group."

"Oh no, that's just me." Tower laughed. "People who argue crack me up. Life doesn't need to be so heavy. Hey man, I'm sorry if I gave you that impression." Tower opened the door for John. "Fact of the matter is, we share lots of good moments. We all laugh and the bond between us is strong. Sure, we're a family with some issues, but we're all grooving along together." Tower followed John out of the building. "To be honest, I think it's the meaningful things Able says in our considerations that really connect us. There are some sweet moments among the tribe when folks share from their hearts. It's beautiful, man. I wouldn't want to raise my kids anywhere else." Tower's eyes moistened up and he swallowed hard.

John turned away to give his host a moment to collect himself. He stopped at a thick maple tree near the front door, where an empty welding tank hung from a limb. A chain held the tank about four-inches above the ground with a foot-long iron rod that dangled nearby. "Yeah, that's our dinner bell." Tower sat down on the same bench where he had left his moccasins. "It gets rung ten minutes before every meal. When you hear the three loud clangs, come running. Cause you do not want to be late and miss the grub. Now, if you hear constant clanging, then there's an emergency like a fire or something."

"Had enough of those." John muttered to himself.

Tower carried his moccasins as he led John up the hill, past the big lawn, and toward the woodshop. He figured he might as well open up a bit to keep the interaction flowing. "For me, I guess it all started my sophomore year. I took a philosophy course with Able. Well... back then he was Professor Rifkin. Anyway, he said some amazing, mind-blowing stuff. Made me question everything." They entered the woodshop through a sliding wood door and Tower hopped up onto one of the workbenches near the radial arm-saw. He placed the napkin and carob cookies on the bench. "Like I keep saying, religion has never been my bag. But Serene, man, she really dug the class. And she wanted to increase my awareness too. You know, beyond basketball." Tower grinned and started in on his second apple. "Man, what a trip! We would rap nearly all night about the far-out things Able taught us that day. Things my parents back in Wisconsin would have freaked out over. They're Lutheran."

"In seminary, we called Lutherans, God's *'frozen'* people." John said with a smirk, but he did not get a reaction from Tower. "You know, like the Jews calling themselves, God's *'chosen'* people. Anyway, Lutherans haven't changed much over the years."

"Yeah well, my folks are very uptight. That's for sure." Tower used his hand to wipe the abundant juice from his beard. If he had not been in a such a rush to complete the tour, Tower would have told the minister how much he actually missed his parents and that they'd pretty much disowned him, and how bummed it makes him feel that the twins hadn't met their grandparents yet. "Yeah, so anyway. Serene and I considered quitting school and heading to India to take a dip in the

Ganges River. Kick around the world for a year or two. Maybe hang-out in Marrakesh. I was stoked. We were making plans and starting to check out maps. Looking at scoring our passports." A broad grin appeared beneath his bushy beard. "Then we got pregnant." A long pause ensued. "Oh, and I blame Jim Morrison, by the way."

"Who?"

"You know. The Doors. His song, *'Light My Fire.*"

John shook his head. His blank expression showed that he was not aware of what Tower was referring to.

Tower sang with his sexy Jim Morrison impersonation. *"The time to hesitate is through. No time to wallow in the mire."* He dropped the voice and simply asked John, *"Girl we couldn't get much higher?* They sang it on the Ed Sullivan show a couple of years ago. And Jim wouldn't change the lyrics. Anyway, we had the record playing the night Serene and I... oh man, never mind." Tower went silent. There was no denying the generation gap between him and the minister. "So yeah... Serene and the twins have changed my life for the better."

"That's wonderful." The Pastor thought of his own unexpected path to parenthood. He quickly shifted the conversation back to the farm.

"How does all of this get paid for?"

"Well, we've got some good businesses. Like that lathe over there makes some far-out wooden bowls we sell in town. And two of our guys are licensed tree trimmers. They're called, *'The Tree Fellas.'* Name was my idea, by the way. They make good bread. Especially when storms roll through Keene and the downed trees need to be cleared. We get a bunch of free wood from those jobs, too. Which is needed, cause we've already cut down most of our biggest trees for firewood." Tower tossed the entire apple core, seeds and all, into his mouth and continued. "That first winter was a tough one. Some members quit and that put a lot more pressure on those who stayed. I swear I did nothing but chop wood all day long." Tower laughed. "Some guy said back in the day, *'Split your wood and it will warm you twice.'* Man, ain't that the truth." Tower straightened his posture and twisted his head in each direction, resulting in two loud cracks. "Oh, we also have a roadside farm stand that does pretty well. Fresh veggies and handmade pottery. We also sell our extra honey and goat cheese at the Co-op in town." Tower hopped off the workbench.

"What's a Co-op?"

"It stands for cooperative. It's like a business owned by its members. Ours is a food store that sells healthy stuff we all dig. Like nuts and grains, you can buy in bulk. Vitamins. Basic hippie stuff at a fair price, cause making a profit isn't the goal." Tower raised his eyebrows. "Can't say that about the other stores in town."

"The townspeople… do you all get along?" John asked.

"Not all. Some folks still aren't cool. Fortunately, a lot of the locals were good friends of Serene's father, so Ruth keeps those relationships going. She knows most of the cops too, and they pretty much leave us alone. Most people in town call us *'Harveys'* cause of the New Harvest name and all."

"Harveys. That's pretty harmless." John said. "Who named the farm?"

"I guess we all did." Tower grinned at his recollection of the event. He had not thought about that night for some time. He pulled down on his long beard again and again, as if each tug brought forth another vivid memory. "We were at Able's house near campus, helping him box up his book collection. Lots of wine, food, and laughing. We had a blast throwing around all sorts of names for the farm. Words like *'love'* and *'peace'* came up a lot. Someone came up with *'Find Your Center Farm,'* but that didn't get many votes. Finally, everyone agreed it should reflect a different way to live, a new way. So *'new'* was a keeper. Then Serene came up with *'harvest'* cause she liked the idea of growing something spiritual for the planet. So, everyone agreed *'New Harvest Farm'* would work." Tower headed for the door. "Of course, Ruth wanted to add, *'A Commonsense Commune.'* Wanted it painted at the bottom of the entrance sign."

"Like a disclaimer." John stated. "So, do you really share everything? I don't think I could do that."

"Pretty much. Although some hold on to the cash they get from their parents. That's their decision, I guess. Able doesn't want folks to feel obligated to give over what is theirs. They can give what feels right to them. All members do get a small monthly stipend though. To spend any way, they want. It's called a *'partner draw,'* because we're all partners in a way. Before the twins came along, my draw went for candy and the occasional burger and fries. Now it's all for the kids." From his vest pocket, Tower pulled out an antique pocket watch and noted the time. "Come on, it's getting late. I want to show you the auto shop." Tower led John out of the woodshop just as Blaze met them in the doorway. "Blaze, this is Reverend Thomley."

"Please, call me John."

"Nice to meet you, John." Blaze made room for the two to pass.

"Why aren't you at the river with everyone else?" Tower inquired.

"I need to put another coat of linseed oil on some bowls. Guess I'll swim after that." Blaze remembered. "Oh yeah, I gave Terra your message. Everything's unloaded." He turned to John. "Are you folks staying the night?"

"Brother, I left some fresh cookies inside for you." Tower hurried John along. He hollered back over his shoulder, "Don't worry man, they'll be staying for a while. He knew what Blaze was fishing at. It had a lot more to do with Malorie than with the minister and his kids.

They arrived at the entrance of the dark garage located on the other side of the woodshop. Tower hit the switch, and the florescent tubes buzzed and blinked on and off in their quest to warm up. He mentioned the five vehicles the farm members shared, not counting the two old buses, the tree service truck, and the step-van. He pointed at the car sign-out sheet that shared a wall with several girlie pinup calendars. Tower joked how the commune's women called the tool calendars sexist and loved to rip them down; only to have our young mechanic put new ones back up. Above the two men loomed a 1967 Ford Fairlane on a hydraulic lift. Its right front wheel laid on the oily floor. A long hose from the air-compressor looked like a black snake coiled over the hand tools scattered in front of them. Tower imagined that Smooch had been hurt by trying to pull off the wheel by himself. Tower told John about their mechanic's bad back and that Smooch should be well enough to install his new starter by the time it arrived in the mail. Tower turned off the lights and they left the garage. He pointed to the green barn across the way and explained that it was named the *"Green Gables,"* after a novel his wife and her sister loved when they were little. Tower went on to inform John that he, Malorie, and his kids, would probably crash on cots in the newly renovated part of the barn. Tower apologized about the walls not being completely painted yet, but guaranteed the brand-new toilet and shower were working fine. They continued to stroll along a dirt road to their right and passed by one of the commune's four outhouses scattered throughout the farm. All had crescent moons carved in their wood doors, and most had been painted in a variety of bright colors. Nearby, a worn path branched off toward the barnyard. It was home to numerous goats, dozens of egg-producing chickens, and a flock of plump white turkeys with pink and bluish heads. Tower informed his guest that turkey was the only meat served at the farm, and he let John know how very much he wished that would change. Tower absolutely loved prime rib. Despite Tower's excitement to show him the cute baby goats in the barnyard, John let it be known that he wasn't a big fan of animals. His allergies were already affected by the musky scents that had wafted toward them from the stalls.

Tower was bummed. In his opinion, the farm animals were the best part of the tour. As a result, the last stop would be at the row of seven A-frames that stood just a few hundred yards below at the bottom of the hill. He was quite sure Aurora and her daughter, Breeze, would have the minister's daughter relaxing in their own whimsically decorated A-frame. Or perhaps they were kicking' back in the handmade hammocks. Each one strung out between the trunks of the mature willow trees nearby. As they walked, Tower provided details on the benefits of building an A-frame. Not only were they easy to construct, but they didn't require windows on the sides, keeping them cool in the summer and warm in the winter. Plus, given the roof's steep pitch, the snow just fell right off. The only downside of the buildings for Tower, was always being forced to stay in the very middle where there was just enough headroom to stand.

John peered above the tree-line in the distance and noticed wood poles bunched together at the top. "What's that over there? Is that an actual teepee?" He asked.

"Yep. I suppose you're gonna' want to check it out." Tower continued with trepidation. "The thing to keep in mind, is... well, that teepee is where we smoke... weed and whatnot."

John did not reply and continued to stare at the unique hidden structure surrounded by lofty pine trees. A long moment of silence passed.

"I feel centered when I'm high. I see things more clearly." Tower turned and faced his guest. "You know, high on pot. Marijuana." Tower smiled. "Have you ever tried it?"

"Well, no." John looked around and got excited about the possibility. "But I'm open to new experiences."

"Right on preacher-man!" Tower extended his arm around John's shoulder and pulled him tight into a sideways hug. "We've got time, before your boys get back, to enjoy a little taste." Tower led John to the entrance of the teepee; he lifted its canvas flap with one arm and made a grand welcome gesture with the other.

John placed a hand on the nearest pole of the teepee to support himself and removed a shoe. "Yes, well, the Lord helps those who help themselves." John's second shoe hit the ground and both men disappeared inside.

11

Bud was still groggy when he barked out the order from his horizontal position on the car's front seat. "Matty, wake up!" With no reply, the older brother begrudgingly sat up and looked for the source of the horn that just woke him. Bud could not understand why there was even a honk since his father's signs were down. He coughed deeply and rubbed his eyes until they adjusted to the bright sunlight. "Wake up Matthew."

The 1946 Chevy tow-truck passed by and pulled over behind the stranded car. Its driver shifted into reverse with a loud grind of gears, and brought the back end of the truck within three feet of the car's rear bumper. He exited the cab, grabbed a wooden tire-block, and made his way through the settling cloud of dust the battered rig had kicked up. Dressed in an oil-stained jump-suit, Able bent down to catch Bud's eye through the rear window of the car. He gave a friendly wave and hollered, "New Harvest Towing at your service!"

"Matty, come on, we're getting towed." Bud peered over the back of the front seat. Empty.

Able put his forearm on the driver's side door and leaned in. "I bet you guys are ready to split."

Bud exited the passenger side door. "Shit! Shit! Shit!"

"Well that's not the greeting I was expec-"

"Matthew's gone, man! My Dad is gonna' kill me." Bud entered the station wagon's back seat surprisingly fast for a person his size. He hoped his little pain-in-the-ass brother would be asleep in the way-back. "I can't believe this! He's gone."

"He's probably taking a leak," Able stated over the car's roof. "Go check the woods there while I hook up the car." Able placed the tire block against the front wheel and crossed between the vehicles. He used the hand-crack to lower the heavy-duty hook and chain. As Bud reached the tree-line, Able hollered out, "don't panic big guy, we'll find him."

"Big guy... why not call me lard-ass?" Bud mumbled to himself as he headed into the thick forest. For Bud, the saying, *"big guy"* was always an insult disguised as a harmless observation. He had heard it for years. *"Hey big guy, guess you'll need your own booth."* Or, *"You're gonna want some dessert, right big guy?"* But it wasn't harmless. It hurt. Bud realized he needed to piss as well, and stepped behind a nearby tree. "Matty! Matty! Come on Matty, we're getting towed!" Bud looked down, startled to find his urine had a light pink tinge. He was about to freak out when the memory of the cherry Kool-Aid provided the answer. He still felt unsteady from the effects of the strong joint and figured he must have fallen asleep. More likely, he passed out completely because the pot had been so much more intense than he was used to. No wonder he didn't hear his brother leave the car. The sudden rustling sounds of a few disrupted animals he couldn't see increased Bud's trepidation. "Matthew?" He raised the volume of his voice and finally found the courage to venture farther into the dark grouping of trees.

Able tugged-on a pair of leather work gloves and made his way to the car's rear end. He knelt and placed a hand on the bumper. Its chrome held the sun's heat and instantly warmed his glove. He reached under the car and placed the chain and its large hook around the automobile's sturdy frame. Able smiled. He sensed the stress of New York City start to melt away. It felt good to be working outside again, and he took a deep breath of the clean, New Hampshire air. He loved nature and always felt at home in the woods. Able returned to the tow rig and cranked the handle of the winch until all the slack in the chain disappeared. He ducked under its taut, rusted links and made his way to the driver's door with a long rope. He could hear Bud's distant calls as he secured the line around the door frame. That was the moment that he smelled the familiar aroma of marijuana.

"Well, I'll be." With a smile, he gave a hard tug until the rope's slipknot held fast. Able inserted the remaining line in and around the car's steering wheel a few times, and tossed the remaining rope toward the passenger's side. He walked around to the other side of the car and tied the rope to the passenger's side door frame. The tight cord would keep the steering wheel from turning in either direction, and ensure that the front wheels remained straight as the car, in neutral, was towed. Able gave a last look in through the driver's side window and caught a glimpse of a handwritten note. It was pierced and held in place by the ignition key. "Hey kid, I found a note!"

Bud bulldozed his way back through the bushes with the familiar twinge up his spine from leaving a scary location behind. As a child, the same sensation would nearly paralyze him on the creepy basement stairs in the parsonage. Bud was huffing for air when he finally broke free of the gloomy woods and onto the sunny shoulder of the road. "What does it say?" he gasped. "Let me read…"

"Keep your shirt on. He's fine." Able handed over the wrinkled paper.

Bud,

Going to get Mom. Tell Sarah not to worry - I took the map.

Let Malorie know I will return her duffel bag.

Tell Dad I found my gumption.

"God damn it! My Dad is gonna-"

"Would you forget about your Dad. Look, it's good he took the map. He's probably hitching the main roads." Able smiled.

Bud stepped back. "You don't understand. My little brother doesn't know how to hitchhike."

"Has he got thumbs?"

"Come on Wade, I'm not kidding." Bud's eyes were filled with concern.

"Wade?" Able replied in confusion.

Bud pointed at the name patch on the blue coveralls.

"No, no, I got these from the shop. I'm Able."

"Able? Guess we'll find that out."

Able smiled. He headed back toward the station wagon to grab the tire block and roll down the rear window to air it out. "Don't worry Bud. Worry is a misuse of the imagination. Now just get in the truck and I'll finish up."

Bud had a hard time heaving his sweaty body up and into the small interior of the cab. He felt the entire wrecker shimmy as Able activated the hydraulic levers of the tow-arm. The truck groaned like an old man with gout until the rear-end of the station wagon was lifted into position.

Able got behind the steering wheel with a sparkle in his eye and asked, "So what happened to your groovy signs?"

"They weren't mine." Anger in his voice.

"Hey, relax." Able pulled the truck and its load out onto the paved county road. He would need to find a wide intersection to pull a U-turn toward the commune. "Okay, let's get this classic back to the farm."

"No way, man. We should look for him now! He could be hurt."

Bud pleaded. "He could be dead in a ditch somewhere."

"Careful now. Our words become actions." Able shifted gears and the truck sped up.

"Are you kidding me? Pull over Wade. Or whatever you call yourself." Bud grabbed the door handle. "I'll find him myself."

"Kid, towing a car is no way to conduct a search. Besides, we can get more help at the farm. Calm down, everything will be fine."

Able's words made sense, and his smoothing voice helped put Bud at ease. Miles passed until Able asked, "so what's it like to be the son of a minister?"

"Well, it stinks actually."

"Yeah, I figured. There was a son of a Rabbi where I grew up. He hated it too. I can imagine it's pretty difficult to live up to all the expectations." Able waited a few moments before he continued. "Hey, can I ask you some questions?"

"Yeah... I guess so." Bud's eyes narrowed, unsure what the hippie's motivation was.

"Does your father like to be the center of attention?"

A tentative laugh escaped from Bud. "All the time."

Able nodded. "Wants everyone to admire him?"

Bud grinned. "He thrives on that."

"Does your father admit his mistakes?"

A grunt escaped from Bud at the absurdity of the question. "You don't get it man - my old man is never wrong."

"How does he react to criticism?"

Bud's expression lightened. "Well, he doesn't take it." He looked straight ahead, and his voice turned to sadness. "But he sure as shit gives it out."

Able nodded with a smile. "Does he exaggerate his own importance?"

"He's a minister for Christ's sake." Bud's voice shot up in volume. "Don't they all? They speak for God Almighty, no less." Bud laughed. He enjoyed the honest exchange with a pretty cool adult for a change.

"How does he treat you?"

"Like crap." Silence played out before Bud spoke again. "Teases me about my weight. Says I can't do anything right. Compares me to... never mind." Bud crossed his arms and slumped farther down in the seat.

"You know what man; I really don't feel like talking anymore."

"That's fine. Whatever you need." Eventually, his passenger drifted off to sleep. Able was not too surprised that Bud shut down so quickly to his questions. Though he wasn't a practicing psychologist, he had experience with students like him. Obese kids who used their weight as a kind of buffer from the outside world. People who eat way too much to fill the vast emptiness felt inside. Able would need more information before making an informal diagnosis, but he was certain the source of the teen's problems stemmed from a poor relationship with his dad. A self-absorbed father with narcissistic tendencies and extremely poor parenting skills.

"Like I should talk…" Able whispered to himself. He felt guilty expecting better behavior from another parent, given the fact that he had just lost custody of his little girl. He worried about the long-term psychological damage his absence would have on her. Not to mention his wife's vicious anger toward him and the harm it may have already had on their daughter. She often berated him in front of the child, quoting the school administration's rules against unwarranted faculty interaction with pupils. His wife insisted his tenure was at risk, stressing the wild weekend parties with students would amount to vocational suicide. He was surprised by her concern, given she had grown to hate the small college town of Keene, New Hampshire. She wanted to return to New York, and admitted she was never suited for country life. She missed the city's culture and excitement. She insisted that their daughter would get a better education there, and benefit from being closer to her grandparents in Manhattan. Able knew their marriage was over. And ultimately, none of it mattered anymore. He was done with her and the college. He was sick of the mean, backbiting politics of the school and the vague threats from the administration. He felt unfulfilled with his career and unhappy, his only friends were teachers, fellow professors who rambled on about their low pay and the laziness of the students. Teaching for Able had become a depressing bummer, something he felt he had been doing for way too long. He had no interest in conducting the same predictable classes year after year until retirement. Followed by what? Old age and death? Screw that! Able wanted to explore in more depth the various philosophies he had taught over the years. To put them to real use. To actually experience an expanded consciousness and share a spiritual environment with people who had the same desire for enlightenment.

Able downshifted to make it up the steep hill. He purposefully took in a few deep breaths. He knew better than to fixate on his own problems, let alone others'. It only brought suffering and dissatisfaction. Or "*dukkha,*" as Buddhists called it. That intrusive anxiety of trying to keep hold of things that are constantly changing. He drove on and focused on his breathing while Bud continued to snore.

On the commune, Serene and Tower's portion of the old farmhouse consisted of a cramped main room, a bathroom with a claw-foot tub with a shower head and curtain, a cast iron stove, and a tiny kitchen with just a sink and a hot plate. Numerous, spent, Jiffy-Pop pans filled the trash can at the end of the counter. Each emitted a two-week stench of burnt kernels and oil. While no one was home, a fine layer of dust had settled on every surface. Like the bus, the ceiling was draped with colorful tapestries from India, and the walls had planks of faded gray barn-wood nailed up on an angle. Along their top, five-inch wide boards served as mini-shelves for dozens of science fiction paperback books. Melted candles of various heights sat on two large speakers located in opposite corners of the main room. They were connected by visible wires to the record player that operated atop an upturned crate. It held the couple's favorite collection of vinyl records: *Steppenwolf, The Doors, Creedence Clearwater Revival, The Rolling Stones, Jefferson Airplane, The Beatles*. More albums were stacked along the shelf on the waterbed's custom headboard.

Serene was surprised how happy she felt to be back in the room where she had spent nearly three months on bed rest. The weeks in Maine had provided a welcome break, but now, with the twins bathed and fed, she loved being home again. To have them snuggled-in on both sides of her body. Soon a deep sleep took hold.

Malorie pulled back the top corner of the bold, daisy-print shower curtain and hollered to be heard above the running water. "Serene, you're so right! This stuff's amazing!" She held up the plastic bottle and read the tiny white text and quotes that filled the blue label. *"Dr. Bronner's 18-In-One Hemp Peppermint Pure-Castile Soap. Family Soap Makers Since*

1858. " With no response, Malorie assumed she was not heard. She rinsed her body of the minty suds and felt all of the day's craziness flow off and down the drain. Her scalp tingled. She wasn't quite sure if it was the strong soap or the aftermath of Sarah's earlier tirade. Malorie dried herself and wrapped a towel around her head. The robe her host had provided smelled of patchouli oil. She stepped out from the bathroom refreshed, and hoped their discussion of motherhood would continue. Malorie saw immediately that Serene and her beautiful twins were sound asleep. Hushed moments of intense longing to be a mother herself crept by, until Malorie could not resist the desire to join the peaceful trio. With absolutely no experience with waterbeds, her attempt to lie down resulted in a sudden fall backwards, and a huge displacement of water. Serene woke with a start.

"Holy shit, you scared me half-to-death!"

"I am so sorry. Are you okay?" Malorie asked; she moved cautiously to scoot up toward the head of the bed without making more waves.

The young mother realized her babies were still asleep and replied, "everything's cool."

Their giggles started low, but grew louder with each gasp for air. The pressure not to wake the twins only added to the hilarity. The women felt the waterbed's surface undulate with each belly laugh, while their eyes brimmed with tears of joy.

"Oh my God, I haven't laughed like that in years," exclaimed Malorie.

Serene caught her breath. "Tower makes me laugh so hard; I've actually peed my pants."

"I'm jealous, you know. He is so in love with you and the kids. You're lucky." Malorie adjusted the damp towel on her head and gazed at the details of the complex tapestry above the bed. "How did you know he was the one?"

"I didn't." Serene said. "I mean, not at first. But when I realized the universe had blessed me with a child and I told Tower I was pregnant his face lit up like the sun. It was so far out. *That's* when I knew he was the one." Serene gently turned her body sideways to face Malorie without disturbing the children. "What I didn't know, was how hard marriage would be. Let alone throwing twins into the mix."

"I wish... I mean, well, never mind." Malorie said.

"What? Go ahead."

"Well, there have been times when I think John is *"the one."* I think."

"Isn't he married?" asked Serene.

"He says it's ran its course."

Serene sat upright. She brought the two swaddled babies together and used the bedspread to construct a fluffy nest around them. "Aren't you worried about the age difference?"

"Not really. It seems to be a much bigger deal for him." Malorie gently positioned her pillow against the headboard to join her new friend.

"What would your folks say?" asked Serene.

"Not much, unfortunately." Malorie felt the familiar tightening in her throat. It happened whenever she had to address the agonizing subject. She stated flatly. "They're both dead."

"Oh, my goodness. What happened? How old were you?"

"Three." Malorie's voice became monotone as she rattled off the four facts, as she always had, when people asked. "It was winter. They lost control on a mountain road. Killed instantly. No one suffered."

Serene's eyes moistened with tears. "How horrible for you."

Malorie shrugged her shoulders. "I was raised by my grandparents." Malorie's vacant gaze indicated that she wanted to remain unemotional. "It happened so long ago. I try not to think about it." Serene brought one of the twins up for Malorie to hold. She knew her daughter's innocence would help soften Malorie's guarded heart.

"Are they your mom's parents?"

"Yeah. My mom was their only child. Their little princess. Both were completely devastated. I found out later that my grandmother nearly had a nervous breakdown. I think she only recovered by keeping my mom's memory alive for both of us. There are tons of photographs all over the house. Baby shots, school pictures; you know… cheerleading, marching band. And every year on my mother's birthday, I'm required to go through her photo album from start to finish. My parent's obituary is on the last page." Malorie paused and sighed deeply. "The local paper used their wedding picture. You can see how excited they were to start their lives together."

"Wow, that's heavy. I'm so sorry."

"Thank you." Malorie gently touched the cheek of the baby in her arms. "Apparently everything I do reminds them of her. The same mannerisms and stuff. I don't remember her at all, but my grandmother makes sure they're still in my life. Sometimes I feel, I don't know, like I'm really not seen for myself. Like I'm a place-holder or something." Malorie's voice took on mock pride. "And sure enough, growing up, each and every Sunday after church, I was required to walk down the block to visit my Dad's parents too." Her smile disappeared and her voice got softer. "Apparently, I have his eyes."

Serene nodded.

Malorie lowered her face to smell the top of the sleeping baby's head. With her eyelids barely closed, she surrendered to the unique sweet scent she had never encountered before. Malorie wondered if having her own baby would eliminate the constant pain, the hollow feelings of loss that her parent's death had resulted in. She opened her eyes and forced her mind to return. "My grandparents have always seemed old to me. All their friends are old. Guess they've rubbed off on me." Malorie's sudden giggle surprised Serene. "And my grandfather never buys green bananas, cause you never know." She leaned back and let out a sigh. "I'm so tired of hearing stories about World War I. How hard it was to live through the Depression. Christ, I've been around elderly people my whole life... no wonder John's age isn't a big deal."

"Able says I'm an old soul." Serene stated with a smile. "I bet you are, too."

Malorie's eyes narrowed. She had never heard the expression.

"Wise beyond your years. He believes an old soul learns lessons from past incarnations. You know, past lives. Anyway, they use that wisdom to make sense of a current life. They're deep thinkers. Drawn to spirituality rather than being materialistic."

"I suppose. One thing's for sure. John's daughter hates me, old soul or not."

"Fathers and daughters, so intense. I know that firsthand. My sister and I fought all the time for our dad's attention. We finally made a deal. She'd help him with the farm work, and I'd cook his meals." Serene carefully swung her legs over the side of the bed with her baby son in her arms. It felt good to stand. "So how long have you been, you know, attracted to him?"

"I've had a crush on him since my freshman year when he took over the Youth Fellowship at church. He's so intelligent and funny. Tons of charisma." Malorie's expression lightened up as she held the baby in her arms. "Then last year, he appointed me the president of the Youth Group. We started to spend a lot more time together. You know, planning the trip to the Holy Land, raising money." Malorie smiled down at the drowsy baby girl in her arms. In a playful baby voice, Malorie cooed in a hushed tone, "And he's such a good kisser, oh yes, he is, yes he is-"

"Hey, don't take this wrong, but he could be a father figure."

"Yeah. Guess it makes sense. But don't you think that's kinda' creepy since I'm well… attracted to him? You know, in a sexual way."

Have you slept together yet?" Serene's eyes twinkled.

"No. But we made out once during the trip." Malorie replied.

Serene pointed her finger at her new friend. "Well, when you do, use a rubber. Better yet, use two!" Both girls laughed.

"I wish they'd let single women take the pill." Malorie raised her right hand, as though repeating an oath. "I would take it every morning. Religiously."

"I'm not sure the Pope would appreciate your wording."

Once again, their giggles nearly woke the twins. Finally, Malorie surrendered to a lengthy yawn, and Serene followed suit. Both laid back down with the babies in their arms, and the sleep they needed took hold.

12

Barbara was starved. The moment the small plate hit the counter in the hotel's coffee shop, she devoured the grilled cheese sandwich and wished she had ordered the fries. Hal sat next to her on a green swivel stool and scanned the most recent gossip in the hotel's in-house newspaper. He glanced over at her and winked.

"Well, you'll certainly fit in."

"What does that mean?" Barbara hoped his comment was not about her ongoing struggle with staying slim. She looked at her watch and turned the reflective napkin dispenser sideways to check the status of her dark mane. The thick brunette hair was the one attribute she really liked about herself.

Hal lowered his voice. "I heard eating is a national past-time here. Fortunately for us, employees get served the same food as the guests. Not as many choices, mind you, but the food is supposed to be delicious." Hal swigged down his last bit of coffee. "And though I don't relish the idea of sleeping in the men's dormitory, the free room and board will allow me to save quite a bit of cash."

Barbara peeked at her watch again.

Hal's expression lit up with a big grin. "Manny really enjoyed our audition, didn't he? He certainly liked you."

"I suppose."

"Now look, he said it's only a suggestion."

Barbara rolled her eyes in disbelief. She knew it was much more than a suggestion.

Hal's voice was upbeat. "Well, anyway. I thought we sounded great. We made it, Barbie Girl!"

"You know Hal, there's something I've been wanting to discuss with-"

"Can I get you folks anything else?" The stocky waitress with the frilly apron hated to interrupt, but her shift was about to end, and her girdle was killing her.

"Just the check, sweetheart." Hal reached for his wallet while Barbara opened her vast leather purse.

"No Hal, I've got this!" Her voice had a trace of anger from the missed opportunity to set her friend straight on the *Barbie Girl* issue. She decided there wasn't time to address it before her appointment at *"Salon Di'Elegante,"* the resort's very own beauty shop located downstairs. Their plan was for Hal to escort Barbara to the salon, and then walk the grounds of the resort. He had never seen an actual indoor pool and wanted to look through the famous underwater window at the guests swimming in the deep end. The duo decided to keep their hotel rooms for the evening and have their luggage delivered by a bellman to the staff dormitories in the morning. The rest of the day would consist of filling out employment paperwork, rehearsal, and finalizing their play-list of songs.

"So, are you ready?"

Barbara responded. "Ready as I'll ever be."

Hal grinned and opened the glass door to the salon. The half-dozen women inside were oblivious, given their preoccupation of reading magazines and having their heads incased in loud hairdryer helmets. "So… is it true blondes have more fun?" He teased Barbara as she entered the shop.

"Guess I'll find out."

Matthew had left his brother sound asleep in the station wagon and walked half-a-mile before he decided to try hitchhiking. He was not sure if he should enthusiastically swing his forearm repeatedly in the direction he was traveling, or appear nonchalant with his thumb held low at his side. Of the three cars that passed, only one slowed down before it drove by. Matthew realized there might be more hiking than hitching ahead of him.

Farther down the road he caught a glimpse of an old wrecker coming around the bend. He worried that it belonged to the commune, and was on its way to pick up the family car. Matthew scurried into the tree-line without being seen, and waited there to see if the truck returned with the station wagon in tow. While sitting in the woods, an idea occurred to him. Matthew used his sketchpad to draw a larger-than-life image of a thumb. Complete with detailed shading, a thumbnail, and defined wrinkles on the knuckle, the drawing looked exactly like a 17-inch thumb, extended up from the bottom of the sketchpad. He left the sheet of paper attached to the pad's stiff cardboard backing so the drawing could be held upright from the bottom. Eventually the same tow-truck passed by with his brother in the cab, and the family car hitched up at the rear. Matthew promptly made his way back down to the roadside with the sketchpad in hand. He felt confident someone would appreciate his artwork.

Matthew's instincts proved correct when the very next vehicle came to a stop. The bed of the white 1965 Ford pickup was fully loaded with cardboard boxes of groceries and supplies. The driver, in his early seventies, leaned across the seat and hollered through the passenger-side window. His docile beagle sat up and panted beside him.

"Well God bless you son!" He grinned a friendly smile of worn-down dentures. "That big thumb is a hoot! Where ya' headed?"

Matthew stepped closer. "I need to get to Keene. To catch a bus."

"Well son…" The driver removed his tattered Red Socks cap and slid his hand back over the remaining gray hairs on his spotted scalp. "I can drop you off in Keene." He checked his Timex watch, its cracked face sat protected on the inside of his wrist. "But I'm sorry to say that by the time we get there, the station will be closed. Keene rolls up their sidewalks around five." The old-timer always got a kick from that mental image.

"Oh, okay. Well, I'd appreciate a lift anyway, sir."

"Toss your bag in back, but mind the hamburger buns." To make room in the truck's cab, the driver placed his clipboard onto the dashboard. Its long list of checked-off groceries reflected in the dirty windshield. Matthew did as he was instructed and hopped into the pickup. The dog sniffed the new passenger's arm a few times and showed her acceptance by laying her head back down on her master's knee.

"This is Ruby. And I'm Pete Curtis."

"Hi Ruby, I'm Matthew. Nice to meet you, Mr. Curtis."

"Mr. Curtis was my father's name. Call me Pete."

The truck accelerated, and the breeze through the window felt wonderful on the teen's face. Matthew smiled. He allowed himself a moment of celebration for the success of his drawing. His artistic skills had often been a source of praise from others but in that moment, he felt even more satisfaction from knowing his art made a real difference.

Simply being brave enough to hit the road alone felt cool too. Until that afternoon, he had always avoided risk. Matthew liked this new sensation of courageousness and hoped it would continue. He turned to ask the driver where he was headed but noticed the hand-carved wooden cross dangling like a fishhook from the rear-view mirror. Pete noticed the boy's distraction and launched into his all-time favorite song, *"The Old Rugged Cross."* Matthew smiled but didn't take the bait to join in. He couldn't believe that of all the vehicles traveling the roads of New Hampshire that afternoon, he would be stuck with a holy roller who loved singing hymns. Pete finished his rendition and started a one-way conversation.

"My wife and I run the mess hall at the Gift of God Bible Camp. It's down on Old Swanzey Road, across from Pisgah State Park. This will be our twelfth summer of serving the Lord there." During the passing miles and across Keene's city limits, Pete described how difficult it was to feed twenty-six hungry teenagers and four camp counselors three square meals a day, not to mention cleaning the pots and pans and shopping for supplies. He went into detail about how he made perfect flapjacks that everyone demanded after the six-am reveille he played over the PA system. Pete stressed that the camp's activities of canoeing, volleyball, leather crafts, archery, and horseshoes always played second fiddle to the study of scripture. In fact, the counselors had to ensure that their kids accepted the Lord Jesus Christ as their personal savior by the end of summer. Matthew listened politely. The pickup finally stopped at the curb in front of Keene's darkened bus station. It occurred to Pete that while sharing his zeal for the good works he and his wife had done, he completely failed to ask the boy what his plans were for the night.

"Young fella, tell you what. You come stay in the boy's bunk house and I'll run you back here in the morning. Our campers won't arrive for the start of camp until the afternoon, so you'll have the whole place to yourself." Pete grinned. "My missus will fix us some grub, too. How does that sound?"

Matthew had not eaten since he shared the loaf of bread with his brother and was famished. Having a place to stay overnight sounded nice too. "That would be wonderful, Mr. Curtis. I mean, Pete." They shared a chuckle and the truck pulled out. Ruby moved toward Matthew and got her buttery velvet ears rubbed with tenderness.

The peaceful river that ran near the commune was indisputably the favorite spot for everyone to relax and clean up at the end of a hot day. The previous summer, farm members had dumped two truckloads of fine sand on a section of shoreline to provide the perfect location to spread out towels and sunbathe. Along its banks, the children giggled while hunting for frogs that they would later race on the beach. Lush leaves filled the tree branches stretched out over the water and provided shade from the hot sun. Colorful bluegills in the shadows darted in and out of the deep pockets among the boulders. The river's quiet current was nearly indiscernible but for the harmless suds from the bars of Ivory soap the bathers used to get clean.

CLANG, CLANG, CLANG, CLANG, CLANG, CLANG, CLANG!

Terra had just climbed up the boards nailed to a tree that served as a ladder high above the river. After driving the long trip back from Maine, all he wanted was to cool off and check the status of his garden. When he heard the farm's emergency alarm, he released his grip on the rope-swing and hit the water. When he surfaced, he noticed everyone on shore hastily collecting their towels and clothing. There was no mistaking the look of apprehension on all of their faces. Even the dogs barked wildly, knowing something was up.

Ruth had been in the kitchen, listening to Feather's unwarranted complaints about her workload when the alarm sounded off just outside the building. During their conversation, the stacks of unwashed dishes didn't go unnoticed by Ruth. She decided to mention it to the group once she found out why the damn bell was being rung in the first place.

Serene and Malorie were still deep asleep when the alarm pierced the silence. The twins woke and began to cry. Serene got off the bed and slipped-on one of Tower's flannel shirts; its long red plaid fabric all but touched the wood floor. Malorie's trepidation had more to do with the wailing baby in her arms than with the alarm itself.

"What should I do?"

"Just hold her like this, tight against your chest." Serene retrieved her son from the waterbed. "Now follow me!" She clung to her baby boy and blasted out of the farmhouse. Malorie, in the borrowed terry cloth robe, struggled to get off the unsteady waterbed with the child in her arms. She quickly realized the baby should be placed on the bed first. Once Malorie stood, it didn't take but a few seconds to pick up the child and leave.

When John and Tower heard the clangs of the alarm, they were on their backs watching their shared smoke curl upward like lingering daydreams escaping through the top of the teepee. John was amazed at how graceful his tour guide stood up to exit. The extremely dazed minister could not quite stand and had to roll over onto his hands and knees in order to crawl toward the bright oval opening of the structure. There in the sunshine, he caught sight of Tower making rapid strides along a path toward the warning bell. John had a difficult time locating his shoes and rather than getting upset like he normally would, he found himself giggling like a child. Once the shoes were found and slipped on, he could not tie their laces. He took his shoes and socks off and that made him laugh even more.

Next to the dining hall the parked tow-truck held the station wagon upright like a massive marlin trophy. Able placed his hand on Bud's shoulder and yelled to be heard above the iron rod's last contact with the welding tank.

"Well done, Bud! You can stop now."

"God damn, that felt good!" Despite his ears ringing, Bud couldn't help but grin widely.

"I knew it would." Able turned and noticed most of the commune members were quickly headed up the lane. "Come on, let me introduce you to the family." Able led Bud over to the six picnic tables nearby and stood on top of one of the bench seats. He spoke up to be heard over the excited dogs. "Hey everyone, take it easy! No need to run, there's no fire. I just have a few things to tell you." As the last members arrived and things started to quiet down, Able introduced their newest guest. "Brothers and sisters, this is Bud."

The minister's son felt obliged to flash the peace sign but held off. The folks standing in front of him had friendly expressions under their wet stringy hair and all were actual hippies living off the land with their kids. That impressed Bud. He returned a humble acknowledgment with a smile, and sat down. Clarity, a young pregnant woman with jet black hair tied up in a towel, stepped forward. Wearing another damp towel around her extended white middle, she moved closer to Bud. He was taken aback by her dark pregnancy line that ran vertically down from her belly button and disappeared under the towel. Her dark eyes grew more intense as she bent forward and searched his face. He could smell the river in her hair and noticed a lot of mud had stuck to her unshaven legs and feet. She sensed his trepidation and sat down next to him.

"You look very tired." Clarity considered herself a healer and was certain many of the young man's chakras were blocked. "You hold a great deal of emotional pain inside." She made a gentle sweeping gesture to the gathering. "You are among friends now. Close your eyes and breath deep." Bud followed her requests. Her open hand passed purposely over his forehead without touching it. Just as he was feeling better and about to inhale again, his sister arrived.

"Buddy!" Sarah called out loudly with affection.

Bud's eyelids flew open and Clarity lowered her hand. A look of disappointment washed over her face. She had just gotten started in understanding the complex needs of her extremely toxic patient.

"Where's Matthew?" Bud looked to Able for help. The guilt of failing to protect his little brother made it nearly impossible to speak.

"That's why we rang the bell" stated Able. "Everything is cool. But your bro-"

"What happened?" Sarah cut off the older hippie and made a beeline toward her brother. Her voice turned strident and her eyes squinted for the truth. "Bud, where's Matthew?"

"He took off." Bud kept his gaze on the ground and tightened his jaw. He dreaded this whole situation and knew his father's wrath would only make it worse. Bud remained silent and hoped he could stay calm and not overreact to the unfair blame he was about to receive.

"I knew it!" Sarah was furious. "I told dad he shouldn't leave you two alone with the car. Is he hurt? Why did he leave?"

Bud muttered. "I told him the story. You know, Mom and Dad. The family fire."

Able stepped off the seat of the picnic table and moved closer to the siblings. "I'm certain your brother is fine." He handed the folded note to Sarah. Her hands could barely hold on to it, given the surprise of Bud's statement. She thought her mother had not told anyone else the secret. Sarah recognized from the paper's thickness that it was a torn page from

Matthew's sketchbook. "He probably scored a ride by now and is on his way to see your mom. Don't panic." Able searched above the gathering for Tower, trusting he had the kid's father close at hand.

Suddenly, a male voice arose from the woods. "Hey everybody, what's going down? What's wrong?" Tower's huge dirty bare feet brought him to the group way ahead of the lagging minister.

"Everything's cool," instructed Able.

Sarah's voice shot out. "My little brother is missing, and you keep saying everything is cool!"

Malorie spoke up. "He's just trying to help."

Sarah glanced at Malorie in her robe and saw the baby in her arms. "Oh, so stealing my father isn't enough? You had to kidnap a baby too?"

"Look, I don't know your name, but you need to calm down" Able said firmly. His weariness from the road had taken over, and he regretted his comment immediately. He hated getting emotional and rarely did. "Miss, no one can see their reflection in running water."

"What the hell does that mean?"

"It is only in *still* water that we see." Able smiled. "It's a Taoist proverb."

Sarah pinched the bridge of her nose to relieve the tension. "Oh my god."

John headed for the gathering in bare feet. His attention was keenly focused on the dirt path beneath him, and on his earlier conversation with Tower. He felt grounded as he walked, and admitted to himself that his feet never felt so alive. Pebbles and sharp rocks were less of a concern than connecting with the earth and the enjoyment of being barefoot. His dress-shirt was unbuttoned, and his tee-shirt trailed happily below, as if it had finally found its freedom in the light of day. With his pompadour disheveled beyond belief, John addressed Bud.

"Where's Matthew?" He turned to face his daughter while clumsily buttoning his shirt. It felt odd that he really didn't care if each button went into its matching hole. John's tongue felt thick and his throat hurt. He coughed deeply and asked, "Sarah, where's your little brother?" The words were slow to exit his dry mouth and he hoped his speech sounded normal to those around him.

Sarah noticed her father's pupils looked odd. Both were huge and covered most of the blue irises in a way that she had never seen before.

"Daddy, your eyes look strange."

"He's fine" Tower mumbled as he sat down next to his wife.

"Daddy, what is that smell?" Asked Sarah.

"I introduced him to a little weed, okay?" Tower's anxious comment resulted in laughter among the members of the commune. "No harm, no foul."

Sarah fell back onto the seat behind her. Her eyes filled with disbelief and the color drained from her face. Bud's reaction took the form of a slow appearing smirk as he realized he would finally have ammunition to use against his old man. Malorie's response was a giggle as she hid behind the head of the baby girl in her arms. The day had been full of so many surprises, but this one wasn't on her radar. John glanced at the happy baby in Malorie's embrace and felt more than just a tinge of paranoia.

"Please give the note to your father," Able told Sarah on his way to a large flat piece of granite nearby. Farm members called it, *"The Talking Rock,"* a foot-high platform used by anyone who wanted to address the group. Able's volume increased. "Please take a seat everyone so we can discuss the situation." They sat down at the familiar picnic tables that often served as a location for their outdoor meetings and meals. The tables had also been used as workstations in the past for peeling fruits and cutting vegetables at the start of every canning process. Old, embedded stains of beet juice were crisscrossed with the dull orange nectar of peaches and apricots. Dark green streaks of trimmed spinach and kale filled the scarred tops of every table. Each stain was a permanent reminder of the hundreds of hours the commune members had labored together for the benefit of all.

"Now look, I know this is a bummer. We were looking forward to a welcome home celebration. But we need to wait on that until we find the minister's son." Able announced.

The group groaned their collective disappointment, though they understood the situation required them to accept the change in plans. Feather was not at all pleased and took off her apron. She tossed it aside in her frustration over the needless preparation she had already done for the party.

Ruth had to speak up. "This is what happens, Tower, when you pick up non-members on the roadside."

"Don't blame me for the missing kid. That's on his brother."

Tower had lost his high and that always made him cranky. "Besides, I was in the teepee with their old man."

Blaze snickered. "Nice cop out, Chief Talking Bull." Malorie laughed along with the rest of the group. She enjoyed the carpenter's sense of humor, and found it made him more attractive. If that was even possible.

Sarah, who was sitting next to her father, suddenly stood up. "My little brother is missing and could be in real danger!" She turned to face her father. Her anger affected her voice by getting louder. "I told you it wasn't safe! And now you're what, high on pot, to boot?"

John remained silent. With a vacant expression, he attempted to put on a sock but could not balance well with one foot high in the air. The image of Anne Bancroft raising her leg to seduce Dustin Hoffman in the film, "*The Graduate*," filled his mind. His sudden, uncontrolled giggling confirmed to everyone present that he was still stoned.

"That's it!" Sarah's cheeks flushed with rage. "I'm calling mom!"

Able hurried over to Sarah and used a softer tone. "Please wait. There's no need to worry your mother. Things will work out." He gently took her hands in his. "I give you my word, we will find him. But you must trust me." Sarah hesitated at first, then nodded her agreement. She saw the sincerity in his kind brown eyes. She could see that Able understood her fear and concern for her brother. He turned away to address the group. "It's pretty obvious John here, nor his car, are in any condition to search for his son. And since everyone is a bit burned out and in need of a hot meal, I suggest we eat first. Then we'll finalize a plan."

Ruth stood and crossed her arms tightly. "Well then, someone better wash the dishes. You know… the ones you ignored while the rest of us were in Maine."

"And someone spaced-out on weeding the garden, too" Tower added in a teasing, tattletale tone. "Didn't water the plants in the greenhouse either."

Terra sprang up from his seat. "What did you say?"

"It's cool man, I'm pretty sure I saved them." Tower said with pride. "Oh, and trash-run wasn't done either, by the way."

Ruth shouted. "Bear, that was your job! What the hell did you do while we were gone? Just hang out at the river and get high?"

"Pretty much." Bear stood up. "What did you expect?" His white skin made the long abundant black hair on his barrel chest and shoulders stand out even more. "Since you've been riding everybody's ass forever."

Silence. Ruth was visibly taken aback. "Yeah, well, maybe it's because I'm way too *"up-tight."* Isn't that how you put it?" Ruth shot a burning glare over the picnic tables at Aurora.

To everyone's surprise, Bear spoke up again. "This was the first real break we've had since the farm got started." Nods of agreement and numerous *"Right-On"* were angrily voiced. Bear's children, Willow, age six, and Gem, age five, had never seen their father so upset. They scurried into their mother's arms just as she was wringing out the last bit of water from her long, strawberry-blonde hair. Despite their father's abundant black hair, both daughters shared the fair complexion and hair color of their mother.

Malorie had to conceal her laughter as a thought came to mind. *"So much for peace, love, and understanding."*

"This farm started long before you and Star got here!" Ruth shouted back. "And it has always taken hard work to keep it going!" With hesitation, Bear sat back down to comfort his girls.

"Well, I hope the animals were fed at least" Aurora said kiddingly to reduce the tension.

"Oh Mom, of course they were" Breeze spoke up and laughed. "I helped milk the goats too. Every morning and every afternoon." Her sweet smile brought the group back to peace.

"Good for you, darling." Aurora gave her daughter a big hug. "I missed you so much."

"Yes, thank you, Breeze." Able stepped back up onto the stone and cleared his throat. "Perhaps we should address all these concerns later. You know… when the kids aren't around."

"No!" Bear stood and raised his voice. "Look man, we need to rap about this now. And I don't care if the kids hear. In fact, it's because of my kids that I want it resolved."

Able got off the stone and sat down on the nearest picnic bench. "Sure man, the Rock is yours." It took a moment for Able's surprised expression to disappear. Bear boldly took his place on the rock and turned to face his shocked audience. In all the years at the farm, he had never spoken from the Talking Rock.

"I generally don't say much."

"You don't say?" Aurora thought her attempt at humor was priceless. "Get it? You don't say?" Her excitement caused chuckles in a few, until Bear's angry reaction turned the entire gathering silent.

"Quiet! I have the Rock now." Bear took a deep breath to regain control of his temper, but everyone sensed it wasn't working. "Let's face facts. All of us work pretty damn hard. Some work harder than others." He looked directly at Tower, then turned his attention toward a girl on his right with a short, Twiggy hairstyle. "And not all of us have a trust fund we can rely on." Bear turned back to address the group. "Anyway, I think those who have been here the longest deserve more than a monthly partner draw. We should get part ownership of the farm."

"Bullshit!" Ruth jumped to her feet. Her reaction was fast and loud. "Who the fuck do you think you are, demanding part ownership of my farm?"

"*Our* farm, sister dear." Serene's soft voice did little to settle her sister down.

"You mean our *family* farm. What don't you get about that?" Ruth headed for the Talking Rock with a voice filled with scorn. "Besides, I thought you hippies didn't want material possessions to tie you down."

"I'm not done." Bear's thundering roar caused his youngest daughter to cower into her mother's lap. Bear's voice instantly became gentle. "Oh no. I'm so sorry, sweetie. I didn't mean to scare you."

Star, with loving arms around her two children, locked her tearing eyes with those of her husband's. "It's okay, Babe. Tell them about your accident. How it changed you."

Bear nodded and took another deep breath. "You all know the fall from that big spruce last winter nearly killed me. In the hospital, while lying in traction, I realized that if I had died, there would be no one to take care of my wife and kids." Bear's voice cracked as his suppressed fears crept up from his huge chest.

Aurora had to speak. "Oh Bear, you know your Harvest family would have stepped up."

"I know that. But it's the long-term future that worries me."

Ruth remained silent with her arms crossed. She had known that this day would come eventually when someone would raise the topic of shared ownership. But she had hoped it would not happen this soon. To make matters worse, it was Bear who had made the request. She really liked Bear. She was always impressed with his work ethic and how he never complained. Deeply respected by everyone on the farm, it would be difficult to sway members from Bear's demand.

Serene walked over to Ruth's side and handed her the baby. Serene was certain Ruth could not remain angry when her baby's coos did their job of distraction. "It's still a family farm sis. It's just a larger family now." Ruth rolled her eyes as she returned the baby to her sister. Without a word, she turned and retreated to her part of the old farmhouse. Serene grinned and announced, "Don't worry everyone, she'll come around. She always does."

Able winked at Bear. "Let's give Ruth some time." Bear nodded and stepped down from the Rock. The few moments of silence that passed provided a pleasant break from the outpouring of emotions. "Okay, let's get those dishes done so we have something to eat on." Able checked his watch. "It's now six-fifteen, so we'll eat at seven sharp and come up with a search plan."

Tower leaned over and kissed the top of each of the twin's heads. He snuggled Serene's neck and teased her in his Humphrey Bogart voice, complete with an overbite.

"Gee Sweetheart, that shirt seems a little big on you." Tower didn't get the smile from his wife he had hoped for, and reached across to Malorie to retrieve the baby from her arms. "Thanks again for helping with the kiddos."

"No problem, we had lots of fun" Malorie replied.

"Apparently, you and the minister had fun, too." Serene scowled up at her husband and turned around briskly. As she headed back to the farmhouse, Tower rushed to catch up, knowing that he'd blown it, with what he thought was just a harmless joint.

During the forty-five minutes that passed before dinner, everyone completed their tasks. Able drove the tow-truck up the hill and parked it at the auto-shop's entrance. He lowered the car to the ground and removed all the rope. John, Bud, and Malorie brought the family's luggage into the nearly finished apartment on the first floor of the green barn. The space was clean, but smelled of primer on the walls. John's queasiness only intensified, so he laid down on one of the army cots and fell fast asleep.

Sarah stayed with Aurora and her daughter, returning to their A-frame, where she was too upset to be anywhere near her father. She borrowed a notepad and pencil from Breeze, and soon a detailed outline of reasons for conducting an effective search emerged. Careful consideration was given to the potential dangers Matthew might encounter on the road. At the top of the list, drivers not seeing him and drifting onto the shoulder. Next, violent motorcycle gangs. Then, the real possibility of falling rocks. And last, although highly unlikely, black bears lurking along the roadside. With those, and more in mind, Sarah wanted the search to start immediately.

The dishes got washed while Terra doubled-checked the garden and the greenhouse. He saw plenty of weeds still in need of pulling and confirmed that Tower's efforts had rescued most of the thirsty plants in the dome. He made time to stop in on Smooch in his A-frame to see how the teenager's back was feeling. The purple glow from three black lights on the pitched ceiling brought to life the numerous psychedelic posters tacked nearby. Because of the lighting, Terra's teeth appeared super white as he provided the farm's mechanic with news about the minister's missing kid and the conflict between Ruth and Bear. Smooch found the story entertaining, but his back was still killing him. He just wanted to be left alone with his bottle of aspirin and his AM/FM transistor radio.

The remaining members of the community changed into dry clothing. In her renovated apartment on the second floor of the barn, Charmed recalled Bear's criticism of her sizable trust fund. Everything in the small apartment looked expensive because it was. The Waverly floral curtains matched the bedspread, and the closet overflowed with the latest in fashionable clothing. Her makeup table was filled with pricey perfumes and the best makeup products money could buy. Charmed had always felt that it wasn't her fault she'd come from a wealthy family. Nor did she set out to have her amazing college professor awaken her spiritual identity. And yes, living on a hippie commune helped in her ongoing rebellion against a very controlling father, and people couldn't deny that she was also working hard to improve herself in her search for enlightenment. Charmed decided to double-down on the unfair treatment by Bear, and to wear the outfits she had set aside for the now canceled party. Buzz, her current boyfriend and one of the two Tree Fellas, was rarely seen in anything but denim, covered in sawdust. To make Charmed happy, he agreed to wear the new colorful Dashiki shirt from South Africa. She knew it would blow everyone's minds to see him in such groovy threads. Charmed suggested the water buffalo sandals from India would look cool with the white bell bottoms, as well. He reminded her how the sandal's leather bands gave him blisters on both of his big toes the last time he'd tried to wear them. She agreed they would just go barefoot as usual, and donned her fashionable tiered patchwork skirt, beaded headband, pink granny glasses, and her new favorite embroidered blouse. Their flamboyant display, as in past events, would later be a topic of conversation among several of the other members of the commune.

At his desk, surrounded by rustic wood shelves filled with books on far-east studies, Able reviewed his map of the northeastern states. He recognized that there were countless roads the boy could have taken, and it was going to make the search a lot more complicated, especially at night. Adding to the difficulty was Tower's poor judgment in turning the minister on to grass. John wouldn't be completely down from his first high for a couple more hours at least. Though Able loved Tower like a brother, this was not the first time he had put the farm in danger with his frequent smoking of grass. Able smiled. At least he used the teepee this time. It was where everyone agreed would be the location for taking drugs on the commune. Children were never allowed inside the beige teepee hidden deep in the woods, and its camouflaged location was a huge benefit when unexpected visitors or the local cops arrived. The most important rule in the teepee involved the taking of hallucinogenic substances. A strict buddy-system was required as a part of guided trips, where a straight person would carefully monitor the drug's effects on the user. It ensured that no one would suffer an overdose; it was certainly not an arbitrary requirement. It was a strict rule that everyone was expected to follow. Able had seen his share of college students over the years who had passed away alone in their dorm rooms just trying to get the best high possible.

    Able folded the map and noticed the sun was starting to go down. He switched off the brass desk lamp and headed out of his one-bedroom office. He decided it would be best for everyone if the search got underway first thing in the morning.

"Are you out-of-your mind?" Sarah screeched like a live version of one of her owl figurines back home. Her voice resulted in a sudden halt to eating dinner at the picnic tables. "It's almost dark! We're just wasting time!"

"To make the right choice *is* to save time." Able stated calmly and continued eating.

Sarah rolled her eyes and flopped back down next to Aurora, who smiled. Aurora understood how Able's numerous pithy comments could grate on one's nerves.

"Darling, he really is only trying to help." She gently patted the top of the girl's trembling hands. "If it were wintertime, hell yes, we would be out there this instant. But if he had to, your brother could curl up under an overpass somewhere and be simply fine for a night. Who knows, he may have already gotten a ride."

"That's just it! What if he got picked up by some crazy person who…" Sarah dropped her head down on folded arms and wept.

Reverend Thomley was not there to comfort his daughter. His search for enlightenment still had him at one with the green army cot in the newly converted room in the barn. Malorie thought she should stay behind and watch over him, but her empty stomach growled for food. She and Bud walked down the hill to the dining hall together and got in line. Once seated at the picnic table outside, Bud was surprised how good the odd-looking soup tasted. He enjoyed dunking the now familiar hearty bread into his clay bowl. He was about to go back inside for seconds of the lentil soup when the girl in the long blue-jean skirt seated next to him suddenly stood up. It took all of Bud's willpower not to stare at the loose gaps in the crochet top where a large bra should have been doing its job.

"Bear's right! We deserved a break and I'm so glad we took one." Harmony's comment didn't surprise anyone. She loved to voice her opinion at every opportunity. Those who had stayed on the farm put down their spoons and clapped for the talkative young lady. She grabbed her skirt and performed a theatrical curtsey. Tensions released when the entire group joined in mutual laughter. Harmony spoke again. "As for the boy, I want to help find him right now." Her impassioned voice rang out, while many in the group nodded their heads in agreement. "Why don't I drive his sister around and look for him? What if he made it to town but can't get a ride?"

"Well, I guess it's worth a try." Able turned to Ruth and asked, "What do you think?"

Ruth was the last one to arrive at the gathering and had just gotten her food. Without looking up from her soup bowl, she shrugged and said, "It's fine with me. But her father should pay for the gas."

"Oh, he'd be happy to, thank you. Thank you, all." Sarah wiped her tears and quickly covered the short distance between her and Harmony. "When can we leave?"

"Hey, I'm going with you." Bud rose from his seat and faced his sister. Sarah could see the anxiety in his eyes, and knew that it was time to forgive him for Matthew's disappearance. She nodded yes.

Ruth had to speak up one more time. "And, though I don't mean to sound too up-tight, but Harmony, if you're going into town, you might want to put on a shawl."

"Gee Ruth, that's so cool of you for thinking of me." Harmony's sarcastic response resulted in more laughter as she led the minister's kids up the hill and toward the motor pool to grab the keys to the VW van.

"Okay everyone!" Able stood. "If they don't have luck tonight, I'll take their father with me in the morning."

Ruth injected, "Between the weeding and trash-run, there's no shortage of chores for the rest of us tomorrow." The group released a heavy moan.

13

Over dinner, Pete doubled-checked the bus schedule for the fastest route from Keene, New Hampshire to Liberty, New York. As he suspected, the boy would need to take a bus to New York City first, and then transfer to a Greyhound headed north to reach the resort. They shared a friendly chuckle over Matthew's situation. It was the perfect example of the classic phrase from Maine: *"Well, you can't get theya from heah."* Pete suggested he stay at the bible camp until the end of the two-week session. He could participate in all the activities at no charge and best of all, he could get closer to the Creator. Pete would then drive Matthew all the way to Liberty to find his mother. Matthew thanked him for the generous offer and said he would sleep on it. But Matthew had already decided. Given his urgent rush to reach his mom, hitchhiking remained his fastest option.

Mrs. Curtis took the empty dessert plates to the sink while her husband and his dog walked their guest to the bunkhouse. Pete handed his old GI flashlight to Matthew. It was olive green and had an angled head like a submarine's periscope. "You'll need this to find the outhouse. Just up the path through the trees."

"Thank you." Matthew clicked the flashlight on and off as Pete headed back down the stairs of the bunkhouse. "Please tell Mrs. Curtis I enjoyed her cooking."

"Will do." Pete reached the ground and turned to face Matthew. There was a twinkle in the old man's eyes. "Oh, by the way. If you hear strange noises coming from the woods, pay them no mind."

"Noises?"

"Yep. Folks quarreling in the distance. Rumor is the forest is haunted." Pete grinned. "We hate the devil, but our campers sure do love a good ghost story. Don't you?"

"Ah, sure." Matthew could tell Pete was enjoying himself and imagined the numerous campfires where his new friend would have scared the crap out of his spellbound audience.

"So back in the summer of 1938, Mrs. Eldora Collins and William Milke were employees at the old Dickson Lumber Company not far from here." Pete gestured over his shoulder toward the state park. "Well sir, they say jealousy was involved and they had a bad argument. One that got out of control. In any event, William grabbed his shotgun and shot poor Mrs. Collins, dead. Story goes he then took a shaving razor to slash his own throat rather than go to jail." Pete placed his cupped hand behind his ear. "Some nights, if you listen hard, you can still hear them arguing in the woods." With a smile, Pete limped away and raised his own voice. "Give some thought to our offer, son. I know you'd enjoy the fellowship."

Matthew entered the bunkhouse and closed the door. Only the cricket's symphony outside continued to make its way through the large screened-in windows. He turned on the florescent lights. Two rows of single beds stood upright along the cedar planked walls. Large gold-painted crosses nailed above all the headboards made the room look like the barracks of modern-day Christian crusaders. Matthew shook his head in disbelief and turned off the lights. He dropped the duffel-bag onto the floor and stretched out on the nearest bunk with the flashlight and the map. His grandfather had also served in World War II and owned the same military type flashlight. There was enough moonlight streaming in from the windows to turn off the flashlight, and unscrew the separate bottom compartment to see if it still held the extra colored lenses inside.

Just like his grandfather's, two round plastic disks, one blue and one red, fell into his hand. The flashlight had a handy belt-clip and an on/off slide switch on its side. Above that, a small metal button for Morse-code. He practiced the S.O.S. sequence, just as his grandfather had instructed him years before. Matthew smiled with the memory of that amusing night in the dark barn with all the cows mooing their confusion. He rolled over and propped a pillow under his chest to remain above the map. He located the town of Keene and followed Route 9 west with his finger to find Pisgah State Park next to the bible camp. He could save a lot of time by simply walking through the park for a few miles to reach Route 63. Next, he would hitchhike south toward Hinsdale and connect with Route 10. He could tell from the map that it could take more than a few days to make the entire trip to Mendelson's. It all depended on getting good rides. One thing was certain, his trusty thumb drawing would be put to the test again.

Matthew wasn't exactly sure what he would say to his mom once he arrived at the resort. Bud made it sound like divorce was a sure thing, and Matthew hoped he was not too late in convincing his mother to stay in the marriage. He had to reach her as soon as possible. Except for his sister, and what he imagined her feelings were of misplaced guilt, he did not care what led up to the marriage or how it all got started those many years ago. His main concern now was keeping everyone together.

Brought on by a full stomach and the long emotional day, Matthew came close to falling asleep. Instead, he stood up, switched on the lights, and emptied the duffel bag onto the bed. He would not need much clothing on the road, so he decided to take just his sleeping bag, the sketch pad, pencils, and whatever food he had. He also set aside the souvenir dagger his father gave to him instead of Bud. His dad had stressed that his brother did not deserve the gift after the whole shoplifting ordeal. Matthew doubted his dad would have wanted the dagger brought on the trip, but he took it anyway. If nothing else, it could be used to sharpen his drawing pencils. Matthew was pleased the duffel bag made him look more like an explorer than just a kid with a suitcase, running away to join the circus. He felt a little more grown up and excited about the adventure ahead of him. He took a moment to write a brief note on drawing paper to thank Pete and his wife for their hospitality, and the flashlight. Matthew promised to take good care of it and return it when he was able. Explanations for why he had left in the dead of night would be given upon his return. He felt the less said, the better. He silently closed the cabin door behind him and headed for the opening in the woods.

Since he did not want the bright beam to be seen by Pete, Matthew opened the bottom end of the flashlight. He removed both disks and inserted the red one in front of the bulb. He was excited to see the result and turned on the light. In its eerie red glow, he moved ahead like a crimson specter traveling through the dark woods. He listened for voices and heard none. Soon, Matthew came to realize that he did not really need the flashlight because the clear sky and moonlight between the trees defined the path he was on. It would save the life of the batteries, as well, so he turned the flashlight off. But twenty minutes later, when the path ended abruptly and the clouds moved in, he realized the shortcut he depended on may not have been a good choice.

Around midnight, rain fell, and he stopped walking. He located a large pine tree with thick branches that provided both cover from the rain and a bed of dry needles on which to place his sleeping bag. The familiar flannel lining of the bag had a woodland sports theme, with a man in waders fly-fishing a stream, a majestic deer with antlers bounding over a log, and ducks flying above two men with guns pointed skyward. When he was younger, Matthew would spread out the soft sleeping bag onto his bedroom floor and read under a blanket tent secured with clothespins. The additional image on the lining, of a fierce grizzly bear standing on its hind legs, had never bothered him until that night beneath the tree. As a result, Matthew quickly zipped up the bag's side and used the flashlight to perform a final check of his surroundings. He knew he should conserve the batteries, but there were so many mysterious shadowy shapes farther in the woods that triggered his imagination. With that, Matthew removed the dagger in its sheath from the duffel bag and placed it within reach near the top of his sleeping bag. He tightened his jaw and summoned the courage to switch off the flashlight. Within a few moments the occasional gentle blinking of fireflies arrived, and Matthew found them comforting. The exhausted teen yawned again. The thoughts of non-stop hitchhiking to get to his mother as quickly as possible made his headache worse. Soon his dry eyes closed, and he fell into a deep, peaceful sleep.

Bud would normally have fought his sister for *"shotgun"* before they climbed into the van. Instead, he sat in back with his trusty poncho draped over his right shoulder. It felt good to have it handy again and to be out looking for his brother. He was also grateful that the beige VW van had not been painted in wild psychedelic colors that demanded attention like the commune's other vehicles. As they drove off, the motor in the rear revved up so loudly that Bud had to scoot forward on the seat to hear what Sarah and Harmony were saying.

"When did I join?" Harmony looked both ways and turned left onto the paved county road. "Oh man, I guess it's been over a year now. Wow, that feels weird to say." She tucked her long, curly blonde bangs behind her ears and adjusted the rear-view mirror to check on her handmade earrings of amethyst crystals. "Back then, I was so different. Involved in the anti-war protests on campus. Lots of crazy distractions. You know, boys and... well, stuff. Anyway, my grades weren't very good. Lots of pressure from my parents to switch majors from music to something practical like accounting. I'd rather die. I was so bummed out to say the least. Then I heard about the farm. I had always been taken with the idea of communes, so I visited. Oh my God, it was so far out! People were kind and welcoming. And those cute baby goats just stole my heart. I quit school and moved onto the farm the following week. My parents were pissed, but they're always pissed off at something."

"I love your name." Sarah turned to Bud. "They toss names into a big pot and the new member gets to draw one. It becomes their Harvest name."

"Fine. I'm gonna' look out this way, you should take that side" instructed Bud as he moved closer to the window on his left. He had more important things to think about than listen to the two carry-on up front.

"It's a bummer you didn't get to meet Smooch. Such a sweetheart."

"That's a strange name" Sarah said.

"Yeah, but it fits perfectly. He joined the farm before I got here. Apparently, he dropped out of high school and got stuck fixing cars at his dad's shop. Able used to take his car there for maintenance and saw how badly the kid was treated by the father. We think there were beatings and that's why his back goes out." Harmony paused to roll down the window and adjust the van's side mirror. She enjoyed having someone new to talk to. "So anyway, Able invited him to live on the farm. The kid was very insecure at first, but once he got away from the alcoholic father, he just opened up. He blossomed. At his naming ceremony, he was so grateful to be accepted, he kissed the forehead of every single person there. Then everyone threw their suggested names into the kettle."

"Hence, the name Smooch." Sarah said. She smiled, but soon found her thoughts returning to Matthew. She hoped that her shy brother was safe. The increasing darkness limited what she could see along the passing roadside, and it added to her fears.

Harmony drove on and soon filled the silence with more details. "Folks come to the farm from all over the country. Did you get inside the bus Tower was driving?"

"No, I was told to ride with Ruth and Aurora. She's amazing." said Sarah.

"You're talking about Aurora, right?" Both women giggled.

"I shouldn't have said that. Ruth has some good qualities." Harmony felt a sudden chill and rolled up her window. She wished she had taken Ruth's advice and taken a shawl. "So, that old bus belonged to Frisco and Sonnet back in the day. He's the one with the long brown beard and ponytail. They were sitting across from your brother with their three kids at dinner."

"That's one hell of a nose he's got." Bud added with a snicker.

"Buddy! That's not nice." Sarah said.

"Yeah, but it's true." Harmony winked at Bud in the rear-view mirror. "Nose aside, he did an incredible job converting the school bus into an actual house on wheels. They sold their pad in Berkeley. Gave away everything that wasn't needed on the bus. And for an entire year they traveled across the country with their kids, baking bread in church kitchens."

"Churches?' Sarah turned to look at Harmony. "You're kidding, right?"

"They would make a deal. If they could park in the church parking lot and bake bread in the church kitchen overnight, they promised to leave the kitchen cleaner than when they arrived. Then, they would sell the bread to the parishioners on Sunday morning. Hopefully make enough cash for more baking supplies and gas. They would travel to the next small town and do it all again. Well, needless to say, not every church was receptive to a poor hippie family."

"No surprise there." Sarah added.

"Anyway, they got tired of living on the road. So, they searched for a commune they could join. They looked at one in Vermont, but the leader was really controlling. He's some kind of failed musician with a really shitty voice. And a huge ego. He demands that each member give over their money upon joining. He also tells them to cut all ties with their families. Oh, and he gets to decide who has a romantic relationship with who. Decides who gets married. And the thing that didn't jive with Frisco the most, is the commune would actually hire migrant workers to do all the hard-manual labor. Not exactly what communal living is supposed to be. Well, as you can imagine, Frisco and Sonnet didn't stay. And they found us instead."

"Who is the big hairy guy?" Bud asked. "He was pretty gruff."

"Oh, you're talking about Bear. Yeah, he stood up to Ruth, for sure. That was a surprise. Normally, he hardly says a word. Sure, he'll smile if you walk by him on the farm, but he won't say hello. Nothing. Can you believe that? I've tried a bunch of times and it drives me nuts. His wife, Sonnet, told me Bear dislikes wasting words that serve no propose. Well that's just fine for him, but I love talking and speaking my mind. In case you haven't noticed." She smiled again at Bud, who nodded.

Sarah found Harmony's openness refreshing compared to her stuffy friends back home. She liked the way Harmony didn't care what other people thought. "So how did they find the farm?"

"Oh, you're gonna' dig this. Turns out, they were shopping at the new co-op in town and noticed a poster in the window made by the commune. It was decorated with an illustration of a magician with a wand pulling a bunny out of a top hat. And the bold heading said, *"Turn-on to the Magic of Life,"* or something like that. At the register, there was a stack of fliers and Bear grabbed one. He had loved magic tricks ever since he was a kid and he got all excited because he thought it was an ad for an actual magic show. They went to the meeting. Well, there were no tricks, but they sure grooved on Able's talk." Harmony caught Bud's eye again in the rear-view mirror. "Guess it was magic after all, 'cause they joined the next day. Out-of-sight, right?"

"They must have been stoned." Bud stated flatly.

"Definitely." Harmony's laughter made Bud smile.

Sarah spoke up. "It's getting too dark on these back roads. Can we try downtown again?"

Harmony nodded her agreement. "We need gas too. There's a station just up the road. Should be open."

The van puttered into the Sinclair, with its giant green dinosaur sign overhead. The vehicle's wheels activated the service bell, and a gangly teenage attendant in an ill-fitting uniform and black high-top sneakers made his way to the driver's window. Like Bud, he noticed Harmony's revealing top as she got out and stretched. Sarah announced she needed to use the rest room and Harmony joined her. The attendant informed the two that there was a restroom key on the counter. Bud yelled to his sister to be sure to get the S&H Green stamps since their dad was paying for the gas. He told the attendant to just fill the tank and not to bother with checking the oil and cleaning the windshield. The attendant did as he was told and reached the station's front door just as the girls returned from the bathroom. He held the door open and Harmony followed Sarah inside. Harmony handed the key, with its ridiculously long piece of wood and chain, to the attendant. Within moments the sound and sight of the van's grinding gears and spinning wheels took everyone inside by surprise.

Ruth was sound asleep in her half of the main farmhouse. The small bedroom was sparsely decorated and had a framed photograph of her and Serene dressed in identical toddler outfits their mother had made. It sat on an oak dresser, near a 4-H blue ribbon pinned on the wall. Ruth had won it for best dairy cow at the Cheshire Fair during junior high. The commune's only phone, other than the one near the buffet line, sat on a small table next to her head. It rang five times before she answered. "Yeah, who is this?" She turned on her lamp and struggled to regain consciousness.

The operator was curt. "This is your local telephone company with a collect call from a Miss Harmony. Will you accept the charges?"

"Yes, I'll accept." She sat up. Harmony's excited voice blasted out of the phone with details of the situation. When Ruth had heard enough, she interrupted. "Sit tight! I'll come get you." Ruth bounded out of bed and donned her overalls, marched around to the building's side entrance, and took the stairs two at a time up to Able's door. She banged on it with a tight fist and shouted, "Tower should never have picked up that crazy fuckin' family!"

The door squeaked opened to reveal Able with a colorful tie-dyed sheet tucked around his waist. He used the palms of both hands to rub the sleep out of his eyes. "*Now* what happened?"

Ruth delivered the news that Bud had stolen the van and demanded that they call the cops. Able stressed getting the heat involved would only bring unneeded attention to the farm. Ruth reluctantly agreed, and headed downstairs to get her boots while Able put on his jeans. As they walked to the auto shop to get the keys to the step-van, he wondered if it was too soon to again bring up the joint ownership of the farm.

Ruth got behind the steering wheel and started the engine. The side mirror captured her exhausted face and she quickly angled it out to take the reflection away. Able pulled the sliding door closed and gave her a sincere smile as he tapped on the window. Ruth slid the side window open.

"I just wanted to thank you for picking them up."

She replied, "Sure, man. I just love being woken up in the middle of the night."

Able laughed. He could always count on her sarcasm. "Have you given any more thought to Bear's comments? About sharing ownership of the farm?" A long moment of silent tension built until Ruth finally responded.

"Not gonna' happen, Bro." She slid the window closed. Her work boot hit the gas pedal and she was off.

Able closed his eyes to keep the dust of the parking lot at bay. When he sensed the air was clear enough, he took in a deep breath and let out a long sigh. It was times like this when he questioned if the commune was worth all the effort. Once again, it was the messy dynamics of human nature that demanded so much of his attention. Conflicts that stemmed from unchecked egos make everyone think their own needs are paramount. And it wasn't just Ruth. In Able's mind, every single personality had demands of their own, and he often felt more like a referee than a fellow human being focused on spiritual growth. He never imagined the community's day-to-day operations would steal so much of his attention away from meditation and studies. As a college professor, there were at least some downtime at night and on weekends to complete those tasks. His love for nature played a big role in his decision to start the commune. He hoped by living on the farm he could revisit the works of Henry David Thoreau and Walt Whitman, and there would be the freedom to take his daughter to explore New Hampshire's White Mountain National Forest. Unfortunately, the farm's never-ending workload put an end to that. As did his soon-to-be ex-wife.

Able returned to the present and knew that the issue of convincing Ruth to legally share the land would have to wait until the current crisis of the missing boy was resolved. As he walked back to his apartment, Able could not help but wonder how much more the commune should accommodate the minister and his troubled brood.

After an hour-and-a-half of driving west on Route 9, Bud felt drowsy and very hungry. When the billboard on the roadside featuring the bright orange roof of a Howard Johnson's restaurant caught his attention, he didn't think twice about taking a slight detour south into Bennington,

Vermont. He loved HoJo's for their famous twenty-eight flavors of ice cream, and though he preferred the fried clams at the Clam Box in Ipswich, Massachusetts, he could make do with HoJo's clam strips. Unfortunately, it was nearly midnight when he read the restaurant hours on the front door. Bud would have to wait until seven in the morning to eat, and he seriously doubted clam strips would be available before noon. Darling Kelly's Motel and Gift Shop across the way looked inviting, with its many quaint cupolas positioned along its lengthy roof line, but Bud needed to save money for the journey ahead. He backed out of the parking space and found another spot farther back, hidden from the road by the restaurant.

There wasn't much room behind the rear seat to lie down in the van, so Bud decided to use the passenger's side of the front bench seat. He liked that he could just slide to his left and start the van if anyone tried to disturb him. The narrow vehicle shifted from side to side as he settled in and leaned against the door. His poncho served as a pillow of sorts, and by tucking his legs in a little, it seemed sleep would soon follow. If only his mind would shut up. Bud couldn't get over his brother's decision to take off to find their mother. He'd even nicknamed Matthew, *"Safety-*

boy," a few years back because he never took risks of any kind. To think Matthew now had the balls to hit the road alone was pretty cool, and Bud was impressed. Still, he could not stop worrying about his little brother and the need to find him as soon as possible. It was now Bud's only mission. Of course, Sarah would be that much more afraid because *both* her brothers were missing. He knew she would be beside herself with anxiety, feeling the panic that comes from not being in control. He smiled, imagining the shocked expression on her face when he peeled the van out of the gas station. He would have preferred a Mustang or a hot Camaro Super Sport over the VW van, but beggars can't be choosers. Bud was not too concerned with taking the vehicle and didn't see it as actually breaking the law. It did not need to be a big deal. Bud grinned as he recalled how spaced-out his father appeared at the recent meeting. Never in a million years did he expect to see his old man stoned on grass. What did not surprise him was how quiet his father had been. Bud had seen that happen many times with the guys he smoked with in the past. Dope seemed to make the most talkative dudes go silent, while the normally shy ones could not keep their mouths shut. He wished he could keep his dad stoned all the time. Hell, they might even get along.

Bud hated to admit it, but he and his father were alike in some aspects. Both had charisma, but used it in vastly different ways. While John's life centered around the church and its devout members, Bud's friends were mainly troublemakers from broken homes. He understood them, and often used a dirty joke or a funny story about his weight to help his friends cope with the sad, shitty cards they'd been dealt. In his own outgoing way, Bud was a minister too. A minister to screw-ups, degenerates, and misfits who had a hard time in school and distrusted authority figures. The ones who smoked cigarettes behind the bleachers and were sent to study hall for breaking the rules. The difference between him and his father was, Bud did it without asking for praise or attention. He was much more subtle in showing his concern for others and in trying to help. He truly detested his father's tendency to turn the attention away from those in need, to fill the hollow need in himself. Bud supported the disenchanted kids around him without asking for anything in return. Bud remembered the questions about his dad that the Able guy had asked him earlier in the day. It was like the older hippie dude knew exactly what his father was like. All those annoying traits that drove Bud nuts. Able seemed to be fishing for additional information and as Bud sat in the van, he struggled with the reasons why the tow-truck driver should even care.

Before long, Bud's mind returned to his usual thoughts on the meaningless of life. It started in his early teens when he questioned the need for the same level of education for everyone. He hated school (particularly math), and knew he was not going to pursue a job that required it. The same was true with reading and science. He liked history somewhat, but had the hardest time memorizing important dates. And though he could recall wars and how people were affected, not having the correct dates led to flunking out on tests as he did on most of the other subjects. There was one black and white photograph from his U.S. history textbook that had a huge impact on him. The photo itself, taken in 1932, was famous, but no one pictured was well known, just eleven scrappy steelworkers sitting on a lone skyscraper beam having their lunch break with the hazy Manhattan skyline behind. Each man probably had a wife and family or maybe a girlfriend, or perhaps none of those. The man on the far right clutched an empty liquor bottle. Each one had their own stories, desires, and concerns amid the Great Depression. Their faces had no trace of fear from falling, but Bud felt sadness at the frozen moment in time. No one remembered their names. No one left to care about their busy lives, with all the challenging demands to make a buck, no matter

the danger. What happened to those men and their worries that loomed so

large in their minds? All were probably dead by the time he saw the

photograph, and that was the moment that Bud really began to see himself

and others in the same way. Everyone has hardships and are suffering.

Some hide it better than others, but no one is really happy. It seemed to

him people were forced to get an education, raise a family, and pay their

taxes, only to get old and die anyway. He, like those men in the

photograph, might be remembered by his immediate family for a while,

but then he would also be gone without much more thought. He often

wondered, why bother to struggle when nothing really matters in the end?

It started to rain, and the van's metal roof loudly echoed each

drop. Bud wished he had one of Tower's joints to quiet his troubled mind.

The front seat was just too narrow to get comfortable, so Bud sat up. He

glanced again at the motel and wondered what a room would cost. He

liked its name and imagined what Darling Kelly would look like. He

imagined what made her so darling. Would she be working the front

desk? Perhaps a beautiful redhead, dressed in a tiny maid's outfit, who

would check him in and personally guide him to a room. Maybe she would turn down the sheets.

"Fuck it!" Bud grabbed his poncho and headed inside.

Five minutes later, and without much fanfare, an old man with hound-dog eyes and withered hands placed the plastic numbered key in Bud's palm. Bud noticed the cigarette machine in the dimly lit motel office and was happy he had enough coins to buy a pack. He walked out and lit up a cigarette. After a few drags, he entered his room with the intention of continuing the Darling Kelly fantasy in the comfort of the bed in front of him.

14

Barbara was exhausted, and turned down Hal's request to celebrate into the night. Instead, she retired to the upgraded room Manny had arranged. She slept soundly until dawn, when she woke feeling disorientated. Something was terribly wrong, but she could not define what was causing the anxious hollowness in her gut. Barbara willed herself out of bed and decided to ignore the dull pain and try to get dressed. The day ahead was planned mainly for rehearsal, so Barbara selected an outfit that was casual and comfortable, but still flattered her shape. It consisted of a bold, paisley print tunic with a v-neckline and a tie-belt of the same material. Her lavender flared-leg pants, made of double-knit polyester, matched the top's primary color, and would allow her to easily move around during rehearsal. Her selection of clothing was limited by John's low salary, and as a minister's wife, her wardrobe was not allowed to make a fashion statement. She was excited to soon have money of her own to buy any new outfit she wanted. Before she closed the door, Barbara took a moment to savor the privacy of the attractive surroundings in the hotel room, knowing that things would be quite different in the women's employee dormitory.

Barbara felt better with each step, and as she approached the bellmen's desk in the lobby, she smiled. "Good morning. I did as you asked and left my suitcase behind." She placed the key in front of the same friendly bellman who had brought her and Hal's bags to their rooms the night before. Barbara read his name tag out loud. "But I'm afraid, Andrew McIntire, Bell Captain, you'll need a forklift." She giggled.

"Oh yes, Miss Thomley, I remember you... and your luggage." His kind eyes met hers with a smile. "You can call me Andy, by the way." He gestured toward her hair. "Hey, I like your new hairstyle. Very becoming."

"You think?" Barbara could feel her checks blush and replied, "I'm still getting used to it." Her slender hands fluffed the full blonde curls at the bottom of her shoulder length hair. "Manny thought the change in color would help the act. And please, call me Barbara."

Andy's smile disappeared. "Yeah, that Manny, he's something else." After a pause Andy's upbeat tone returned. "The grapevine says you nailed the audition. Congratulations Barbara."

She did a little jump of excitement and clapped her hands with her slender fingers extended backward. "Oh, I can't wait to start!"

Andy loved her sincere, childlike enthusiasm and it caused a noticeable delay in his response. The moments that followed were fully charged with an undeniable attraction to each other. Barbara noted how completely different Andy was from John. His strong build and rugged good looks of reddish hair, together with a thick strawberry blonde mustache, reminded her of a bold Celtic warrior, an appearance she found extremely exciting, having all the attributes her bookish husband didn't have.

Andy glanced at his watch to hide his boyish grin. "Hey, you know what? The employee dining room is still serving breakfast. You should go enjoy it while I start the forklift."

Barbara released a hearty laugh. She found his sense of humor extremely sexy, and was pleased to see the lack of a wedding ring. "Thank you so much, Andy. I will." She removed a tip from her purse.

"No need, you're one of us now." He retrieved a one-page, color map of the resort from the stack on the counter and showed her the fastest route to reach the employee dining room. "I'd be happy to give you the complete tour of the grounds later on. I get off at three." He waited anxiously for a reply. "There are certain things you should know about this crazy place. And the folks you should be wary of." His face showed disappointment when she informed him her entire day would be tied up in rehearsal. Andy's expression lightened up considerably when Barbara made it clear a raincheck of his tour would make her very happy.

The map proved invaluable in finding the employee dining room located behind the vast kitchens and near the giant smokestack that rose above the maintenance building. She ventured inside where Leonard, an older heavyset man with a Brooklyn accent and black orthopedic shoes, led her to a table. As he filled her coffee cup, Leonard provided, as he always did to new employees, his lesson on kosher food and why the hotel didn't prepare or serve meat where dairy food exists. It became obvious to Barbara that he took great pride in his duties of waiting on the staff and operating the burnishing machines that polished the hotel's silverware.

"The hotel has two of everything." Leonard topped off her cup. "Two separate kitchens, each with its own pots and pans, freezers, stoves, china, dishwashers, and most important, clean shiny flatware, which is my specialty, Madam." With a smile and feet pointed outward, Leonard waddled away to another table like an odd, cheerful penguin.

There were only a few employees in the room because most had already eaten their breakfast and started their workdays much earlier. Barbara enjoyed the rich flavor of the dark coffee and took the opportunity to think about her kids. She hoped Sarah had a good night's sleep and was ready to tour Keene State College in a few hours. Barbara looked forward to hearing the exciting details of the graduation and her opinions of the three colleges Sarah visited. In hindsight, Barbara wished she had stayed to enjoy her daughter's achievement with her. She recalled how handsome Bud looked in his dress-shirt, and was thrilled he'd washed his long hair for his sister's big day. When he was a toddler, Buddy loved baths and dressing up for church. She smiled, remembering the Tom Thumb wedding he took part in with the neighbor's daughter. He looked so cute as the toddler groom walking his little bride down the aisle in his tiny top hat and cane in hand. But as the years went by, and *Little Buddy* became *Big Bud,* he cared less and less about his appearance. Barbara took another sip of coffee and hoped the weight loss camp would help with her son's self-confidence, but she knew firsthand how much pleasure Bud got from eating. It would also prove to be difficult for the staff when his appetite demanded attention and he turned belligerent. She worried that just when he needed food for comfort the most, it would not be available.

Barbara imagined Bud and John sharing a small hotel bed last night with arms crossed, both afraid to pass over the invisible center line. She could not remember the last time she witnessed any type of affection between them. Not one hug or pat on the back from John in years. That made her sad, so she quickly switched to pleasant thoughts of Matthew. She could see him drawing something beautiful on his sketch pad. She was thankful he had the creative outlet to keep him occupied while John and Sarah checked out the various college campuses. Barbara doubted that Matthew had sleeping on the hotel floor in his sleeping bag last night, but that would all change once Bud was dropped off at the camp.

The coffee in Barbara's empty stomach was not doing her any favors, and she ordered a poached egg with rye toast from her new best friend, Leonard. She was pleased that everyone seemed so friendly and welcoming at the hotel, but wondered what the handsome bellman meant when he said there were some people to avoid. He was certainly one she would not. Her order arrived quickly, and she enjoyed every bite.

"Just coffee." Hal's voice came from behind Barbara; its harshness surprised her.

"That chipper bell-captain told me I'd find you here." Hal flopped down in the chair across the table from Barbara. "So much for sleeping in." He yawned and stretched his arms. "Guess who called my room? Manny. He says we are very good. No need to rehearse." Leonard placed the empty cup in front of Hal.

"Well that was nice of him." Barbara smiled. She waited until Hal's cup was filled and the waiter walked away. "And?"

Hal rubbed his swollen eyes. Removed his reading glasses and a piece of paper from his shirt pocket. It had a scribbled list of hotel names. "Manny wants me to drive all over and size up the smaller hotels. I really don't feel up to this, but thank goodness I had the bell-captain mark their locations on my map." Hal looked down at the list. "There's the Stevensville Hotel and Kutsher's. The Pines. The Nevele, which by the way, is the number 'eleven' spelled backwards." Hal took a sip of coffee. "The bell-captain said it was named after a group of eleven women, all schoolteachers, who found some waterfall on a picnic back in the last century." Hal rubbed his stiff neck. "Anyway, Manny wants the nightclub at The Browns Hotel checked out this evening, as well."

Barbara pushed her coffee cup aside. "Well, that doesn't give us much time."

"There's no *'us.'* You're going to take a cab to the Accord Hotel and meet Manny on his way back from the city. He wants you to see our biggest competition." Hal glanced down at his list again. "You'll have lunch, then cocktails by the pool. Dinner at six, followed by the live show in the Imperial Room. He's pretty sure Buddy Hackett was booked. If so, Manny will introduce you. Apparently, they go way back."

"Really? Oh, I love him." Barbara's expression opened wide with excitement until she saw none in Hal's swollen eyes. "He can be funny…"

"The kitchen is about to close." Leonard interrupted with a weak smile. He wondered how this lovely woman could stand being around such a rude man. "So, if you wanted anything more-"

"Just coffee. How many times-"

"Thanks Leonard. We're fine, dear. Thank you." Barbara's sweet voice softened Hal's hostile tone. "What is wrong with you? He's just doing his job for goodness sake."

Too many martinis the night before and the guilt of picking on the breakfast waiter showed on Hal's tired face. He removed a couple of bucks from his wallet to leave a tip. "Listen Barbie Girl, I'm sorry. You know, it's been a crazy couple of days. You go and have fun." Hal stood up. "I'm gonna' squeeze myself into that stupid small car I bought." He placed the back of his hand alongside his mouth and whispered. "And hopefully, I'll find a restaurant on the road that serves *bacon* with their eggs." He winked and pushed his chair in.

Barbara removed her compact from her purse to check on her new hairstyle. "Hal don't worry. We'll get into a routine and you'll make plenty of money." She applied fresh lipstick and smiled. "Besides, we're going to meet lots of new people." She stood and fastened her arm with his. "What could go wrong?" They left the employee dining room with Barbara excited to show Manny what a team player she was.

Breakfast at the commune had been eaten quickly so the search for the minister's son could get underway. John felt stiff from sleeping on the hard army cot and was not thrilled to be awakened so early. The warm oatmeal in his stomach comforted him until Able gave an update on Bud and the van. It resulted in an intense wave of guilt in the embarrassed father, and he apologized to the group for all the unfortunate inconveniences he and his children had caused. He assured everyone that the missing vehicle would be returned soon. Able thanked John for his comments and stressed that the van wasn't stolen so much as borrowed. He pointed out that Bud only took it so he could find his little brother. Able went on to outline in detail the plan he had created.

At first, Blaze was not pleased to hear that he was directly involved in the search and mentioned he had various projects to complete in the woodshop. Many of the farm members smiled at each other, knowing the real reason he was hesitant to leave the property. Blaze had a sense of why Able picked him, and it did make him nervous, but once it became clear to the handsome carpenter that the new girl would be riding with him, the risk almost seemed worth taking. He and Malorie would travel in the Ford Fairlane after he repaired its tire. Since she knew what Matthew looked like, it made sense for them to go in one car, while Able and John headed out in another. The two groups would ultimately aim west for the resort in the Catskills and check in periodically with the farm by pay phone along the way. Meanwhile, Ruth would man the telephone in her room and keep everyone posted, while making detailed work schedules for the coming weeks. Sarah would continue to sleep-in to recover from the long and frightening events of the night before. She would stay behind on the farm in case Bud returned with or without their little brother. The remaining members of the community would pull weeds in the garden under the watchful eye of Terra, while Bear and Tower completed the overdue trash-run to the dump.

Outside the dining room, Able asked John to wait in his car while he tracked down Blaze for a few instructions and to give Malorie the road map. John slipped into the front passenger seat of Able's blue, Saab Monte Carlo and ran his hand gently across the leather dashboard where the rear-view mirror was surprisingly mounted on top. He had never ridden in a foreign car, and he was quite impressed with the wood inlaid of the steering wheel. John's thoughts turned to his oldest son and his recent antics. The positive comments Able made about Bud did little to keep John's familiar feelings of disappointment at bay. Bud had failed to keep an eye on his younger brother and then, made matters worse by stealing a car from their friendly hosts. Not borrowed, stole. Simple as that. Bud's bad behavior did not completely surprise John, but Matthew's decision to take off had knocked the minister for a loop. What in the world was his son thinking? Why would he run after his mother and not want to stay with his dad? The nagging questions were causing his shoulders to tense up, and the dry discomfort in his throat did not help matters. He would have gone back inside for a cup of coffee if it had existed. Instead, there was only a strange tea made from something called chickweed that smelled almost as horrible as it tasted. John looked down at his shoes and vaguely recalled the strange feelings from the evening before. The heightened sense of wonder he experienced while walking barefoot on the path. Perhaps more important than letting go of the fear of being without shoes was discovering that he did not need to be the center of attention during the meeting. John shook his head in disbelief. That was not at all in his character. In fact, he had thought about conducting a morning prayer for Matthew with the members of the commune taking part, but the opportunity never presented itself. He wondered how long this new willingness to just be quiet and take things in stride was going to last.

"Sorry about the wait, Reverend." Able opened his car door and got behind the wheel. He had switched from leather sandals to canvas tennis shoes, and changed into a white Oxford shirt, tucked into khaki slacks. His long, black ponytail was hidden up inside a straw hat. All choices were made to put his passenger at ease.

"No problem. I was just admiring this fine automobile of yours." John gently rubbed the dashboard again.

"Ah yes, the last vestige of being a college professor." He reached around and grabbed his seat belt. "You probably haven't used a shoulder harness before." Able clicked the belt into place. "The Swedish designers were airplane builders before they switched to cars." As John repeated the motions of securing his belt, Able noticed how clean and soft John's hands appeared. It occurred to him his own hands had been in the same condition during his entire career at the college. With his callused right hand, Able shifted into first gear on the column and grinned at his dirty fingernails with the realization that his car truly was all that remained of those cushy times in higher education. With each manual shift, the car's speed increased, and both men grinned at the engine's loud acceleration. Never one for small talk, Able yelled to be heard. "So, what's your trip?"

"I guess once our car is repaired, we'll probably drive to…"

"No, no, I meant your *trip*, your thing. What gets you going? Excited?"

John's laugh had a trace of embarrassment. "Oh yes, of course." John rubbed the stubble on his face. He was not used to not shaving first thing in the morning. "Well, of late, I've become very curious about reincarnation."

"Bet that wasn't covered in seminary" Able replied with a wink.

"Amen to that." Both laughed and relaxed into their seats.

"Did they teach you *anything* about eastern religions?" Able slowed down for the stop sign ahead.

"No, not really" John answered.

"That's a bummer. But not surprising." Able faced John. "Hey, I could give you a quick overview." He turned left at the intersection. "While we look for your son, of course."

"You mean, sons." John kept his gaze on the road ahead. He knew both his boys were probably far away by now, and for the first time, he worried about them.

"When it comes to many eastern religions, belief in reincarnation is a key aspect of their doctrines. And yet, their traditions and concepts in that area can differ." Able stated.

John nodded. It was obvious Able had slipped back into his more formal professor persona. John wasn't feeling up to hearing a memorized lecture, so he inserted quickly, "So which religion rings true for you?" He scanned the dense woods along the passing roadside.

"Well, they all have some wonderful merits." Able wished he could have continued with his standard lesson because it felt oddly good to be teaching again. "I guess if I had to choose just one, I'd say Buddhism. Although it isn't a religion, per se. It's more of a practice, like yoga. It encourages meditation as a means to enlightenment. Of course, meditation is not unique to Buddhism, but with it, you can actually achieve mindfulness." Able turned to smile at John and was greeted with a perplexed expression.

"What does meditation have to do with reincarnation?"

Able knew from his brief conversation with Bud in the tow-truck that it would be hard for the teen's father to acknowledge there were major gaps in his knowledge. As a result, Able tried to keep his answers straightforward without sounding condescending. "Well, each life we live is meant to bring us toward enlightenment. In Hinduism, they believe the soul carries on after death and is then reborn. Each life is filled with choices and decisions, which are just actions. Those actions result in karma. In most Eastern religions, karma dictates the next life."

"So, no such thing as heaven?" John asked.

"Not necessarily." Able smiled. "There is a heaven. It just takes a number of lifetimes to get there. Good deeds in each life eventually leads to enlightenment, and that ends the painful cycle of life and death, known as Samsara."

After a long pause John replied. "Well, if that's true, I know a lot of Christians who are going to be shocked when they die."

Able nodded his head in agreement. "I always wondered about the heaven Christians believe exists. Do they really think God wants to hang out in heaven for eternity with souls who haven't advanced, let alone reached enlightenment? No, I think that would be more like hell for him. Or her." Able sped up to pass the slow-moving car ahead of them.

The joint John had shared with Tower late the day before continued to have a foggy influence on his mind. "I'm still not seeing the connection. Maybe it's all those foreign words."

"Okay, let's try something else. Have you ever heard of Abraham Maslow?" John's blank face showed he was unaware. "He's a famous psychologist who pioneered the work of humanistic psychology. Where a person progresses from being motivated by basic needs, like food and safety, to fulfilling one's greatest potential. Maslow called it the process of self-actualization. Of course, from the scientific papers I have read, he limited his study only to psychologically healthy people. You know, folks who had full use of their capacities and talents in the first place. But I do believe Maslow was on to something there. You know, when it comes to personal growth."

Science had never held much interest for John, and his eyes glazed over with an attempt to process the additional information. "Seems like just going to heaven would be a lot less complicated."

"True." Able decided to make the conversation more personal. "Hey look, take me for example. I'm not fully self-actualized... yet." His brown eyes twinkled. "And I certainly haven't reached pure enlightenment. But I do meditate every day. It's like I have a tangible skill I can rely on." Able sat up straight and squared his shoulders. "I simply focus on my mind and body. Paying attention to my breath, while being aware of my feelings and thoughts." He glanced again at John to make certain he was listening. "By acknowledging those things as they come up, and then letting them go, I get in touch with my higher-self. I get that much closer to being self-actualized." His voice turned cheerful as he playfully tapped the side of John's leg. "Can't you see man? With the practice of meditation, anyone can attain enlightenment. Even you, John."

"I doubt it." John frowned and stared straight ahead.

Able thought it best to allow the minister some time to mull things over. He wondered if John could handle the concept that people create their own reality. That people's attitudes will always form their experience. That there is actually no past or future, just the wonderful present, and that human beings can only think in a linear fashion because of their brain's limitations. As he drove on, Able doubted that John would embrace any of the topics. A lone diner eventually appeared on the right side of the road. With its shiny metal siding and rounded corners, the long skinny building looked like a train's dining car stuck on a gravel lot without the wheels to escape. Able noticed the phone booth near the entrance and pulled in.

"Perhaps we should call Ruth. Establish contact." He gathered coins from the vehicle's ashtray and tried one last approach. "You know Reverend, given your Christian background, you might enjoy reading books about Edgar Cayce. He was a psychic and a healer who believed in past lives but he was also a devout Christian. I taught a course on him back in the day. He believed that dreams were-"

"I'll need to look into that" John interrupted without much emotion. The idea of getting some real coffee had stolen his attention.

Able turned off the car's engine and released his seat belt with ease. "Cayce also believed that people choose their parents before they incarnate."

John struggled to unfasten his belt. "For what purpose?" Finally, the belt gave way.

"To learn particular lessons." Able thought of his own young daughter. He missed her sweet face, and his voice choked up a bit. "And not just for the child. But for the parents too." He cleared his throat and regained control over his emerging sadness. "Take your son, Bud, for example."

John's eyes narrowed as he turned to face Able. "What about him?"

"What if he chose you to be his father this time around? Maybe there is something only you can do for him. Maybe there is something he's meant to teach you, too. Who knows, maybe the roles were reversed in a past life. Perhaps he was your father." Able smiled at John's shocked expression. "Cayce called it karmic memory. A way to ensure spiritual growth. And it's not limited to Bud but includes all your family members. Your wife, too." John reached for his door handle to exit the car. He needed air but Able was able to lay a hand atop John's shoulder. He stayed in his seat. "Reverend, maybe you shouldn't see your relationship with Bud as a burden. See it as an opportunity to correct whatever went south in a previous life." Able gave John a reassuring squeeze and got out of the car.

Inside the phone booth, Able inserted a dime and noticed the preacher sat motionless, obviously lost in thought.

15

Matthew knew he needed to get up, but the warmth of the sleeping bag under the big pine tree convinced him to stay put much longer than he'd planned. The confusing shock from what Bud had told him the day before seemed to have lessened during his sleep. And as he laid there, the new information brought clarity to some things in his past. He'd never understood why both sets of his grandparents never really talked to each other, other than at holiday gatherings. They always stayed on opposite sides of the room and limited their interaction to discussions of the weather. Matthew realized that the blame and shame over the events of that night of the fire had to have been difficult for all involved and had created a wedge between the two families. Matthew thought about Helen, his mother's mother, and the strict religious beliefs she held. Her views on sin, particularly premarital sex, were well known by everyone in the family, and no one more than Sarah. He recalled that when she hit puberty, Sarah was forced to listen to endless lectures from their grandmother on the importance of waiting for marriage before she had any intimacy with a man. And though his grandfather never mentioned the ordeal to him, Matthew wouldn't have been surprised if Glen didn't find some humor in having a young, want-to-be minister involved in his daughter's shenanigans. Matthew knew the pressure his parents must have been under had to be intense to do the right thing. There would also have been a rush to get married to avoid gossip, and so both must have felt trapped just as their futures should have been wide open. Matthew realized that his mother's constant sadness, which he tried so hard to lift, was actually tied like an anchor to an event he had nothing to do with. What if his brother was right? What if they never really loved each other? What if they only did what was expected of them? What if they now just wanted to give up and get a divorce?

A squawk from a showy blue-jay nearby reminded Matthew of his mother's attempts to rouse him from bed at home. He smiled, unzipped the bag, and rolled out onto the sharp pine needles. He was thankful that he had kept his clothes on. Matthew wondered how she would react to his taking off on his own. He knew, of course, that she would hold his father entirely accountable for the danger their youngest child was in. But

Matthew did not feel he was in danger. In fact, just the opposite. He felt like he was finally maturing, becoming his own man. And now with the sun up, along with his confidence, he figured the hike ahead through the forest should not take all that long. He just needed to head west to reach Route 63, and then he could start hitching again. First though, he needed to eat.

The idea of graham crackers and fruit cocktail sounded pretty good and he removed both from the duffel bag. After scarfing down two crackers he realized there wasn't a can opener. "Damn it!" He could picture the electric can opener at home sitting on the counter, with its modern avocado color that matched the kitchen stove. It had been a Mother's Day gift from the family, and he realized how useless it would be in the woods. Matthew came up with a plan and located a rock he could use as a hammer. He retrieved the dagger where it sat near the sleeping bag and removed it from the sheath. He found a large boulder and placed the can on top. With his stronger right hand, Matthew held the blade upright with its point on the inside edge of the can. He used his fingertips to keep the can in place.

Three facts appeared in clear focus as the rock he held came down toward the top of the dagger's handle. One, the razor-sharp blade had no business facing him. Two, using a round rock to strike a rounded handle was stupid. And three, it was too late to stop.

Launched like a catapult, the can flew into the faraway bushes. The dagger skipped back and sliced down through the tender flesh between his thumb and index finger. Matthew pulled his hand back and heard the dagger tumble noisily to the ground. A quick peak at his hand showed the damaged white tendon in contrast with his seeping, bright red blood.

"Oh Shit! Oh Fuck! FUCK!" His screams filled the woods as he searched for something to stop the flow of blood from heading down his forearm. His dad's tie would have worked as a tourniquet, and Matthew was pissed, he had left it back at the cabin. The pain came on suddenly, as did the rush to faint. He took a deep gulp of air and held it as he forced a panicked removal of his shirt, made even more difficult because he could not move his damaged thumb toward his index finger. At last, he clumsily wrapped the shirt tight around his hand and brought them together. The fabric instantly turned red and he raised his arm over his head. He saw the need for something cleaner than his shirt, and with his good hand, tore numerous sheets of fresh paper from his sketchpad. Matthew painfully removed the soaked cloth and laid the folded paper over the wound. The makeshift bandage absorbed the pulse of new blood as he wrapped his hand with a dry, unused section of the shirt. He felt dizzy and extremely thirsty on his slow return to the sleeping bag. He laid down on his side and cringed. It was not the pain. He could handle the pain. Matthew brought his damaged drawing hand close to his chest and wept.

Sarah woke up with a jolt. She knew something terrible had happened to her little brother and she needed to act immediately. She glanced at the clock on the windowsill in Aurora's A-frame and could not believe she had slept in. Granted, the day before had been intense and exhausting, topped off with Bud's stupid choice to take the van late last night. But Sarah had never overslept a day in her life. The bed of folded blankets and quilts on the floor where Aurora's daughter, Breeze, had slept, was empty, as was Aurora's single bed across the way. Sarah reminded herself to thank Breeze for giving up her bed and taking the floor. At that moment though, she desperately needed to pee and left the A-frame for the nearest outhouse. Never having used one, her reaction to opening the door was visceral. The intense smell of human waste caused her to gag, and she pushed the door closed with both hands. She thought about the green barn where a toilet was available, but forced herself to go inside instead. Sarah sat down and prayed out loud. "Oh Lord, give me the strength to face the challenges before me. Amen."

Sarah exited the small structure knowing for certain that Matthew was hurt. She could feel it tugging on her heart and her panic grew with each step. She entered the dining hall to get help, only to find a message written on the large chalkboard.

ALL HANDS-ON DECK!

Everyone needed for weeding...

7:00 am - <u>NO EXCEPTIONS!</u>

Terra - Garden Manager

Sarah heard the clang of metal and scurried around the corner toward the noise. At the far end of the buffet serving counter stood Clarity. The expectant mother was placing lids onto stainless steel chafing dishes. Sarah hesitated to get her attention as she recalled Bud's interaction with the mysterious woman the day before. The strange way her open hand hovered in front of her brother's face looked like an attempt at mind reading, and it still gave Sarah the creeps. She was not quite sure what to make of the dark, gypsy-like woman.

As if she could hear Sarah's thoughts, Clarity suddenly turned and smiled at the minister's panicked daughter. "What's wrong, darling?" She made her way along the counter and gently caressed Sarah's cheek. The tender touch brought forth the tears Sarah had been trying to hold back.

"My little brother is hurt bad." Clarity embraced her as another wave of emotion caused the teen's shoulders to shake.

"Trust your instincts, darling." Clarity placed Sarah's bangs behind her ears. "Now just slow down and take deep breaths." She gently used a clean portion of her stained apron to tenderly dab at Sarah's tearful eyes. "You know our bodies can discern the truth long before our brains."

Sarah sounded defeated. "My father says female intuition isn't the best use of reasoning."

"Of course, he does. He's a man." Clarity smiled. "All men know deep down they don't have our skills." She took Sarah's hand. "Now follow me. Let's get you something to eat."

"There isn't time!" Sarah's fears fed her impatience. "I can't explain it, but I feel my brother's nearby. He is really hurt! I just know it." She leaned her back against a wall and slid down to the floor with knees bent upright. She surrendered her aching head onto her crossed forearms and sobbed. Her voice was childlike and hardly audible. "I need help finding him."

Clarity untied her apron and struggled to lift the material up and over her extended midsection. "Let's get you that help. Come with me." She tossed the apron aside and reached down to assist Sarah in standing. Together they left the dining hall, headed for the garden. Along the way, Clarity told Sarah about Able's plan to locate Matthew. While the news her father and others were conducting a search was good to hear, Sarah knew for certain a search nearby was what was needed.

Scattered throughout the garden, small groups had formed based on their topic of conversation. Harmony, Star, and Feather had just decided what wild animal they would be if they had the choice. Thirty feet away, Charmed and Buzz continued their discussion on the meaning of each other's dreams from the night before. And on the far side of the garden, Frisco and his wife led their kids in a folk song to make the tedious chore of weeding more enjoyable. Their pleasant voices caused most of the farm's dogs to doze off in the shade of the nearby tractor.

"Oh look, it's Sarah." Breeze sprinted between two rows of green pepper plants to greet her. Along the way she passed Serene and Luna, careful to avoid Serene's twins, each snuggled in their own wicker basket. Aurora stood and stretched her back. She smiled at the sight of her free-spirited daughter leaping over the last row to welcome their new house guest. At the top of the hill, Clarity gave Sarah a warm, parting embrace, waved to Aurora, and then headed back to the kitchen to finish preparing lunch for everyone.

Sarah's red swollen eyes made her feel self-conscious, but it didn't stop her from relaying her fears about Matty to Aurora. She asked if she could use the commune's mimeograph machine to make missing person fliers. She said that Harmony had mentioned the machine the night before during their search and hoped it would be okay. Sarah assured

Aurora she had plenty of experience mimeographing the church bulletins at home and could do all the work herself. While Breeze was quick to volunteer her help in hanging the fliers in town, Aurora was not so sure they would be effective. She did not voice her doubts but recognized that the fliers would at least keep Sarah and Breeze busy for the afternoon.

"Somebody must have seen your brother." Breeze's voice was filled with optimism. "Let's go tell the others." Breeze linked her arms with the arms of her mother and Sarah. Together they cheerfully high-stepped in unison like Cancan dancers over each row of plants. The garden filled with surprised laughter and whistles at their lively display. The dogs joined in with excited barks and wagging tails.

Terra emerged from the greenhouse dome determined to find out what was causing the commotion in his garden. He was already pissed because his damaged big toe had slammed against a heavy compost bucket earlier that morning. He cupped his hands around his mouth with fingertips caked in dirt and yelled "why aren't we weeding, people?"

His condescending tone did not surprise Aurora. When it came to the garden, it was completely his acre of land to rule over, and everyone else was simply a worker-bee to be bossed around. "We're calling it quits for now," Aurora hollered back. The comment surprised the other farm members and they happily gathered into a tighter group. By then, the three hours of bending over in the morning sun had dampened everyone's enthusiasm. Aurora told them of Sarah's idea and asked for their help with posting the fliers in town.

Terra started his slow limp down the hill to address the distracted crew. A gust of wind swept over the garden and blew his long stringy red hair straight back from an already receding hairline. His thin frame barely held up the one strap of his tattered overalls. The other strap hung down toward his pale, bare feet and added to his scarecrow appearance. "You know folks. Every weed robs a vegetable of the vital nutrients it needs." He grabbed a handful of dandelions and held it high, as if it were important evidence in a trial. "I still can't believe you ignored these when I was in Maine. Had I known-"

"Take it easy, man." Aurora cut him off. "It's gonna' get done. Just not today." She took Sarah's hand and led her along the row past Terra.

Terra's ruddy face got even redder. "What could be more important than this garden?"

Sarah turned and focused her steely eyes on the hippie. "My brother's life." She continued up the row behind Aurora for a few more steps and stopped. A desire to be more like Harmony, to be more outspoken, took control. She glanced over her shoulder and let it rip. "So, fuck off, man!"

From the moment they left the farm, Malorie sensed Blaze was anxious. He frequently adjusted the rear-view mirror to check the reflection of the road behind them. His hand would return and grip tightly around the steering wheel. At times, his thumbs would break free to nervously tap along the top.

Malorie had to say something. "You know at this speed the kid will be middle-aged by the time we find him."

A forced grin appeared below his dark sunglasses. "I'm obeying the speed limit for your information." Blaze wore his favorite tie-dyed tee-shirt that people said brought out his blue eyes. His long blonde hair stayed in place with a braided leather headband. Malorie made a strategic decision to wear a white blouse without a bra. Its tails were tied in a loose knot to reveal her toned waist. Blaze imagined untying the knot more than a few times as their mutual attraction simmered on the back burner.

Malorie kicked off her sneakers and sat crossed legged, thankful she wore comfortable blue jean shorts for what may be a long drive. "Blaze is your Harvest name, right? Because of your hair, I'm guessing." He smiled and nodded. "What's your real name?"

His head tilted back, and he released a needed laugh. "You ready for this? It's Lonnie. Named after my uncle."

Both smiled. "Blaze is much cooler," Malorie stated. "Of course, I hate that your hair is prettier than mine." He lowered his sunglasses and winked at her. She continued to wonder what was making him so nervous and recalled the moment Able pulled Blaze aside before they left. Both looked extremely serious. Perhaps Blaze was still reacting to their intense conversation. Malorie doubted his current behavior had anything to do with her, given all their previous easygoing interactions. She decided to finally address it. "Hey, are you okay?"

"Yeah, well, sorry. I shouldn't get you involved." Blaze lowered the sun-visor to ensure the car's registration was tucked inside. It was not. "Shit!"

"What's wrong?"

"Do me a favor. Check the glovebox for an envelope. Should say registration on it." Malorie did as she was told and found the paperwork. Blaze's clinched jaw relaxed.

"Worried we're gonna' get pulled over?" She returned the envelope to the glove box and put her bare feet up on the dashboard. "It won't be for speeding." He released a laugh. Malorie opened the map and laid it against her legs. She noticed a piece of folded paper with the name, "Blaze," written across the top. It was held in place by a paper clip. "Hey...it's a note for you. Want me to read it out loud?"

"Yeah, go ahead." Blaze knew who wrote it.

Malorie's cleared her throat. "The famous novelist, Robert Louis Stevenson, once said, 'Sooner or later everyone sits down to a banquet of consequences.'" Malorie gave him an inquisitive look and continued reading. "Blaze, you know your choice was right. Trust in that and you'll be fine." Malorie put down the note. "What is this all about?"

Blaze took off his shades and turned to speak directly to the beautiful girl next to him. Unlike the other chicks he got close to, he never told them his secret and felt he could say anything to Malorie, and she would accept it. "Well, I'm a draft dodger." Malorie held his gaze and saw the pain in his eyes. She nodded her understanding. "I prefer draft *resister*. But I doubt the cops will make the distinction." They drove on in silence, both consumed with their own thoughts. "So yeah... anyway, about six months ago I split from home for Canada. New Harvest Farm was as far north as I got."

"Where's home?"

"Florida. Grew up in a dinky little town in the middle of the state. My dad is a guard at the Sumter Correctional Institution. He's not a big fan of dudes who break the law." Blaze accelerated without realizing it. "Guess that includes me now."

Malorie brought her feet down from the dashboard and tucked them under her folded legs. She sat higher in the seat to give him her full attention. "Was it hard... to leave?"

Blaze took his time to answer. He used his fingers to smooth down his thick blond mustache. It had become a comforting ritual he performed to keep his buried feelings in check. "My older brother, Mark, joined the Marines the minute he graduated from high school. He was gonna' kick ass and take names." Blaze smiled. His brother was the local football star and used the phrase often. Blaze returned the sunglasses to his face. "Mark was killed in combat. Second week in Nam."

"Oh my gosh, I'm so sorry."

"It hit all of us pretty hard. My little sister, Jan, probably the most. They were really close." Blaze cleared his throat. "When my draft notice came a year later, she pleaded with me not to go. So did my mom." His voice became a soft whisper. "God, I miss them." Suppressed emotions from being unable to call home and hear their voices filled his chest. He missed his big brother too. It was hard to breath and Blaze worried about his ability to stay focused on driving. He reached over to turn on the radio but Malorie stopped him.

"Don't." She carefully removed his sunglasses. "You need to get this out." Malorie saw an opening on the roadside ahead and pointed at it. "There. Pull over."

By the time the sedan stopped, any vulnerability in his voice had been replaced by anger. "Of course, my dad didn't waiver. No surprise there. He made it crystal clear it was my duty to serve."

"Did you try to talk to him?"

Blaze nodded and turned off the engine. "Yeah, I told him I wasn't afraid. That I would go if the war made sense. If it was worth dying for. But it isn't." He glanced again at the reflection in the rear-view mirror and adjusted it. "He expects all his boys to do their part. Just like he did," Blaze sighed. "What's ironic is my dad joined up three months before Germany surrendered. He was being trained in Kentucky to be a tank mechanic but never saw any action." Blaze grinned wide. "Unless using a tank to blast a local deer to smithereens is considered action."

Malorie replied, "Oh, that's gross."

"Of course, as kids, we loved to attend all the parades. We waved flags and cheered for the floats he and his buddies built down at the VFW." Blaze switched to a southern accent. "Yes ma'am, my patriotic daddy just loves the USA." His accent disappeared. "He sure as hell tried to make me feel guilty." Malorie placed her arm along the top of the front seat and her hand came to rest on the back of his neck. The cool gentle touch of her fingers caused an outpouring of pain neither one saw coming.

"Sometimes the shame gets so bad." Anguish took his voice away. Malorie leaned across the seat and pulled him toward her. Her arms wrapped around his broad shoulders and she cradled his head against her body. She remained silent and allowed Blaze to release some of the emotions his difficult choice had caused.

As his breathing slowed down and he regained control, Malorie asked, "Which do you feel the most? The guilt your dad placed on you for not serving or the shame you put on yourself?"

Blaze took a moment to think about her question. "As far as guilt goes, I've come to see that's my dad's problem, not mine. And shame, I made the hard choice not to go over to Vietnam and kill innocent people. There's no shame in that." Malorie's smile conveyed her agreement. "At this point though, it's the fear of getting arrested that I worry about the most. I know the fear has changed me. I can feel it draining me and Able sees it." A moment of silence passed. "But what he doesn't know is how dangerous it is for resisters in prison. My old man would come home from work with horror stories. Turns out the inmates hate child molesters and draft dodgers the most. Both are beaten whenever possible. And unfortunately, the guards, including my dad, see no problem with that."

"Wouldn't it be safer to stay on the farm?"

Blaze reluctantly sat up. "The hiding is killing my spirit. Simple as that. It's time to face my fears." With a deep breath, he continued. "Able said my choice to avoid the draft was ultimately braver than going to war." Blaze started the car. "He said it's time to take control, and that getting off the farm, looking for the preacher's boy, was a good way to start."

Malorie stared at her new friend and felt a surge of appreciation for what they had just shared. It felt good to provide the trust he needed to open up. She hoped they could get closer and the thought of losing that connection scared her. "Maybe I should drive. Just in case."

Blaze turned and smiled. He leaned forward and tenderly kissed Malorie's cheek. "Thanks. But I need to do this."

16

Bud didn't want to pay for parking, so he left the van near the Diamond Restaurant, not far from the bottom of the steep hill that led to Mendelson's Hotel. Twenty minutes later the exhausted teen sat in front of the hotel on a wooden bench outside the indoor pool. The hike up had been difficult and sitting there allowed him a chance to cool off and catch his breath. Bud noticed a discarded New York Times newspaper next to him on the bench and he separated the front page from the rest of the paper. He stayed clear of its center fold and slowly tore it vertically straight down without any variation in the tear. Next, he turned the second page horizontally and got quite different results. The separation was as jagged as a mountain range with its unpredictable and crooked path ripped down the entire page. Bud smiled. His grandfather's assessment of him sure hit the nail on the head.

The obnoxious horn of Hal's convertible startled Bud. He knew instantly it was the choir director behind the wheel by the goofy grin.

"Fancy meeting you here!" Hal shouted with an exaggerated wave and pulled his car along the curb. "What gives, big guy?"

Bud folded the torn sheets of newspaper with the remaining pages and wedged them down hard between two wood slats of the bench. He stood and stepped toward the car. "Where's my mother?"

Hal was put off by the brusque response. "Why? Is there a problem?"

"My little brother is missing. He's hitching here to talk to her. Have you seen him?"

"Not yet."

"So where is she, Hal?" Bud's tone had an edge. He had always sensed Hal's inappropriate attraction for his mother.

Hal was still hung-over and was not feeling well at all. "She's at the Accord Hotel, meeting with our director of entertainment. But I doubt-"

"Fine. Take me there." Bud opened the passenger's door and lowered himself sideways onto the seat. It took some effort to slide the seat back and swing his legs into the car.

"Look here, son. I'm not feeling so great. Just need to lie down a bit." Hal was not sure what to say next, but sensed that being kind was probably the best strategy. "Listen, why don't you come with me? We can talk in my room." His bloodshot eyes were a clear indication Hal's hangover wouldn't be over for several hours. "Thank God it's air-conditioned." Bud nodded his agreement and Hal drove forward a short distance where two valet attendants opened both car doors. He left the key, with its guest ID tag, in the ignition and faced Bud. "I don't have an employee parking spot yet so I'm enjoying this perk while I can." The unlikely pair got out of the car and wearily made their way inside.

Matthew located the dented can of fruit cocktail in the bushes. His hunger was getting nearly as bad as his thirst. Though he hated to even touch the dagger, he used it with his good hand to pry open the slight hole in the top of the can. The new slit was just big enough to suck out what remained of the sweet syrup. To get to the fruit itself required using his feet to hold the can in place and then forcing open the can's top with the tip of the dagger. The flavor of peaches, pears, pineapple, cherries, and grape halves never tasted so good. Matthew felt his entire body tingle from the sugar hitting his bloodstream, and he welcomed the renewed energy the delicious fruit provided.

He made his way back to his sleeping bag and sat down with crossed legs. He set the empty can aside and debated whether to eat more gram crackers or to save the rest for the long haul. Matthew could feel his hand bleeding again and hesitated to remove the stained paper bandage to examine the cut. He had some real concerns about bears smelling his blood, or worse, a mountain lion, though he did not know for sure if they existed in New Hampshire. He laid back and stretched out on the sleeping bag to think about his options. Should he keep going or stay put, hoping someone would rescue him? Trudging on through the dense woods would certainly take much more energy than just remaining where he was. If he got to a road, how would Matthew hitchhike without freaking people out? Could he even hold his thumb-drawing with his cut hand? If not, could he hold the drawing with his good hand while hiding the bloody wad of cloth behind his back? Matthew came to the funny realization he was more concerned with frightening a driver than getting help for his injury. The humor gave way to a serious insight about himself. How many times had he ignored his own needs for the needs of others? His mother came to mind. Her happiness was always his priority, but Matthew knew the time had come to put himself first.

"I'm staying right here!" Matthew found comfort in hearing his voice and he liked being under the big pine tree. It provided some cover from the rain and its thick limbs gave him a sense of being protected. His unusual view of the spiraling branches above, with their numerous pinecones, would have made an interesting sketch. He would have used a tight crosshatch for shading, and it would also bring out the rough texture of the bark. A painful sadness washed over him. Would he lose the one thing that made him unique? The talent which allowed him to fully express himself? What if his hand didn't mend and he couldn't hold a pencil? The thought was too difficult to consider. Matthew needed a distraction and redirected his thoughts to a long-standing regret. If only he had joined the Boy Scouts when he'd had the chance. Not just for the survival skills, he could certainly use in his current situation, but also for forging friendships with boys his age. Matthew recalled how hard he tried to get his dad's permission to join the scouts back in sixth grade. He provided a list of benefits and he had his mother's support, but John only voiced his concerns about the demands scouting would have on his own busy schedule at the church. Matthew knew it had much more to do with John's uneasiness in the woods, though having spent no time there himself.

Matthew rolled onto his side and removed the box of Carnation Instant Breakfast packets from the duffel bag. He read the instructions. *"Empty packet into a large glass. Stir in 1-cup of cold milk and enjoy."* "I would if I could" he said out loud. Matthew envisioned the pond he had skirted by on his journey the night before and felt confident he could find it again. Twenty-minutes later, what he thought was a pond looked more like a lake. The water near shore was brackish above the dead leaves and mud on the bottom. Matthew stepped around the tall cattails onto a few exposed boulders that took him farther out where the water looked deeper. With the empty can in his good hand, he squatted down and filled it up. His thirst was nearly quenched after drinking two full cans of cold water, though in his excitement, much of it spilled onto his shoes and on the rock. On the third attempt to fill the container, both his feet slid down off the sloped face of the boulder. The cold water was a shock. He lost his breath and the ability to keep his right arm above the water. When his head resurfaced and he gasped for air, the upright can appeared as a friendly buoy marking a channel back to shore.

Drenched, Matthew returned to his tree and stripped off all his clothing except his underwear. He was not comfortable being fully naked and knew the underwear would dry quickly on his body. He draped the clothes over bushes along with the torn section of shirt he used to secure the folded drawing paper. Tenderly, Matthew removed the wet pink paper and cleaned off the remaining blood in and around the deep wound. He could not tell if the edges of the opened skin were red from the excess blood or the start of an infection. A small amount of fresh blood oozed up from the bottom of the cut and the familiar sense of wooziness suddenly hit him again. He laid back and worked hard to control his feelings. He was scared but knew panicking wasn't going to help. He folded a fresh compress of paper and covered the injury again. It stuck in place and he decided to wrap it later when the fabric was dry. Matthew knew nourishment was key and was thankful he'd had the foresight to refill the can before leaving the lake. He used his teeth to hold the packet and his good hand to tear it open. The brown powder had a nice chocolate scent and he used a stick to stir it in. The lack of milk didn't matter, and he guzzled it all down except for some of the chalky mix stuck on his teeth. His used his tongue to swirl it away while the dizziness faded. Matthew felt a little bit better until the sound of thunder in the distant caught his attention. He thought about lightening and remembered a Danish saying his grandmother used. *"Bad is never good until worse happens."*

Sarah turned the handle of the mimeograph machine toward her in a steady rhythm while the fliers landed gently onto a neat stack. Breeze quickly removed the top page from the output tray and used her breath to blow-dry the ink. She crossed the dining room to show the finished product to the others. Messy peanut butter and jelly sandwiches were put down and hands wiped clean with napkins before the flier made its way among members of the commune. The pleasant vibe in the dining room changed immediately when Ruth entered.

"What is going on?" She stopped in the middle of the room with her clipboard in hand. "Shouldn't all of you be weeding?"

Aurora met her head on. "We're going to post fliers in town. The garden can wait."

Ruth went silent as she spotted the equipment. "And you thought it was okay to just take that from Able's office? Without his permission?"

Serene was breast feeding one of the twins. With a full mouth of her sandwich, she joined in to reduce the tension. "Relax sister. I'm sure Able would approve." Her mumbled words delighted the group with everyone laughing but Ruth.

Tower stood to help Serene swap out the twins and spoke up. "You know what Ruth? I didn't asked permission from the college when I borrowed that shit in the first place." More giggles ensued.

"Well, I just got off the phone with Able. They haven't found the boy but will keep looking. No word from Blaze yet, but that's no surprise." Ruth picked up the flier and read it to herself. "You know, he's probably long gone by now. What makes you think people in town would have seen him?"

Clarity walked over and put her arm around Sarah's shoulders. "Sarah feels strongly her little brother is hurt. That he's actually close by." She gave Sarah a warm smile. "We all agreed to support her intuition."

Breeze approached Ruth. "Here, I'll take that."

Ruth handed over the flier and tore off the top sheet from her pad of yellow legal-size paper. "Okay, fine. Well, here's the work schedule for the rest of this week and next." She waved it over her head. "There's lots to get done, people!" Ruth walked to the bulletin board near the start of the buffet line and forcefully tacked it up, then grabbed a sandwich and stormed out. Aurora took the flier from her daughter and made her way over to the bulletin board. She thought about the missing boy and wondered if Sarah was correct about his being injured. In a quiet voice she stated, "first things first." She laid the flier over the detailed schedule and tacked it in place.

Hal's deafening snore filled the hotel room while Bud nabbed the claim check off the bedside table. At the valet parking counter, where car keys of all the guests dangled by hooks on the wall, Bud parted with a crisp five-dollar bill. He knew the large tip, with the matching claim check, would guarantee success in obtaining Hal's car. While he waited, Bud asked for directions to the Accord Hotel.

"Yes sir. Just turn right at the bottom of the hill. Take Route -17 South. You can't miss the billboards."

The sports car became a red streak as Bud took off. "Now we're talking." When he reached the highway, he turned on the radio and tried various stations without success. He wanted something along the lines of *"Born to be Wild,"* by Steppenwolf, or *"Jumpin' Jack Flash"* by the Rolling Stones, but it seemed any signals from rock and roll stations were lost in the surrounding mountains.

After twenty-minutes of pushing the top-end of the highway's speed limit, Bud slowed down and cruised up the long entrance road to The Accord Hotel. With its numerous tall white buildings of glass and concrete, Bud was impressed with its more modern appearance than that of the old-fashioned hotel he'd just left. His plan was to find his mother quickly. Get in and get out, fast. Handing over more cash for valet parking was not an option. He may need it for buying gas to continue his search for Matty. Bud proceeded slowly past the busy main entrance without being noticed and decided with the second approach he would simply find a small spot between two big sedans. Fortunately, most of the Accord's wealthy cliental owned large luxury cars and they were parked everywhere. Bud sneaked the Spitfire between a long black Cadillac and a yacht-sized Lincoln Continental. He took the key inside.

The lobby was stunning with its wide three-tiered stairway surrounding a beautiful water fountain made of blue and white marble. The rich-looking wood handrail was supported by polished brass railings, each with a decorative sphere on its top. Bud hesitated walking across the fancy floor with its black and white checkered pattern. Instead he moved back against a sidewall and stood still behind a display of lush tropical plants. From there, he got the lay of the land without being seen and watched the well-dressed guests enjoying themselves. A familiar laugh from the top of the crowded stairway caught Bud's attention. With the second laugh, the blonde woman's head tilted backwards and the man she was with leaned in to nuzzle her neck. The blonde wore a black cocktail dress and appeared upset. She pushed the man away, then started her descent alone. It was not until the couple reached the second tier that Bud realized the blonde woman was actually his mother. Bud emerged from his jungle hideaway like a bull elephant and charged for the stairs.

"What the hell is going on?" Bud shouted and grabbed the railing. Every conversation in the active lobby fell silent as he climbed the stairs. Barbara made her way past other guests with her high heels clicking on the hard marble. Bud arrived at the first landing and stood before his surprised mother. "Jesus Christ, what's with the hair?"

Before she could explain, Manny interrupted. "Barbara, who is this punk?" His voice was low in volume but filled with malice. He pulled Barbara's upper arm backward to force her behind him but the sudden move knocked her off balance. Her ankle twisted and she would have fallen down completely if Bud hadn't reached forward to catch her. He gently helped his mother to stand and turned to face the stranger in the silly silk ascot. It was puffed up just like the man's ego.

Seeing his mother in pain along with the mounting fear for his little brother finally caused the dam that kept his rage inside to burst. "I'm her son! Asshole!" Bud reached over to grab the man's lapels, but the sheer force of the move became a powerful shove instead. It sent the wide-eyed man down the remaining stairs. The collective gasp from guests in the lobby confirmed to Bud that everyone would insist it was not an accident.

"Mom, come with me now!" Bud placed her arm around his neck and carried most of her weight on his hip. At the bottom of the landing, Manny, on his back, groaned in pain from a dislocated shoulder. With Bud's help, Barbara limped past and was relieved to see Manny was alive with no blood in sight.

"I was warned about people like you," Barbara wanted to yell so everyone could hear, but the agony in her severely sprained ankle kept her voice above a whisper. "Wished I had asked more questions."

Manny sat up cradling his arm. "Damn it! Someone call hotel security!"

17

Matthew bent over and vomited again. It was a lighter shade of brown because most of the powdered mix had already come up. Earlier, the rain had forced him to collect his damp clothes from falling in the lake; he stuffed them into the duffel-bag to keep them from getting wetter. Though the pine tree helped somewhat to shield his campsite, he could tell everything would get soaked over time. If the sky would clear up, he planned to use the blade of the dagger to reflect the sun to signal a plane if one happened to fly over. Still in his underwear, Matthew felt a chill and crawled back onto the bag. He folded half of it over his chest. He felt much weaker, and his thirst more intense since throwing up. He knew he was starving, and his fears were getting worse. He was fearful that the sharp pain in his empty stomach would get unmanageable unless a miracle of some sort occurred. The idea of a miracle struck him as odd, because until that very moment, he hadn`t thought in those terms. The hope had always been that hikers in the woods would come find him.

They would have food and water. They would rescue him. Then

something his grandfather once said popped into his mind. *"There are no*

atheists in fox holes." Matthew remembered Glen had gone on to say,

"But I sure as hell became one when I climbed out."

Matthew laid back and thought about the stories his grandfather

had told about going off to war. How right it had felt to leave home to

face the Germans. Enemies of America and God-all-mighty. Glen felt like

he and the young men in his unit were about to do something profound.

The conflict would be holy, almost spiritual. Good versus evil. Then the

landing in Normandy happened. His fellow Marines were cut down in a

senseless massacre on the beach, and how that awful carnage shook him

to the core. What kind of God would let that happen? What purpose did it

serve? He started to think maybe there was not a God at all. When Glen

returned home to the States, he hid his new doubts from his wife, a

devoted, God-fearing Christian. Glen knew talking about his change of

heart about religion would have been a waste of time. His wife had deep

beliefs she had clung to since childhood. Beliefs that were reaffirmed by

the Gospel, then taken as gospel. He knew that when his wife's beliefs

were shared and agreed upon as real with others at her church, those beliefs were reinforced. He understood her faith felt validated over the years and as a result, her beliefs ultimately felt real. Factual. For his wife, any doubts of God's existence had simply ceased to exist. But for Glen, who witnessed the horrible deaths of so many brave soldiers slaughtered before his eyes, all bets were off. For his grandfather, anything spiritual outside of nature was man made. He believed in the power of nature and how the beautiful earth could always be relied on. If there was a god, it could only be found in the magic of the seasons and in the bounty the earth provided. Glen loved being a farmer and felt lucky to have survived the war. He was thankful and honored to simply work the land.

A squadron of mosquitoes landed on Matthew's exposed legs. Though his hand throbbed in pain, he got completely into the sleeping bag and closed the zipper until only his face was exposed. He felt even weaker than before. He was dizzy, too. Matthew wondered if he should pray. To plead for God's help. Instead, he called out to his loving grandfather. "Please Grandpa, I need you." The words did not sound loud enough so he tried again. "RESCUE ME, GRANDPA! PLEASE!" The exertion caused a swift rush of blood to his head. He blacked out.

Tower stopped the commune's colorfully painted school bus in front of the Woolworth's Five-and-Dime store on Main Street. The vehicle was too long to pull into the angled space at the sidewalk without its back end sticking out into the street. Aurora chose the location so she could purchase the scotch tape needed to hang the fliers in store windows. She was the first to get off the bus, followed by Breeze, Sarah, Charmed, Buzz, Feather, Harmony, and Fresco with his daughters. Fresco thought having his young children in tow would soften his wild hippie appearance. Tower closed the bus's folding door and drove on to find a side street with enough space for him to park.

"Breeze, give everyone a handful of those." Aurora turned to face Feather. "Take your fliers and put one on every car out in the middle, there. You won't need tape. Just use the wipers to hold them against the windshield." Feather headed out to complete her task. Aurora went into the store, while the remaining farm members waited outside and talked among themselves. It didn't take long to notice the looks of suspicion on the faces of townspeople passing by.

Harmony said, "You know, straight people in town may not be willing to help. If that happens, don't argue. Just go to the next store."

"She's right" Buzz added. "It would be a bummer to cause a scene." He looked at his girlfriend, known for her short fuse. "That means you, Charmed." His smile pissed her off.

"He's a kid, for Christ's sake. I can't imagine anyone wouldn't want to help." Charmed tried to laugh it off. "Then again, we're those evil *Harveys* living on that sex-crazed commune. Very scary." Everyone laughed, but in the back of their minds, being in town could prove to be dangerous if they were not careful.

Aurora armed each team with a roll of tape, and they went their separate ways. Frisco and his daughters giggled as they ran for the town's old-fashioned ice cream parlor. His daughter's reward for helping. Breeze wanted freedom from the adults, particularly her mom, and crossed the street to post her first flyer in the pet store. Harmony led Sarah to the bus station while Buzz and Charmed headed for the Co-op, knowing they would be well received. The long wood bench in front of the Co-op was also the location where everyone would meet once their fliers were distributed. All wore shoes or sandals, aware of the strict rule requiring footwear to enter the shops.

Pete Curtis grimaced in pain as he got out of his pickup. His bad knee was swollen again, but he needed to deposit the bible camp's tuition checks at the bank before it closed. He told Ruby to be a good dog and left her in the cab with the windows down. Pete liked that his hometown of Keene, New Hampshire was once known for having the widest paved Main Street in all the world. With its numerous angled parking spaces in front of the stores, and in the center of the street itself, he could always count on finding an empty spot.

On his slow return to the truck he saw a young female petting his dog through the driver's side window. Pete called out. "Her name's Ruby!"

Feather quickly stepped back. The fliers pressed between her body, and the truck fell to the ground. "Oh shit!" Despite his painful leg, Pete wasted no time helping the young lady collect most of the sheets of paper from the pavement. "I am so clumsy! Thank you, thank you."

"Nonsense. I startled you." The elderly man winked and handed

Feather the sheets he'd collected. He kept one to read out loud. "Missing. Fourteen-year-old Matthew Thomley. Last seen hitch-hiking west... on Route-9." Pete locked eyes with Feather. "Oh, my goodness. That boy was at our home last night!"

"Sounds like Kismet to me," Able said with a happy grin. The minister had just hollered that he recognized his son, Bud, getting out of a small car just a few vehicles ahead of them. He seemed to be having an argument with a blonde woman in the passenger's seat. John unhooked his shoulder harness and raced up the sidewalk. Able pulled his car over to the curb and took a moment to admire Mendelson's beautiful flower beds. He hoped the younger son was already inside the hotel and the hectic search could end. Able just wanted the commune to return to normal with its twice-a-week considerations, which in his mind, kept everyone centered and in tune with one another.

"Bud! What were you thinking?" John asked in a loud voice but immediately regretted it.

"Nice to see you, too." Bud opened the door for his injured mother. "You still high, Dad?"

"What does that mean?" Barbara asked as Bud helped her to stand.

"Barbara?" John's mouth dropped. "God! Your hair? You're-"

"Yes. I'm a blonde now." Barbara turned to Bud. "Pull Hal's car over. Obviously, there's lots we need to discuss." She leaned on John's arm while Bud did as he was requested. It felt odd to be touching her husband again. Familiar, but not comforting, given her realization that their marriage was over. Once the car was parked, Barbara moved away from John and leaned on its fender, keeping her weight on her good foot.

Able pulled over and drove forward to park behind Bud. He joined the group on the sidewalk and introductions were made, along with an update on Sarah and the plan to find Matthew. They were about to discuss how to locate him, if he were already at the hotel, when a car runner from the hotel's Traffic Department approached, out of breath, and informed them they couldn't park along the curb. Able pointed out

Barbara's swollen ankle and the need for immediate medical attention.

The attendant wiped his sweaty brow. "I'll notify the bell desk, sir. They keep a wheelchair handy for this type of thing." He did not get far before Barbara spoke up.

"Be sure to tell the Bell Captain it's for Barbara. The *"recently unemployed"* singer." She glared at Bud, then glanced over to smile at her husband. "Yes, Andy will be happy to help. I'm sure." John's eyes narrowed to understand what she meant.

Able saw emotions were running high and continued to take the lead. "Look, I'm going in to call the farm. I'll find out if Blaze has located your son yet. If not, he may be here. Let's hope."

Bud cleared his throat and spoke up. "Hey man, I left your van at that Diamond Restaurant down at the bottom of the hill. The key's in the ashtray. Sorry about taking it."

Able gave Bud a forgiving smile. "If I had a kid brother who was missing, I'd do the same thing." Able tapped on the hood of the sports car and winked. "Hell of an upgrade." Bud enjoyed a hearty laugh and Able walked away. He turned around when he heard his name.

"Hey Able. If I don't see you again, I think you're pretty cool."

Able returned a peace sign and went farther up the sidewalk toward the hotel entrance. Bud put his hands on both sides of his mouth and called out loudly. "Tell my sister not to worry! If Matty isn't here, I'll find him!"

"Keep your voice down for Pete's sake" Barbara scolded Bud. "You're like a bull in a china shop." She knew she should be solely concerned for Matthew's safety, but if it were not for Bud's hasty actions, she would still have the job doing what she loved. Barbara was certain she could have handled Manny's unwanted advances, too, but the horrible scene at the Accord had changed everything. Her thoughts turned to Hal and how disappointed he would be. She wasn't sure how to tell him. Would they just return to East Fields for the summer? Or try to locate another opportunity for performing, they certainly would not use Manny as a reference. Barbara tried to rotate her ankle, but the pain was too severe. She worried it was more serious than she thought.

"Barbara! What happened?" Andy's voice pulled her out of her thoughts. She looked up to see him speeding toward her with a wheelchair tilted back on its rear wheels.

"Oh, you're a sight for sore eyes." Barbara gushed. She stood up and pivoted around to make it easier for Andy to place the wheelchair behind her. "It's a long story. One I'd rather tell you in private."

"Hi there, I'm Reverend Thomley, Barbara's-"

"Minister." She inserted. "Please, Andy. Take me inside." Her sad eyes pleaded the message louder than her voice.

"Don't worry, I got you." The Bell Captain smiled and had Barbara headed back to the hotel entrance before John could respond.

Bud did not hesitate. "Well, that was weird." He walked around the convertible's front end and squeezed himself behind the wheel.

"Where are you going? I need to speak with you." John stepped closer to the car. "Look son, I don't approve of what you did but I'm impressed with your concern for Matthew." Bud's eyes opened wide with surprise. John had to admit he could not remember the last time he actually gave Bud a compliment. "In fact, you have been very brave." John took a moment to collect his thoughts. "I know I've been hard on you and I'm sorry. I love you, son. I promise to do better."

Bud's chest got tight. His eyes started to tear up. He was about to reply to his dad when an angry male voice shouted from an opened window on the fifth floor.

"Hey, that's my car! Stop that kid, he's stealing my car!" Just moments before, Hal had slammed his phone down when Manny told him he wanted Barbara and her son arrested for assault.

"Dad, I love you too. But I gotta' split!" Bud shifted into first and peeled out. The high pitch noise cleared a path through the frightened guests and staff.

After the fliers were distributed, Tower called Ruth before they left town. He told her they'd found someone who had seen Matthew. Tower's plan was to swing by the Bible Camp on their way home and retrieve the few items the boy left behind. As he sipped lemonade inside the camp's mess hall, Tower admired how spacious it was. If the farm didn't build a dome, the building he was in would be just the right size and shape for the new dining hall the commune needed.

Mrs. Curtis took it upon herself to make lemonade and have her campers serve it to their unexpected guests. The exotic scent of patchouli oil and the sheer clothing on the hippie women did not go unnoticed by the flustered teenage boys. Pete Curtis returned from his office with everything folded neatly in a stack. "Matthew didn't leave much behind. Just an extra pair of jeans, a tee shirt, a tie, and this note." Pete knew Sarah was the boy's sister and handed her the folded piece of paper.

She read it out loud. "Dear Pete, thank you for your hospitality. Please tell Mrs. Curtis, her pie was delicious." It was obvious to everyone in the mess hall that Mrs. Curtis was touched by the compliment. "I also appreciate your kind offer to drive me to my mother. But I need to start hitchhiking ASAP. Thanks for the flashlight, too. I'll return it when I can." Sarah's trembling fingers held the note against her chest. She spoke quietly. "Thank you, Mr. and Mrs. Curtis, for helping my little brother." When her tears fell, Sarah excused herself and hurried out of the building. Aurora wanted to follow, but sensed that Sarah needed time to be alone.

Pete's dog, Ruby, wagged her tail happily against the floor of the porch. The thumping sound helped Sarah to stop crying and she sat down on the first step to rub Ruby's head. Suddenly, the dog bounded down the stairs and stopped at the bottom. Sarah could see in Ruby's gentle brown eyes an intelligence trying to communicate with her. She felt pulled from the step and followed the dog until they reached an opening to a path in the thick woods. Ruby laid down on her back and waited for a belly rub. Sarah smiled and knelt on one knee to oblige. Near the dog's head, an odd blue disk in the soil caught her eye. She picked it up and didn't give it much thought on her way back to the mess hall. That changed immediately when she showed it to Pete.

Blaze and Malorie pulled into a truck stop to get gas. He parked next to a phone booth and called Ruth at the farm. Malorie sat on the sedan's trunk to catch some sun while she waited for an update on the search.

"Well, of course, Ruth gave me crap for not calling sooner" Blaze called out on his return to the car. "The good news… she heard from Able and they located the older brother at the resort where the mother is." He leaned back against the car to feel her leg's warmth. "And apparently, Aurora, with everyone's help, hung missing fliers all over Keene. Turns out some old dude came forward. Said he and his wife had put the kid up for a night."

"Well that's a good sign." Malorie smiled and took Blaze's hand. "See, things are gonna' work out." The tender moment between them fell apart when two police cars, with their sirens and lights on, sped by on the road. The heavy garage door slammed down and surprised the young couple. Moments later, the "*We're Open*" sign on the front door was flipped over to "*Sorry, We're Closed,*" and all the lights inside went dark.

"Hey mister, what's going on?" Blaze yelled out.

The shop's owner ran for his pick-up truck. "Can't really talk right now. I'm a volunteer down at the fire house." He backed out and rolled down his window as he got closer to Blaze. In a panicked voice, he added, "Really bad accident. Some kid speeding in a stolen car and lost control. Rolled it bunch of times."

Matthew could barely move, but the need to vomit again forced him out of his wet sleeping bag again. He felt his damaged hand was bleeding more, on what he hoped would be his last trip into the nearby bushes. Still in his underwear, the numerous insect bites on his body were swollen and bleeding from his scratching for relief. The rain continued to fall as Matthew scurried back for the sleeping bag. It was his only protection from the relentless bugs, and once he got in it, he curled into a tight ball. Matthew's intense hunger and thirst brought a misery he knew he could not handle much longer. The very real possibility of dying there under the tree occurred to him for the first time. He thought about his mother and how devastated she would be. Sarah would certainly flip-out and probably never get over it. Bud would be angry at him for being so stupid and for making the wrong decisions. Of course, his father would grieve for a while. Then over time, his minister dad would rationalize it as being God's will. Matthew knew he should write a letter to his family, but the handwriting result from using his left hand would look childish. More importantly, the letter would be an acknowledgment of his failure to survive.

The slow-moving dark clouds passed over him. The rain had ended, but Matthew's fears about death had not. What it would feel like, since his chances of survival were getting slimmer. Could reincarnation be a real thing? He felt the need to keep all options open. Where would he go when his body was dead and was left behind? Would there be a waiting period for his spirit before starting a new life? Would he get a longer life next time, since the current one ended so early? That seemed only fair. Even with his questions unanswered, Matthew admitted to himself that reincarnation seemed a better option than just falling into a black void of nonexistence, never to be loved again.

Dusk fell and the sounds of the woods increased in volume. Matthew distracted himself with thoughts of things he would never get a chance to experience. Dating. The love of a wife. Sex. Children. Grandchildren. Creating more art. The sadness felt heavy on his chest. Time passed slowly until a loon gave its spooky call from a far-away lake. The odd sound caused him to stick his head out of his damp cocoon to hear better. Matthew mumbled to himself, "what's next? Ghosts?" He remembered Pete's story and chuckled. Nothing but the crickets, so he laid back. Then came the faint bark of a dog and distant voices. "Is that singing?" The closer the noises came; Matthew recognized the lyrics of a song he'd learned in Sunday school.

"Hide it under a bushel? No! I'm gonna' let it shine. Let it shine, let it shine, let it shine." Sung together by the Christian campers with their flashlights and the hopeful hippies of New Harvest Farm, the cheerful sound got closer. Matthew thought he was hallucinating, when suddenly, Sarah and Ruby hurried toward him through the trees. He knew it was all very real when the dog's wet tongue licked his face and he heard his sister's scream for joy!

4 years to come

18

"Let's hear it for the college graduate!" Breeze announced from atop a wooden chair. Applause and whistles erupted among the invited guests at Aurora's Blissful Bakery on Main Street in Keene, New Hampshire. Sunlight streamed through the numerous hanging spider plants held by crochet ropes in the shop's bay windows. Bouquets of colorful flowers in old milk bottles brightened each small table along the walls of exposed brick. Through the door, came Sarah Thomley. Her new contact lenses felt uncomfortable but that didn't keep her smile from beaming beneath the graduation cap. Barbara followed her into the bakery and doublechecked her modern shag haircut of brunet hair in the mirror near the door. Matthew skipped the mirror, knowing his underperforming mustache was nearly invisible compared to the others in his senior class. The Thomleys found their name tags on the special round table decorated with twisted crepe paper and sat down.

"Speech, speech!" Aurora called out from behind her display counter filled with pastries and cookies. The savory smell of apple pies and freshly brewed coffee teased the intimate gathering.

"Wow. What can I say?" Sarah took off her cap and stood up. "Okay, first. Thank you all for coming." She enjoyed the happy grins on the faces of her fellow journalism students at Keene State College. "Thank you, Mom and Breeze, for making this graduation so much better than my last one." They exchanged smiles knowing that their efforts had paid off. "And then there's my second mom, the amazing, Aurora, who has encouraged me over the years to be more assertive." Sarah's wave beckoned her to come forward. Her voice got louder. "So, get over here, woman!" Aurora, in her bright tie-dye apron, put her oven mitts down and dove into Sarah's opened arms.

"Enough speechifying. It's time to chow down!" Tower's remarks caused the usual laughter and the party got underway. Sarah's college buddies entertained Matthew and Barbara with tales of their classroom hijinks while Serene, Tower, Breeze, and Aurora caught up.

"It's so far-out to have Tower's parents living nearby." Serene said as she placed a scoop of vanilla ice-cream on top of a slice of pie. "They just love watching the twins." Serene slid the tray of plates to Tower, who served them to a nearby table. "His folks are so proud of us for buying the house in town. And they're thrilled he took the coaching job at the high school."

Aurora divided another pie into eight pieces and asked, "how's Ruth doing?"

Serene laughed. "I think the honeymoon's over for my dear sister. That fisherman she married in Maine has a much bigger drinking problem than she'd thought. She wants to divorce him but knows he'll take half of what's left from her share of the farm."

Breeze returned with a near-empty carafe of coffee. "Guess who works at the Co-op now?" The assembly line of desserts continued as they listened to the grown teenager. She stood four-inches taller than her mother. "Well, from what I hear, Buzz has moved back to Keene. Charmed finally dumped him and is moving to Hollywood to be an actress. Must be nice to have rich parents." Breeze smirked at Aurora. "Of course, I wouldn't know."

"Very funny. Is everyone ready for some more good news? I got a nice letter from Able." Aurora pointed to the bulletin board behind the cash register. Colorful postcards from dozens of Asian countries filled its cork surface. An envelope was tacked in the upper corner. "He says he is done traveling. He's found a Tibetan Buddhist Monastery in India and is staying put to study." Aurora removed the letter. "Listen to this. It's so Able." Aurora cleared her throat. "In closing, as the Buddha once said, *'You should not believe my teaching out of faith, rather through investigation.'* Give my regards to all. Love and peace, Able." Aurora carefully returned his letter to the envelope for safe keeping. "God, I miss him."

"I miss him, too." Tower added. "But keeping us crazy hippies corralled on the farm just wasn't his bag."

As always, their conversation turned to the fallout of Able's leaving and the farm being sold. Harmony and Feather split for Woodstock and never returned. Terra moved to a large commune in Tennessee to manage the garden. Bear and Frisco felt betrayed by Able and loaded their families into a caravan of the farm's buses and headed west. Smooch went along for the ride, knowing his mechanical experience would be needed. Not one word had been heard from any of them.

Aurora spoke up. "So, it looks like Malorie and Blaze are expecting another baby. They found a bigger house outside of Toronto with a yard for the kids. Blaze will continue his work helping draft resisters get settled in Canada."

Eventually, Sarah's friends from school hugged her and said their good-byes. Serene and Tower left to rescue his parents from their kids. He took a leftover pie as payment for their babysitting, but everyone knew his folks would never see it. Aurora was tired and plopped down next to Barbara, while Breeze poured a final refill of everyone's coffee. Aurora noticed Matthew held his cup with his left hand and kept his right hand under the table. That was not a complete surprise given Sarah's updates on the failed surgeries.

"Say, Matthew, your sister tells me you have a summer job lined up." Aurora said.

Yeah, I'm looking forward to it." His mother sat up in her chair and he added, "Oh god, here it comes."

"Not just *any* job." Barbara could not wait to brag. "He'll be painting at The Rocky Neck Art Colony on Cape May." Barbara reached over to caress Matthew's cheek. "His art teacher at school showed Matthew's work to an artist friend there. He is very impressed. He said Matthew's drawings from before the accident were fine but his new paintings, using his left hand, are so much better. He said his natural talent with a brush has freed him up to be a great artist."

"Mom please-"

"It's true, honey." Barbara's happy eyes glistened. "Andy and I are so proud of you."

"Sarah, what's your dad up to these days?" Breeze asked.

"Well…" Sarah noticed her mother's eyes rolled. "He said he'd be here today if he can get away. Two big weddings, with not much time in between so I'm not holding my breath." She sipped her coffee. "I guess becoming a Unity minister has worked out well for him. And his new wife." Sarah's half-smile hinted at her own mixed emotions regarding the younger women he met at the church. "Unity is so much more progressive than the Methodists and the large congregation seems more accepting of his-"

"Agenda?" Barbara spoke under her breath.

"Mom, he's trying his best." Sarah replied.

Barbara glanced at her watch. "We should get going." Barbara stood abruptly. "I want to check on things at the cemetery before we get home."

"Oh, that's right. My condolences on your mother's passing." Aurora rose to her feet and gave Barbara a warm embrace. "This must be a painful time for you."

Barbara released a laugh. "On the contrary. Now that's she gone, Andy moved in and is bringing our family farm into the twenty-first century. She'd die twice if she knew my Scottish lover and I are happily living in sin."

"Oh, that's gross!" Matthew announced as he headed for the door.

Breeze meet him halfway and handed him a large collective bouquet of flowers taken from each table. "Here, these are for your grandmother."

The setting sun cast a subtle pink glow on Barbara's family plot in the cemetery, giving it a warmth that was not there during Helen's rainy funeral. Matthew did not attend the event three weeks prior, for fear he would break down in front of his grandmother's numerous church friends. It felt good to be there with just his mother and sister, in case his difficult emotions spilled over. Barbara and Sarah replaced the wilted flowers in the vase with fresh ones while Matthew stepped behind his grandfather's headstone. With his good hand, he reached into his pants pocket and held the blue disk Sarah had found in the woods. It had become a cherished token he always carried with him. Matthew placed his injured hand on the cool granite and closed his eyes.

"Thank you."

"Come on, you two. Let's take the rest of the flowers to Bud." Sarah's cheerful voice came from a paved path that led up a newly landscaped hill. The light from the sunset turned into a beautiful deep hue of orange as she waited for her family to join her. They walked together over the ridge and were greeted by a simple metal sign that dangled from a chain crossing the path.

CLOSED FOR

RE-SEEDING

Sarah tenderly caressed her fingers around Matthew's damaged hand and spoke in a reverent tone. "Looks like NOOT to me."

Matthew nodded his agreement. "The natural order of things."

All three quietly giggled and came together with arms around each other's shoulders. The sign had served its purpose.

The End

Thanks to:

Amanda and Hayden, our beautiful adult children, for their love and encouragement.

My sister, Debbie, and her son, Forrest. Two highly creative people who hold a special place in my heart.

Susan Flowers, professional editor, who made certain the sentences were free of errors.

Frank Giannangelo, for providing his much-needed input and improvement.

Made in the USA
Middletown, DE
20 February 2021